TERRE HAUTE

TERRE HAUTE

Will Aitken

DELTA
FICTION

A Delta Book
Published by
Dell Publishing
a division of
Bantam Doubleday Dell Publishing Group, Inc.
666 Fifth Avenue
New York, New York 10103

Design by Richard Oriolo

The trademark Delta® is registered in the
U.S. Patent and Trademark Office.

Library of Congress Cataloging in Publication Data

Aitken, Will.
    Terre Haute : a novel / by Will Aitken.
    p. cm.
    ISBN 9780385298728
    I. Title.
PS3551.I95T47 1989
813'.54—dc20   89-32505
                                                  CIP

November 1989

Printed in the United States of America
Published simultaneously in Canada

14672180430 01

For the Garside boys,
Bruce, Paul, and David

This book was made possible in part
by an Explorations Grant from the
Canada Council for the Arts.

Ils ont vu les Pays-Bas,
ils rentrent à Terre Haute . . .

T. S. ELIOT
Lune de Miel

TERRE HAUTE

NOVEMBER

*T*hey stand near the top of the hill looking down at the unfinished house. The setting sun turns the 2×4 skeleton gold. He tells her he couldn't have done it without her. She smiles, tears in her eyes. Everybody else thought he was crazy, wanting to build a house like that. She was the only one who believed in him, in his genius. He cups her chin in his hand. They kiss.

I don't see why it can't work out. Kirk Douglas and Kim Novak look so perfect together. They both have the same tarnished blond hair, the same sparkling white teeth —even their skin's the same deep rich gold. He has that neat dent in his chin and when she smiles she looks just like a Siamese cat. But they're married to other people so they'll always be Strangers When They Meet.

The girl at the Orpheum refreshment counter has

this pink birthmark the shape of South America running from her left eye all the way down her neck. When it gets really busy at the refreshment stand Chile and most of Argentina turn purple.

"What'll it be?"

"Buttercup, big Coke, Clark bar and a jumbo box of Root Beer Barrels. Please."

Coke foams over the paper cup's brim. "How come you're not home watching TV like everybody else?"

"I got tired of it. It gets boring after a while."

"It's history is what it is—that's what my daddy says." She pops open a collapsible tray and loads in my stuff.

"Movies are better."

She looks at me like I'm weird. "I guess."

The second half of the double bill is *Advise and Consent.* Mother got it from the Book-of-the-Month Club a couple of years ago. If it's anything like the movie nothing happens, just a bunch of men in suits sitting around talking politics. I'm thinking about leaving when the young senator gets a phone call. From an old army buddy. He goes to a bar to meet the guy. The bar's in a basement and it's pretty dark. The army buddy isn't there, just all these men standing around a piano. They stare at the senator. A couple of them smirk. He runs back out into the street.

Back at his office—the Washington Monument's right out the window—he goes into the bathroom and looks at himself in the medicine-cabinet mirror. His eyes look big and scared and his face is all sweaty. He opens the medicine cabinet and takes out his straight razor.

DECEMBER

*M*other rubs the fabric between thumb and forefinger. She turns back the sleeve to check the lining. "Good quality, but don't you think the color is a little . . ."

The clerk lifts the suit off the rack. Soft green, almost heathery, it changes color slightly as the clerk drapes it over his arm.

I want it so much. "If you think it's too . . ."

"Perhaps not." She checks the double stitching of the lapels, tugs at the buttons, crumples the trouser leg to see how quickly it springs back. "Why don't you try it on?"

I come back from the dressing room and mother stands back, arms folded, head tilted to one side. "It has a good line. I'm still a little worried about the color. It seems, well, don't you think it's flashy, Jared?" She turns to the clerk. "Do you think we could take it out into the sun?"

There hasn't been any sun all week but all three of us stand on the sidewalk in the gray afternoon light, crowds of Christmas shoppers plowing past us. Mother asks me to turn. I turn. "It does bring out your eyes." She tugs lightly at the points of the vest.

Back inside she supervises as Harry the alterations man kneels at my feet, pinning the cuffs. He stands up, knees cracking, and makes chalk marks for taking in the jacket. Maybe my diet's working. Mother wanders over to the counter and gives the brass tie tree a spin. She slips off half a dozen. She's moving faster as she approaches the Wall of Shirts. The clerk watches as she matches up ties and shirts—wine-red silk with a burgundy button-down pinstripe, emerald tweed with a wheat-straw spread-collar tattersall. The clerk gathers up the shirts and ties and she turns back to me, face flushed, pupils bright and tiny as tackheads. She looks over the shop. Her eyes light on a headless mannequin wearing a tan overcoat.

"You really think your Burberry's going to be warm enough for the winter?" She runs her hand over the nap, unbuttons the coat and strokes the swirly satin lining. The clerk helps her ease it off the mannequin. "See how this does. I think it's just the thing for that suit." She's right. It's perfect.

"Real camel's hair," the clerk says as he helps me into it, "not some cheap blend of wool and camel's hair." I stand in front of the three-way mirror, trying to hide how much I love it.

"I don't know," mother says. The clerk watches her closely. "The buttons are a little . . ."

"I know exactly what you mean, Mrs. McCaverty. We have some nice leather-covered ones in the back."

"Do you?" She smiles so her teeth show. That hasn't happened in a while.

"I can have Harry sew them on when he does the other alterations."

Back out on the sidewalk, holding the black-and-gold Bemelman's bag full of shirts and ties and the lizard belt she tossed in at the last moment, I think about steering her past Hanover's to point out the pair of oxblood cordovan wingtips I noticed last week. But she looks tired. A good spree usually will perk her up for the rest of the day. I can tell she just wants to get home. She's worried to death about her collie bitch. Yesterday Lady Jane threw up on the Persian rug in Father's den and today when we got up there were puddles of piss and diarrhea all over the kitchen. Mrs. Krapo took a fit.

"I'll walk you to the car," I offer, but she says no, she knows I want to stay downtown. She looks like she'd rather be alone anyway. Her eyes are all pouchy and her mouth's set in the usual narrow line.

I hurry along Wabash Avenue, trying to catch glimpses of my reflection in store windows. I always expect to look different after I've bought a lot of things so it's always kind of a disappointment when I don't. I stop for a second to check out Berkowitz Fine Leathers' Christmas display. Underneath the tree, surrounded by briefcases, purses and vanity cases, there's a small calfskin jewelry box, very plain, with gold trim edging the lid and a gold rectangle stamped on the lid itself. A small white card propped against the box says $49.95, Monogramming No Extra Charge. It would make a great stocking stuffer. I've got to have it but how can I get mother to see it?

Sometimes I think if I could just have this or that thing—a suit or pair of shoes or sweater or jewelry box—I'd be finished, perfect. Wouldn't have to buy another thing. No one would be able to touch me then. But it seems like there's always something else. At this rate I'll never be complete.

Fannie May's Sweete Shoppe is packed with old ladies in veiled hats and fur-collared coats drinking hot chocolate. I'd love to go in for an apple cruller but no way. I said I wasn't going to eat anything today and that's that. Osco Drugs is a temptation too. A cherry Coke always seems to pick me up when I'm feeling a little down, but the clock over the door of Vigo Federal Savings and Loan says four thirty-five as I turn onto Seventh.

Slope's heavy brass-plated doors have long narrow windows set into them. Brasswork screens cover the windows, the brass curved to look like reeds swaying in the wind.

After the doors the entry hall's a disappointment: the gray doors of the four-passenger elevator to the left; to the right a brass scroll dedicated to the memory of Chauncey R. Slope, the jeweler who gave Slope's to the town. Straight ahead three tiers of black marble stairs mount up to the galleries.

Slope's is a gift the town has never taken to. Which is fine with me because it means the place is almost always empty, even on a Saturday afternoon.

The permanent collection isn't much. There used to be a Rubens called "Abraham and Isaac" but a couple of years ago the tag came down and a new one went up reading SCHOOL OF RUBENS. It still hangs in the hall at the top of the stairs though, and it's still my favorite painting in the whole place. Isaac, stripped to the waist, hands tied behind his back, bends over the white sacrificial slab. The angel's holding back Abraham's sword. Hard to tell from the expression on his face if Abraham's relieved or disappointed.

No one at the sales desk so I head straight for the South Galleries. The galleries themselves are prettier than a lot of the art. Long high-ceilinged rooms with gray or black marble floors, and instead of windows, whole walls of glass brick so the light comes in pale and watery. Big palms in brass tubs stand against the walls, fronds casting webby shadows on the paintings.

A full-scale plaster cast of Michelangelo's "Pietà" stands at the very center of the Long Gallery. It's smooth and pale gold, like beeswax. I run my fingers over Christ's cool toes. Sometimes I think it would be nice to lie across Mary's lap too.

I glance about at the pictures. Same ones that have been up all fall. "Indian Encampment," a Remington so varnished over it's hard to make out more than the setting sun and a couple of blurry tepees; "The Fourth of July" is kind of neat because it's this fat nude sitting in an armchair looking out a window—over her plump shoulder a Fourth of July parade is passing by; the Bierstadt of the Hudson River is cold and gloomy, swirling gray water like a reflection of the gallery's gray marble floor.

I'm heading for the Glass Gallery when I notice a new display set up in the library alcove. The wood-and-glass cases usually hold snuff boxes and delicate perfume bottles or ivory-and-silk fans. Every time a rich old lady dies she leaves all her knickknacks to Slope's.

The new display's different: letters, photographs and small books covered in grainy leather. A typed card taped to one of the cases reads THE LIFE AND TIMES OF CHAUNCEY R. SLOPE: A MOVEABLE FEAST. His bust

stands in the hallway outside the director's office, right
next to the bronze Mercury balancing on a ball, wings on
his cap, wings on his feet. The bust looks like any old
guy, big bald dome of a head, mustache like a little
fringed curtain, thin lips stretched into a semi-smile.
Leaning over the case I check out his baby pictures and a
family tree done in India ink on a length of curling parch-
ment. I'm about to move on to the Glass Gallery when a
brown-tinted photo catches my eye. A young man sitting
on a beach. He's got on one of those black bathing suits
that look like long underwear cut off at shoulder and
thigh. His dark hair's long and swept back off his forehead. The card says CHAUNCEY R. SLOPE, THE BEACH
AT DEAUVILLE, 1923. I can't believe it. He looks so
handsome, profile set off by the dark sea.

His diary lies open in the next case, along with some
letters on thin blue paper. His writing's long and slanted
and hard to decipher, the words like small boats sailing
into the wind. One page though is neatly printed in block
capitals:

> I LOOK ON LIFE AS A CHAMBER WHICH WE
> DECORATE AS WE WOULD DECORATE THE
> CHAMBER OF A WOMAN OR YOUTH THAT WE
> LOVE, TINTING THE WALLS OF IT WITH SYM-
> PHONIES OF SUBDUED COLOR AND FILLING IT
> WITH WORKS OF FAIR FORM, AND WITH
> FLOWERS, AND WITH STRANGE SCENTS, AND
> WITH INSTRUMENTS OF BEAUTY—PATER.

Imagine having a father who said things like that. Imagine calling him Pater. Really old-fashioned but kind of
neat.

The letters aren't very interesting. Written to his
mother mainly. A couple are to somebody named Theo,

which sounds like a boy's name but the letters make me think it must be a girl's nickname. Lots of talk about love and lots of descriptions of the sea. The sun rising from it, the sun setting into it, sometimes the sun just hanging there in the sky. Pretty awful.

In the last case a three-page biography of Chauncey R. Slope. Depressing. Nice at first though. Rich parents, sent abroad to study—Oxford, the Sorbonne, Heidelberg, all before World War One. Paris, Berlin, the Riviera afterward (but no mention of what he did during the war). "The Great Crash of 1929 led to a reversal of the Slope family fortunes. Chauncey Slope returned from abroad in 1931 and for the rest of his life devoted himself to rebuilding the family enterprise. In 1942 he established the Rosamund Hatter Slope Foundation for the Arts, in memory of his beloved mother. The Slope Gallery opened in 1946, one year after Chauncey Slope's untimely death."

Untimely. Christ. The guy was fifty-six. What I can't figure out is how he went from being the handsome young man in the brown-tinted photo to the old guy on the pedestal outside the director's office. I'd rather shoot myself than end up looking like that, especially after starting out so well.

The Glass Gallery's pretty junky. A lot of it's like the stuff Grandmother Fortman keeps on the sideboard in her dining room—ruby glass goblets, Belleek and Waterford decanters and candlesticks, tinted or clear glass twisted into swans or gondolas or something. But on a plain black pedestal at the center of the Glass Gallery stands a vase that gives me a chill every time I see it. Nearly two feet high, it's perfectly clear, a little wider at the brim than at the base. On one side a shimmering school of fish swim upward. Near the base an unopened oyster lies half buried in the ocean floor. On the other side a naked boy glides downward across the glass. Silvery white, he's part of the glass but also stands out from it, not etched but like he was blown along with the rest of the vase. I don't know how they did it. Maybe he was carved on after the vase was blown. It's called the "Pearl-fisher."

I close my eyes and run my hand over the slick glass. My fingers know the raised swimmer by heart—his wet curls and smooth brow, the edge of the knife clenched between his teeth, the arching back, the star-shaped indentation at the base of his spine, the way his thighs . . .

"Please don't touch the . . . why, Jared Mc-Caverty!" Mrs. Mandle stands in the doorway. She smiles and most of her face disappears so that all that's left are these great big horse teeth and a lot of wrinkles.

"Hi, Mrs. Mandle. No one was at the sales desk when I came up."

She touches the big yellow velvet bow at the neck of her dress. "You gave me quite a scare. I didn't recognize you at first. I thought you were someone who had just wandered in. My, but you're growing so tall." She clicks her false teeth twice. The small yellow bow in her hair bobs up and down. "Sometimes we get the strangest characters in here, you know. They slip right in and you don't even know they're there until you go to close up and—"

"I didn't realize it was so late."

"You take your time. It's just going on five. Charles won't be coming for me till half past."

"That's okay, Mrs. Mandle. I was just going anyway."

I follow her back to the sales desk. Same old stuff in the sales display case: pewter candlesticks, delft tiles on small brass easels, a greenish bust of Nefertiti, a black Maillol bather perched on a rock. A rack of postcards stands on top of the display case—The Great Paintings of the World.

I spin the rack to see if there's anything I don't have already. There isn't. I'm flipping through the print bin when I notice the Christmas cards.

"Aren't they lovely?" Mrs, Mandle looks up from counting the cash box. "They just came in today." They're beautiful. Only two designs—the three Magi on their camels, dripping jewels and silk, set against a crimson brocade background, and an angel in a white feathery robe blowing a long gold trumpet, surrounded by a border of antique gold. Mrs. Mandle lowers her voice to a whisper. "You know who painted them? Mrs. Kennedy. Watercolors you know. So talented. Of course she must have done them before he was . . . before she lost him. So terrible. Both of them so young and those two beautiful children. Like a bad dream."

I have to have them. "How much are they?"

"Twelve dollars a box."

"Maybe I'll just take the angel. It's nicer anyway."

"With your member's discount I could let you have both boxes for twenty. And it's for a good cause. UNICEF, I think, or was it UNESCO? It's there on the back."

She carefully writes out the receipt, tongue pointing out the corner of her wrinkly mouth. "The new director comes Monday. I hope you're planning to come to the welcoming reception Friday."

"Have you met him, Mrs. Mandle?"

"Oh, yes"—her false teeth click again, twice—"when he flew in for his interview. He's ever so nice.

From the East too, of course, but nothing like Mr. Bilodeau. Nothing at all."

Mr. Bilodeau was the old director. He and Mrs. Mandle never really got along, not after he tried to abolish the sales desk. ("We're running a museum here, Mrs. Mandle, not a flea market.")

"Yes, he's a very pleasant man. Quite knowledgeable too. I'm sure you'll like him."

Mrs. Mandle takes forever making change, getting half of it from the tin cash box, half from her purse.

I'm halfway down the long stairway when she calls after me. "Don't forget the reception, Jared. Six to nine. Semiformal."

Grandmother Fortman's house is one of the big old columned-and-balconied places over on Yew Terrace near Indiana State Normal University. Only place on the block that isn't a frat house. Looks just like one though—all it needs is a pair of neon Greek letters over the double door.

Saturday's Brigid's day off so Grandmother Fortman lets me in herself.

"Not on the lips," she says as I bend to kiss her. She's terrified she's going to die from somebody's germs.

I follow her into the front parlor. The fire's crackling in the grate. She always keeps one going from late August to early June. The room's heavy with heat.

Grandmother makes a big deal of sitting down in her overstuffed platform rocker. Takes about five minutes she's so unsteady.

"Your mother called to say Sally's coming to pick you up but so's Christmas." Grandmother rattles her throat at her own joke. "I don't know how you people live the way you do. Crisis and chaos all the day long, people rushing hither and yon and now your mother with that poor old dog. Why she doesn't have it put down is beyond me. It's against nature to let a dumb animal suffer so long."

Wish I'd taken the bus. I always forget how truly awful she is until I'm in her house half a minute.

"Don't fidget the antimacassars, Jared. Last time you were here you bent every pin nearly in half. Took Brigid all afternoon to straighten them out.

"And don't go playing with your bangs. Twisting and pulling at your hair like that you'll be bald by the time you're twenty, just like your grandfather. You grow it long in front like that just so you can play with it, don't you? Makes you look like a girl. Maybe you ought to have been born a girl. Then you could grow your hair as long as you wanted."

No good talking back to her. She just finds something else to pick at.

"You getting fatter or is it that sweater? I worry your little belly's going to keep getting fatter and fatter till it pops. Then where will you be? And that big bottom of yours, sticking out like the back end of a bus. Can't you hold it in, honey? Only one worse than you is that Sally. She came in here the other day in a skirt you wouldn't believe, so short you could see the top of her nylons. If I had legs like that I'd want to disguise them, wouldn't you?"

Nothing to do but ride it out. She wears down eventually. I've got ways of passing the time till she does. One is, I sit quietly and look around the room figuring out what I'll take when she finally croaks. Not the mother-of-pearl picture of Westminster Abbey over the mantlepiece. Slope's probably gets that anyway. And not the Chippendale dining-room set I can see through the doorway. Sally's already laid claim to that for her trousseau. I want the things nobody else cares about—the feather painting hanging over her rocker of a little dark-skinned boy leading a flock of geese, the lacy silhouette of plumed ladies taking tea in an old-fashioned room with striped wallpaper and maybe the set of paperweights too, except for the ugly modern one with the real rose inside.

A second way of passing time at Grandmother's is watching it. Or more like not watching it. I tell myself I won't look at the eight-day clock quietly whirring on the side table until five minutes have passed. Or ten or fifteen. I usually get it right on the nose.

"I don't know where that girl has got to." Grandmother cranes her neck around to see the clock. "That's the trouble with both of you. Has anyone ever seen such a brother and sister? No sense of time, keep a body waiting forever. What do you care? You're young, you've got all the time in the world."

When she gets onto time it's clear she's running down fast. Pretty soon it's not the time I waste but the time she waits.

"You children don't know how lonesome I get here. How slow the time goes. The days when nobody comes to call at all." No use reminding her people don't want to come because when they do she always tears a strip off them. For not coming more often, for playing with their hair, biting their nails, eating too much or not enough. But it'd take a pretty stupid person to point this out to her because anytime anyone criticizes her she breaks down and cries. She's bound to cry anyway, of course; it's part of the visit. Today I try to head her off at the pass.

"You know you have a lot of visitors, Grandmother. And you go out a lot. To church and Eastern Star and the D.A.R."

"Oh, honey, I know." She's softening fast now, lower lip quivering. "People are so good to me. Ever since Fred's been gone they go out of their way to carry me here, fetch me there. And me so feeble they have to creep along by my side." In the twenty years or so since Grandfather's been dead she's never learned to drive. Too late now anyway, but she never even tried. Once in a blue moon she'll call a taxi.

"I've tried to lead a good Christian life. It hasn't always been easy. It's horrible having to depend on people all the time for the least little thing. Makes me feel so old and useless. But people are so good. I only hope I can be deserving of their goodness. Your poor mother . . ."

That's my cue. I excuse myself and hurry out into the hall and up the front stairs to the bathroom. When she gets onto mother it's cloudburst time for sure. First she talks about how perfect mother is and always was and then to prove it she always winds up by reading the essay mother wrote back in college called "My Mother." Grandmother keeps it in a small silver box on the low table next to her chair. It's been unfolded and refolded so many times it's closer to lace now than paper. Grandmother starts out in her quavery voice: "My mother was thirty-six when her first daughter, Marianne, was born. Marianne was three when she died of diphtheria. Every night my mother prayed that she would be allowed to have another child. My mother was forty when I was born. The doctor warned her she was too old to bear a child safely but my mother . . ." It's right there that Grandmother starts weeping and can't go on. At least not right away.

I stay up in the bathroom for as long as I dare, opening cupboards and taking the lids off decorative boxes and jars of cold cream until I'm sure she's finished.

I flush the toilet for authenticity's sake and head back downstairs.

Grandmother's wiping her drooping pickle of a nose with a black-bordered hanky. Sally sits on the leather hassock at her side, a comforting hand on Grandmother's trembling shoulder.

Sally drives home fast, hitting three lights in a row on the tail end of yellow. Doesn't say a word till we reach the city-limit sign.

"You're such a shitty little coward, Jared Mc-Caverty. Leaving Grandmother alone in a state like that." She thinks she's so cool because she's in high school and has her driver's license. No point in trying to explain I left the room before Grandmother pulled out the essay and her hankie.

"McCaverty, what's the drill?" Miss Tilley coughs a little. Not a wet cough like she's got too much phlegm but a dry one like she hasn't got any.

"Special homeroom study hall, Miss Tilley, so you can finish your grading."

"Carry on, McCaverty. I don't want to hear a peep out of anyone till the bell sounds."

She opens her black spiral gradebook and starts in on a pile of bluebooks. I'm about two paragraphs into the principal exports of Paraguay and Uruguay when she raises her big head. "McCaverty, it's hotter than Hades in here. For God's sake give us some air." I get up from my desk and use the stick with the iron hook at the end to open the top panels of the tall windows a little way.

Miss Tilley was in the army back in the war and a lot of that's stayed with her. She's about as wide as she is high and loves bright colors. Her lipstick's cherry-red and a little off her lips, her suit jacket's magenta with big puffy sleeves. The chartreuse skirt with gold threads running through it looks like it belongs to a suit jacket, only not the one she has on. She missed the first six weeks of the semester. Sick leave. When she came back she looked pretty much the same except her skin hangs differently now, like slipcovers so old they've gone loose on the chair.

Today, like every day since she's been back, she's got a scarf knotted around her neck. Yellow-and-orange streaks and splotches on some kind of filmy material. When she swallows or coughs the knot bobs up and down and the scar shows. It's pretty long and deep enough to fit a pencil point in and trace it down. She uses lots of powder on it. Only makes things worse. The red edges show through the white powder like a second set of lips. Vertical ones.

"What are you staring at, McCaverty?"

"Nothing, Miss Tilley."

"You're supposed to be studying."

"Yes, Miss Tilley."

She puts down her chrome-plated fountain pen and surveys the class. "Martinson, your spine is not a noodle. Bopp, for your sake I hope that's your cud you're chewing and not Beechnut. And Fitzhugh, you know better than to put anything smaller than your elbow in your ear.

"Just look at you all. A sorry bunch if ever I saw one." She leans back in her chair like she's really starting to enjoy herself. "I'm not saying this just to devil you. If you don't shape up now, I worry about what's to become of you in later life. I want you to think about your lives and where you're headed instead of just grazing around like beasts of the field. I know you think I'm just an old woman who doesn't know anything but if there's one thing I've learned in my sixty-odd years on this planet it's that . . ."

The door opens. A little guy comes in. Miss Tilley cocks her head back to survey his entrance. He stops midway between the door and her platform.

"Is that how you enter my chamber?" She's smiling real big.

"Huh?"

"Huh! Are you man or beast?"

"What?"

"I asked a simple question."

"Ma'am?"

"That's better. At least now we know you've got some manners. Now tell me, how does a gentleman enter a lady's chamber?"

He thinks about that a while and then answers in a voice so low only Miss Tilley and the front row can hear. "I don't know."

Miss Tilley lowers her voice too—to a stage whisper that bounces off the back wall. "A gentleman knocks before entering a room."

The little guy tries a small smile. "Yes, ma'am. I'm Randy . . ."

Miss Tilley waves one puffy hand in the air in front of her. "I'm sorry but I don't hear you. I can't even see you. Not until you enter my room in the proper manner."

The little guy stands there a moment like he can't believe this is happening. Then he looks at the rest of us for the first time, like he's expecting some kind of help. We look down at our books. Most of us. He turns on his heel and walks out the door, carefully closing it behind him.

We wait an eternity. Then: *rap-rap-rap,* like wood striking wood. The door's glass panes rattle.

"Enter!" Miss Tilley calls, looking pleased. He comes in and walks over to the edge of her platform. He's trembling a little all over.

"And who might you be?"

"Randy Sparks, ma'am." His voice is even lower than before. Close to a growl. "They sent me up from the office."

"And why did they send you up, Sparks?"

"I'm new, ma'am. A transfer student."

"You are, are you?" She pauses and we wait for her to say something really mean, but she doesn't, probably because he doesn't look like he's ever going to cry. "Welcome to the 9B3s, Sparks, best homeroom in the whole school. Sit yourself down next to McCaverty there. He doesn't bite. You'll show him the drill, won't you, McCaverty?"

"Yes, Miss Tilley."

He sits down, scrunching way down in his seat and stretching his legs out as far as they'll go, which isn't very far, but far enough so I can see his shoes—black, pointy-toed, scuffed, with built-up heels, Cuban heels, the kind everyone wore back in the seventh grade when the Continental Look was big. The socks are the worst though, green and fuzzy, like moss growing up his ankles.

Miss Tilley looks over the top of her steel-rimmed half-glasses. "If you're going to be a 3, Sparks, a 9B3, you're going to have to take better care of your spine than that. The vertebrae are delicate things, almost like . . ." *Hack-hack-hack,* she starts coughing like a dog with a chicken bone caught in its throat. Her jowls flap up and down and her face goes really red. Tears run down her powdered cheeks. *Hack-hack-hack.* Suddenly the red drains right out of her face. She stands up, sway-ing a little. She can hardly talk. "Carry on, in silence, while I . . ." She starts coughing again, bending nearly double as she staggers out the door.

Everybody starts talking at once. Jimmy Stripling leans across the aisle and knocks Sherri Watson's books to the floor. Ronnie Leyman makes farting noises by cup-ping his hand under his armpit.

Randy Sparks is sitting up real straight now, hands folded on the desktop. He doesn't have any books or notebooks. They're small hands, monkey hands. Not pale, white and long-fingered like mine but light brown with stubby fingers and pink nails. I watch the second hand on the clock over the blackboard and tell myself the next time it passes twelve I'll say something to him. It passes twelve three times. "She's not so bad, once you get used to her. She's like that with everyone."

"She think she's hot shit or what?" His lips pull back so it's hard to tell if he's smiling or snarling. His teeth are tiny and milk-white, like two rows of sweet corn.

"You're from around here?"

"Nah."

"Where you from?"

"Michigan. Ann Arbor. Moved here Friday." That explains a lot. Maybe that's how they still dress up in Michigan. Not even Continental when you get right down to it. Just plain hood. Too-tight, too-short black jeans, no belt. Paisley shirt looks like someone ran it up on a sewing machine. The buttons are too far apart and the collar's more like a big wrinkle than a collar. He wears the top button buttoned too, like a farmer.

"You don't know anyone around here?"

"Nah, but I'm used to it." He juts out his chin. I try

to picture how he'd look in a Princeton cut, short in back
and on the sides, long and swept to one side in front.
Probably wouldn't work. His hair's way too long and
awful thick, too, curling down over his shirt collar in
back, curling around his small brown ears, spilling in
loose curls over his forehead. Strange color—dark brown
and yet almost gold everywhere it curls, like a jar of dark
honey held up to the light.

"You move around a lot?"

"Ten schools in eight years." He pulls back his lips
again and wrinkles his nose.

"Wow. How come you move around so much?"

"My mom's a teacher."

"What kind?"

"University. She's just got a job at Indiana State
Normal. Somebody died. That's why we had to move
here in the middle of the year."

"Really?"

"No, I just made it up to entertain you." He turns
and looks straight at me for the first time. His eyes are so
narrow you have to look close to see what color they are
—pale brown with flecks of green and gold. "What's so
funny?"

"I don't know."

"Oh." He hunches down in his seat again. His shirt
puckers across his shoulders. If it's washed one more
time, next time he yawns or stretches it's going to split
right down the back.

"What's she teach?"

"Music."

"What kind?"

He stretches his legs out and looks over the edge of
his desk to see if his feet are still there. "What do you
mean, what kind? Music's music."

"I mean does she teach a certain instrument or something?"

"Piano and harp."

"Really?"

"That all you ever say?"

"I've never known anyone who played the harp."

"Lots of people do."

"I guess. You play an instrument?"

"Not anymore."

"You used to?"

"French horn. In Ann Arbor. They had a real orchestra at my school."

"We've got a band. They're always looking for people."

He curls his lip. "Great. Always wanted to march in a parade."

"What's your father do?"

"He's dead."

"I'm sorry."

"No big deal. He died when I was two."

"Oh." Still. Life must be pretty lonely for a guy with no father, a guy who lives with his harp-playing mother, moving from town to town, from school to school, never staying in one place long. Must be hard for a guy like that to make friends. Must be rare for a guy like that to have even one good friend.

I wander downstairs at eleven, wondering why no one called me for church. Sally's at the kitchen table, putting away a loaf's worth of French toast. The radio's blaring gospel and Mrs. Krapo's tearing around the room, beads and cardigans flying. She always wears at least three men's sweaters over her Sunday black, which is about six inches longer in back than it is in front. Lay-

ers of pink, baby-blue and white petticoats hang down
well beyond the dress, almost grazing the tops of her
translucent plastic high-heeled galoshes. Within, her
white patent pumps show like bones in an X ray. Once
she took the galoshes off and right away caught cold so
now she wears them all day every day. The beads, like the
sweaters, come from Woolworth's, clacking strands of
lumpy pink pearls, blue crystal chunky as rock salt,
smoky rhinestones. Three strands minimum weekdays,
Sunday beyond counting.

"You ready for some French toast too, Jared?" Mrs.
Krapo smiles, showing worn-down ridges of gray gum
and three stubby teeth.

"I think I'll just have tea and toast. Where is everybody?"

"Tea and toast—you a growing boy?"

"Jared's on a diet," Sally mumbles, a trickle of syrup
running down her chin.

"Diet!" Mrs. Krapo throws her hands in the air and
spins around so her petticoats flare way out. "Not in my
kitchen. Sit right down there, Jared McCaverty. There's
still enough scrambled eggs and hash browns to fill you
up without fattening you out."

"Why didn't somebody call me? It's almost noon. I
could have slept all day."

Mrs. Krapo slides a willowware plate in front of me.
I reach for the catsup.

"God, Jared, you are so sick." Sally throws down
her napkin, scoots her chair back noisily and heads for
the back stairs. I'm sick? In five minutes she'll be up in
our bathroom shoving two fingers down her throat.

Mrs. Krapo leans against the big black range, cup of
coffee in hand.

"Where is everybody?" I help myself to some cornbread.

"Your father's out in his workshop. Your mother's
in her room. Sleeping I hope. She had a terrible night.
Terrible. When I got up she was asleep on the daybed in
the morning room. And with no cover or anything. She'd
spread the afghan over Lady Jane, who was stretched out
there on the floor beside her, dead as a doornail.

"I made her come into the kitchen where it was
warmer. You could tell she didn't want to leave that dog.
Wouldn't take a bite to eat either. Oh, I wish you could
have seen her, Jared. She looked that sad."

I spread a dollop of Mrs. Krapo's strawberry preserves across a rectangle of warm golden bread. "Is Lady
Jane still out in the morning room?"

Mrs. Krapo shakes her head. "I called Clyde right
away." Clyde's our yardman. His shack's down at the
end of the orchard, close to the tracks. "He came up in
his own sweet time and carried Lady Jane out to the
compost heap, complaining to beat the band."

"He left her on the compost heap?"

"Not on it. Next to it. All covered up and everything. Promised he'd bury her this afternoon. His rheu-
matism's acting up. Again." Mrs. Krapo clucks her
tongue.

I climb the stairs to my room, cornbread holding me
back every step of the way. I can hear Sally retching in
our bathroom.

I lie on the window seat a long time. The willows
around the twin ponds look gray and dead. A white film
of ice covers the twin ponds like the skin on cold soup.
The grass is no color at all.

Finally I get up and go over to my desk. I lay out my

new Christmas cards in two neat stacks, angels on the right, Wise Men on the left. Angels for friends, Wise Men for all the rest. I get out my calligraphy pens and a bottle of gold ink.

I sign all the Wise Men first. They look pretty good —a big slanting J, tail hooked at the end, the M and C fat with loops. Then I do the envelopes—Grandmother Fortman, Grandma and Grandpa McCaverty, Miss Tilley, Mrs. Mandle at Slope's.

That leaves the angels. I make a list of fourteen girls at school who'll think they're wonderful. Boys? Last year I handed out thirty cards and got sixteen back, all from girls. Most of the guys don't give out cards at all, and the ones that do don't to me. Jimmy Herscowitz, the president of the student council, passed me an envelope in study hall last Christmas. I thought my popularity was really on the rise. When I looked inside it was the card I'd given him shredded to confetti.

I start to address an angel to Randy Sparks but blow the C. Too flowery. He might think it was weird anyway, getting a card from somebody he's just met. I tear up the envelope. Then I tear up the card. I tear up four more cards and four envelopes just to see how it feels.

Sunday lunch is late and pretty quiet. Sally and I sit on either side of the dining room table pretending we can't see each other. When Father finally comes in from his workshop he's wearing an old lime-green dental gown with grease all down the front. He wouldn't come to the table like that with mother here, but she's still in her room.

"You think I should go knock on her door and see if she wants anything?" Sally says to Father as Mrs. Krapo offers around a platter of fried chicken.

"I think she's better off left alone," Father says, spearing the biggest leg on the platter with his fork.

"You could stand outside her door and bark and whine. That might bring her out."

Father turns to me, knife in hand. "Jared, someday that mouth of yours is going to get you into a lot of trouble."

He says that a lot. The other thing he says a lot is, The mouth is the filthiest orifice in the human body. I know that's hard to believe, considering the competition, but he claims there are more different strains of bacteria in the mouth than anywhere else.

After lunch he goes back out to his shop. Sally takes mother's Buick and heads off to cheerleader practice. I go back up to my room.

Don't feel much like studying. American history is so boring. No kings or queens or beheadings or anything. Don't feel much like reading either. *Silas Marner* gives me a pain. Finally I go down to Father's den and sit down at the piano. With one finger I pick out "The Lover's Concerto," which is actually by Bach. It sounds nice, even if the piano hasn't been tuned in my lifetime. I open the piano bench and root through the sheet music, most of it from when Mother still played: "You Made Me Love You (I Didn't Want To Do It)," "Bewitched, Bothered and Bewildered," "Mood Indigo," "But Not For Me." And a thick purple book called *Easy Classical Favorites,* all of which look pretty hard to me. I can read music and pick out bits of songs I like but that's about all.

Near the bottom of the stack I find a tattered copy of "Stormy Weather." Mother played that a lot when I was little. I pick out the melody with my right hand. "Don't know why, but I'm feelin' kind of blue, stormy *wea*-ther, since that man and I . . ."

I plunk through the melody four, five, six times. Then I start in on the left hand. Even by itself it's hard, with all that syncopation. I don't know how long I've been loping through the same four bars when the door opens and mother comes in. She's wearing her long blue quilted robe.

"I wondered who could be playing." She smiles with her lips pressed together. She comes over and rests one hand on my shoulder. I try not to squirm but it's so creepy. She never does that. Never. Nobody does in our family and I'm happy to keep it like that.

"I was bored."

"It sounds nice. Especially the melody. Real feeling to it."

"You think so?" I look at her sideways. Her eyes are a little puffy but she seems calm.

"Yes, it sounded very smooth."

"It really needs tuning."

"Still, it sounded nice."

"I was thinking . . ."

"Yes?" She leans in close.

"I was thinking I might like to take piano."

"Really?" She looks down at my hands resting on the yellowed keys. "Do you want me to give Mr. Buhasz a call?"

"Not Mr. Buhasz. He's for kids. I want a real piano teacher."

She suddenly cocks her head like she's listening for something. A dog barking, for instance. "Yes, I can see that. I suppose you are a little beyond Mr. Buhasz."

"I'd like to learn Bach and Mozart and stuff like that."

"That might be nice." She's losing interest, I can tell. Her eyelids slowly droop to half-mast. "I know Jane

Prince's daughter takes from Dr. Program at Indiana Normal."

"Someone at the university might be good," I say. "I can ask around at school. Someone must know."

She seems happy with that. She gets up and trails toward the door. "You ask around, Jared." The door shuts softly behind her. I can hear Rex and Louis hurrying to her side, tags jingling. They weren't house dogs until Lady Jane got sick. Now it's hard to turn around without falling over them.

Miss Tilley trundles across the room and sags into her chair with a big sigh just as the late bell rings. Her lipstick's so far off today it's like she's got a whole other mouth. Behind the plum-and-orange scarf the scar looks rawer than usual.

"Something catch your eye, McCaverty?"

"No, Miss Tilley."

"If there's nothing to look at, don't look. Didn't your mother ever tell you that?"

"No, Miss Tilley."

"Then she wasn't much of a mother if you ask me."

Everybody giggles at that until she pounces again. "What about the rest of you? Exams coming up and you still have time to lark about?"

Books open, pencils are taken up, heads bend in silence. I have to know.

"Miss Tilley?"

"What is it?" She rears her head back like an old horse about to snap.

"You forgot to call the roll."

"Thank you, McCaverty. Mustn't forget the drill. Discipline is all." She coughs twice. Sounds like she's got her phlegm back. "Write that down everybody. Discipline is all." She opens her black leather gradebook. "Abernathy, Anselm, Billings, Bolling, Bopp, Cadman, Dollard . . ."

She reaches the end of the roll and snaps the book shut.

"Miss Tilley?"

"What is it, McCaverty?" She looks real tired.

"You forgot Sparks."

"Who?"

"Sparks, ma'am. The new boy."

"Oh, him. He was a mistake, McCaverty."

I won't ask. Won't give her that satisfaction.

She smiles. Lipstick on her teeth too. "Gone to the happy hunting ground."

I sit real still, gritting my teeth.

"You know where that is, McCaverty?"

"No."

"No, what?"

"No, ma'am."

"He's gone to the 9B9s."

The 9s! It must be a mistake. The 9s aren't accelerated. They aren't even normal. The guys all take shop and the girls get homemaking and secretarial science. Slow kids. Mainly Negroes and what Grandmother Fortman calls PWTs—Poor White Trash. Has to be a mistake.

"Don't know what the front office was thinking of when they sent him here," Miss Tilley says, wrinkling her nose like there's a bad smell. "Before they even had his test results. You ask me, it's a hell of a way to run a railroad." She stops for a second and stares right at me. "Excuse my French. Let's get on with it, McCaverty."

I open *Masterpieces of World Literature:*

From the bank and from the river
He flashed into the crystal mirror,
"Tirra lirra," by the river
Sang Sir Lancelot.

It isn't fair. Meet somebody you like, somebody who could be your best friend, and something like this happens. I can't believe it. I'd like to take my book and throw it at Miss Tilley. I'd like to run out of the room, slam the door so hard the glass shatters and the whole room's sprayed with it, people with glass in their eyes and sticking out of their skin. Blood everywhere.

I look down at my book:

And sometimes through the mirror blue
The knights came riding two by two:
She hath no loyal knight and true,
The Lady of Shalott.

Mrs. Mandle stands at the top of the stairs looking like a wrinkled little girl, big teeth gleaming, black velvet bow bobbing in her silver curls. Her lace-trimmed black velvet dress falls to just above her puckered knees. Her white knee socks sparkle with sequins, her black patent Mary Janes catch the light.

"Isn't this exciting, Jared?" She takes my camel's-hair coat and hands it to her husband Charles. "You've met Charles, haven't you?" Charles smiles vaguely toward the ceiling and shuttles off toward the cloakroom. Charles used to run the bar at Slope receptions until Mrs. Mandle decided they'd better hire professionals.

"You must see the guest book." Mrs. Mandle's voice is light and breathy. "One hundred three entries and it's not even eight yet." The guest book is Mrs. Mandle's special province. At the end of every week she goes through it copying out entries from the Comments section onto little file cards she keeps "for future reference." Most of the comments don't amount to much: "Why don't you have another show of covered-bridge paintings?" or "The palms in the Long Gallery need dusting!" At the end of the week she also carefully erases obscenities and other insults scrawled by groups of schoolchildren dragged through Slope's by their teachers. One hundred three signatures is more than Slope's usually gets in a good month.

Charles comes back, still holding my camel's hair, looking confused. He whispers in Mrs. Mandle's ear.

"You'd better go in and mingle, Jared," she says, "There seems to be some problem with the hangers."

I edge into the Central Gallery. It reeks of hairspray and cigar smoke. Board members, members-at-large, honorary members, ordinary members—they all stand packed together, women in long silky gowns or short sparkly ones, men in good dark suits, one or two stuffed into rusty-looking dinner jackets. Waiters in short white coats crisscross the black marble floor carrying silver trays clinking with champagne glasses. A big Christmas tree stands at one end of the room, flocked white and dotted with gold electric candles. At the other end the big refectory table's pushed up in front of the door to the library. Two men stand behind it pouring drinks. That's one of the best things about these boring receptions: I can get a drink without anyone asking how old I am. Usually everyone's too potted to care.

I'm squeezing my way toward the bar when a big hand clamps down hard on my shoulder. "Jared, my boy . . ."

Senator Cyrus "Cy" Proffitt's red bulldog face looms over me.

"Hello, Senator Proffitt." He's a golf buddy of Father's. He's only a state senator, not the real thing.

"So who do you think it's going to be this year, Jared—Honey Creek or Tech?"

"Gosh, I don't know, Senator Proffitt. They look pretty evenly matched to me."

He moves his huge head in close so I can smell the bourbon on his breath and count the pores on his swollen nose. He grabs my upper arm and wrenches it. "Don't you believe it, my boy. Tech's going to whip their fairy asses." He's breathing heavily, sweat streaming down his flabby cheeks. If he fell down dead of a heart attack right there on the marble floor I'd spit on his bloated corpse.

"You may be right, Senator Proffitt."

The bartender eyes me suspiciously. "What'll it be, sonny?"

"Chivas on the rocks with a splash." That shuts him up.

I take my drink and stand between two potted palms, back to the room. Brushing back a palm frond I examine a landscape. A nightscape really, very dark, all the colors running together and not much as colors to begin with. The hills are flat brown, dim blue streaks make a river, purple clumps and clots are bushes and trees, specks of yellow scattered like salt are stars. The tag says HIGH DESERT AT NIGHT: TAOS (1960). Letting the palm frond snap back in place I move on to the next one. More brown, less blue and purple. THE DARKLING PLAIN: TANGANYIKA (1958). Through the crowd I can make out another whole wall hung with dark paintings. Totally depressing. The frames are nice though. Not like any frames I've ever seen at Slope's, where every picture's usually surrounded by gobs of goldleaf plaster. These are almost not frames at all, just the thinnest bands of silver and gold.

The smoke in the room's thickening. People seem to be enjoying themselves. Lots of them are laughing loudly. No one's looking at the art, which is just as well. A woman in a shimmery gold dress does a little dance in front of the Christmas tree. Step, step, kick, step, step, kick. She stumbles and falls into the tree but two men right her before she does any real damage. The woman kisses the two men, leaving red smudges on their shiny cheeks.

"There you are, Jared." Mrs. Mandle glides up in her Mary Janes. "I do want you to meet our new director. Now where can he have gone?" She takes my hand and tows me through the crowd. Her fingers are bony and cool. "He's been so keen on meeting you, you know," she calls over her shoulder.

We find him in the Glass Gallery, standing next to the "Pearlfisher," champagne glass in one hand, cigarette in the other. An ashtray overflows onto the "Pearlfisher" 's pedestal. The Cardinal sisters, in identical red dresses, form a half circle around him, laughing at something he's just said. Two of the Cardinal sisters, Bennie and Cynthia, are married but everyone still calls them the Cardinal sisters anyway. Ned hasn't gotten married yet although she almost did. She was engaged to Dr. Vaccaro, who was a chiropractor and a real runaround. They found him last summer in his ransacked apartment, shotgun wounds in his throat, shoulder and left buttock. The coroner ruled that Dr. Vaccaro had killed himself in a fit of double-jointedness.

Ned looks like she's gotten over it. She's laughing even harder than Bennie and Cynthia, head thrown back, blond hair swishing across her bare shoulders like a horse's tail switching flies.

". . . like this piece of art-deco trash." The new director points his cigarette at the "Pearlfisher." The Cardinal sisters laugh again. Mrs. Mandle uses her bony elbows to cut through their circle.

"Mr. Clay? Mr. Clay, I'd like you to meet—"

"Yes?" He exhales a big cloud of smoke right in Mrs. Mandle's face. Then he smiles like he's just remembered who she is. "Come and join our little circle, Mrs. Mandle. Enjoying yourself?"

"Not as much as some." Mrs. Mandle gives him her biggest smile and clacks her false teeth twice. "This is the young man I was telling you about."

He glances at me. The Cardinal sisters peer over his shoulder looking like they wish I'd go away and take Mrs. Mandle with me.

"This is Jared McCaverty, Mr. Clay."

"Oh, yes. How do you do, Jared?" He puts out his hand and I shake it, making my grip as firm as possible. Father says there's nothing worse than a dead-fish handshake. Which is exactly what Mr. Clay gives me. "This really is a pleasure. Your parents are on the board?"

"No, they're not." This time he actually looks at me, head to toe and back again.

"Jared was Slope's first student member, Mr. Clay." Mrs. Mandle says.

"Yes, yes, of course." Mr. Clay glances back at the Cardinal sisters. "Our youngest member."

Bennie whispers something to Ned. Ned whoops.

Mr. Clay gives them a look. "I'm sorry, Jared. I'm so bad at names. Not a very good start for a new man, is it? Mrs. Mandle was telling me all about you this afternoon. Our first student, uh, member."

Ned whoops again, but softly.

"You signed on when you were only eleven, if I remember correctly."

I nod.

He looks me up and down again, taking in my drink. "And now you must be what—seventeen?"

"Fourteen, Mr. Clay."

"Goodness, they grow them big here in the Midwest. That's a lovely suit you're wearing. Almost heathery."

I don't think I've ever heard a man use the word *lovely* before. But then Mr. Clay's from the East. There's also a slight twist to his voice, like he's italicizing every second word.

"Well, Jared"—Mr. Clay takes my arm and steers me toward the doorway—"I'm sure you know far more about Slope's than I do so why don't you give me the nickel tour."

Mrs. Mandle steps out of our way, looking pleased.

"You'll excuse us, ladies," Mr. Clay calls back to the Cardinal sisters, who have drawn together into a knot of blond hair and red silk.

He leads me back into the Central Gallery. His blond hair, not brassy like the Cardinal sisters' but more like wheat, falls down over one eye. He brushes it back with a long-fingered hand. "I was wondering how I'd ever get away from them. Who on earth are they?" He bends his head close to mine. His voice is raspy and low.

"They're the Cardinal sisters, Mr. Clay."

"I know that. But who are they and why on earth do they still dress alike at their age? All that red. Like a Poe story."

I laugh.

"You know the one I mean?"

" 'The Masque of the Red Death'?"

"You read that in high school?"

"I'm not in high school yet. Junior high."

"Is that so, Mr. McCafferty?"

"McCaverty, Mr. Clay."

"Very well, McCaverty. Now why don't you call me Julian? All these *misters* make me feel old."

I didn't mean it like that. Actually he looks really young although he could be as old as Father I guess. It's hard to tell with grown-ups. Imagine having a name like Julian.

He stops in front of one of the paintings with the thin gold-and-silver frames: TOLEDO AT DUSK (1961).

"So what do you think, Jared?" He takes out his cigarette pack. Not a pack, a box. Red foil with gold lettering and trim. Dunhill. Never seen anything like them.

"The frames are neat."

"Aren't they though? I chose them myself. But the painting, young man, what about the painting?"

"It looks kind of muddy to me."

He looks up at me over the flame as he lights his cigarette. His Dunhill. His eyes are gray, pale gray, almost no color at all.

"Muddy, eh?" He blows out a stream of smoke. "Muddy! You can gaze on this, on this dark night of the soul, on this bleak embodiment of human despair, on its sheer pictorial expressiveness, on the exquisite barrenness of the composition, and all you can say is *muddy*?"

His eyes get big and his nostrils twitch. He starts to walk away from me. Then he smiles, teeth yellow and streaked as the keys on mother's piano. "Muddy it is, Jared. But please don't say it too loudly, for these"—he makes a sweeping gesture with his Dunhill to indicate the entire gallery of dark paintings—"these are the, how shall I put it, the handiwork of the estimable Lucille Cabot-Bostwick and she's standing right over there." He tilts his head in the direction of a small gray-haired woman whose beige dress hangs on her lumpy body like a potato sack.

"Who's she?"

"Lucille Cabot-Bostwick is a bright new talent on the American art scene. Not by any means on account of what you see displayed before you here but rather because of her grandly hyphenated name." He lowers his voice to a respectful whisper. "You know, of course, who the Cabots are?"

"The Cabots only talk to the Lodges and the Lodges only talk to God."

He gives another flash of the piano keys. "For a young fellow you certainly do get around. And her husband's the venerable Charles Worthington Bostwick, advisor to three Presidents and special envoy to the United Nations."

I look back at Lucille Cabot-Bostwick sipping her champagne. She still doesn't look like much.

"And this"—he gestures at the room at large—"is my inaugural show at Slope's. Mrs. Cabot-Bostwick may not cut an overly impressive figure, although that frumpy dress practically screams old money, but her husband is grateful for whatever attention one gives her. You'll notice he's not in attendance tonight. We display her muddy paintings for a couple of months and in the spring Mr. Charles Worthington Bostwick sends us a genuine Titian. Not a major Titian, mind you, not even a very large one, but a genuine Titian nevertheless. A lovely young girl. Obviously patrician. Not a redhead, alas. In fact her hair's nearly as dark as yours, but her veil, young man"

—one beautifully manicured finger taps my lapel—"her veil is pure Titian red, with Venetian gold trim."

"A real Titian!" Sure beats School of Rubens.

"And that, Mr. McCaverty, is what the museum business is all about. Tit for tat, so to speak."

I look about the Central Gallery. "That sure puts this in a totally different light, Mr. Clay."

"Doesn't it though?"

He heads over to the bar and comes back with another Chivas for me and a glass of champagne for himself. Then he drags me through the rest of the galleries, demanding to know what I think of this or that painting or statue. Most of the time he tells me what he thinks before I get to say anything at all. He takes an absolute fit over the "Pietà." Sometime later, after my third Chivas, we end up back at the sales desk.

A skinny young woman's sitting right on top of the desk. I'm about to warn her that Mrs. Mandle will snatch her baldheaded if she catches her sitting there like that when Mr. Clay says, "And now, young man, let me introduce you to the prize of the collection. This is my wife, Dorcas."

Dorcas. Her hair's shorter than mine, her green beaded dress's shorter than Mrs. Mandle's. She looks a lot younger than Mr. Clay. Her handshake's a lot firmer too.

"Hello, Jared. You showing Julie the ropes?"

Julie! I can't help giggling.

"Aren't you sweet." She italicizes as much as he does. Her face is sharp and kind of pointy, like a little fox's. She turns to Mr. Clay. "Got a fag?"

He offers her a Dunhill and lights it carefully with his red-and-gold lighter. He lights one for himself too. They exhale elegantly, blowing narrow streams of smoke above their heads so that the two streams intertwine. It's neat when married people have something they enjoy doing together.

The past couple of days Miss Tilley has been feeling so poorly she sends me down to the office with the attendance slips. I don't mind. Anything's better than sitting in that stuffy room listening to her cough. Lately she's been bringing things up. She acts like she hasn't but then she takes a hankie from her purse and dabs at her lips. It's pretty clear she's not just dabbing—she's depositing.

I make it a practice never to go straight down to the office even though Miss Tilley must know it takes ten minutes tops to get there and back. When I slip back into my desk half an hour or even forty-five minutes later she never says a word. Yesterday when I got back she had her head down on the desktop and stayed sound asleep until the bell rang. I won't say what was left behind on the desktop when she finally raised her head.

Sometimes when everyone's in class and I'm out wandering the corridors the school's like a ghost ship, mysterious and echoey. Today it's nothing, just long dim hallways smelling of sweat and steamed cafeteria food. Today even the glass-fronted display cases full of brass and silver trophies and faded team photos don't do much for me. Boys in old-fashioned basketball uniforms, tracksuits, football jerseys. Boys with big grins and slicked-back hair and knotty arms. Lots of them must be dead by now. The Honor Roll over the main staircase lists in gold letters the ones killed in both wars. A mural runs on either side of the stairs. On the right-hand wall men stripped to the waist work in front of a great fiery furnace. Huge gears, pulleys and levers nearly crowd the men off the wall. On the left side of the stairs the same men are wearing khaki uniforms and they hold bayonets to the throats of fat men in black tailcoats with big diamond stickpins in their striped ties. The fat men hold up their hands. Their eyes bulge. They look like scared pigs. The artist's signature is down in one corner along with the date. The signature has faded almost to nothing but the date's still clear: 1919.

The office is at the top of the stairs. I knock on the frosted-glass door. No answer. I open the door and there he is, sitting on the bench.

"Hi."

He looks up. No one's behind the wooden counter.

"Where is everyone?"

He nods toward the inner door, the frosted glass printed with black letters: DR. IRWIN VANDERKROON, PH.D., PRINCIPAL. "In there."

"Are you in trouble?" He's wearing exactly the same thing as the first day I saw him—faded paisley shirt, pegged black jeans, pointy-toe shoes. The 9B9s certainly haven't done him any good. Hoods every one of them.

"Got caught fighting." He turns his head so I can see his cheek. It's red and slightly swollen. His left eyelid droops. A purple scab, oval and raised like an Egyptian scarab, has formed on his forehead.

"What's the other guy look like? I . . . I wondered what had happened to you. After the first day I mean."

He looks down at his pointy shoes. "I got put in with the dummies."

"I'm sorry."

His chin shoots out. "What for?"

"Because I don't have anybody to talk to now."

"You'll get over it."

He can be so rude. "What are they going to do to you?"

"I don't know. Suspend me probably. They—"

Dr. Vanderkroon's door opens and Mrs. Hemp comes out, glasses spinning on a beaded chain. "You can go in now, Sparks."

He stands, hitching up his pants. "See you."

"See you."

He saunters through the doorway. Doesn't even look afraid. More like he doesn't care one way or the other.

Mrs. Hemp smiles at me as I hand over the attendance slips. "What a day, Jared. Poor Dr. V. Some days I just don't know how he stands it. Just one thing after another. And some of these kids. Honestly, I just don't know."

I agree with Mrs. Hemp that Dr. Vanderkroon has a rough time of it. The old turd. When I get back to homeroom Miss Tilley's wide awake and hacking away.

Father dresses down to go shopping. Thinks he'll get a better deal if people think he can't afford much. Even has a special shopping get-up—baggy old maroon trousers, shiny at knees and crotch; navy-blue high school football sweater gone at the elbows and lint balls all over; mud-colored moccasins, Indian beading half off; the doe-skin jacket he bought in Jackson Hole, Wyoming, the year I was born, pockets so bagged down with clock parts and tiny screwdrivers they gape like hungry mouths; old moleskin hat with the brim turned down and a yellow feather in the band. None of this ever fools anyone—everyone in town knows who he is and how he spends. Cash on the barrelhead from the thick stack of bills he keeps in a ratty old pigskin wallet.

To complete the look he drives the old wood-paneled station wagon he ordinarily uses only to haul antique clocks he's picked up at auctions. And he always insists on waiting till Christmas Eve to shop.

"Why Dr. McCaverty, what a surprise. And Jared too." Frida, the head saleslady at the Bon Ton, bustles up and down the racks and along the display cases pulling out half a dozen suits and dresses, an armload of purses, cascades of scarves and belts, gloves and jewelry.

Father chooses the plum wool suit, an indigo knit ensemble and a royal purple cocktail dress. From long experience Frida knows he buys only from the purple spectrum. I think she throws in some bright greens and the occasional red just to make him feel like he's choosing. She's preselected the accessories, so they match up quickly. Out comes the wallet. "If she doesn't like them she can always bring them back?" He asks that every year. "Of course, Dr. McCaverty." Frida waves us out the door. Eleven minutes from entry to exit. A new record.

Out on the sidewalk I automatically head for Swan's Way to help him pick out stuff for Sally, but he stops. "I've already taken care of Sally's Christmas. I think we'd better split up now." Fine with me. He's obviously off to pick out stuff for me. Anyway, it's embarrassing walking around downtown with someone dressed like that. "You want to meet up back at the wagon in an hour or so?" He says it like he hopes I won't.

"That's okay. I've got a lot to do. I'll take the bus home."

The bus terminal stinks like a giant urinal. An old Negro lady sits with two little kids on a wooden bench under the grimy front window. The kids are asleep. She looks like she's about to cry. Maybe she's just tired out too. I'd hate to be poor.

I walk over to the magazine stand at the far end of
the snack bar and pick up an *Argosy*. On the cover a
blond girl in a torn white dress is chained to a post. The
headline "ZULU CAPTIVE!" runs in red across her
thighs. I put it back and take down a *Sun Era* from the
top shelf. People playing volleyball, deck tennis, shuffle-
board, and every one of them—fathers, mothers, kids—
buck naked. Kind of exciting but kind of gross. I look
over to see if the old man who runs the snack bar is
watching. He's filling the salt shakers. I reach up to the
top shelf again and take down a *Physique*.

The guy on the cover looks about eighteen. Blond
and tan with beautiful teeth, he leans against a tree, arms
stretching above his head to clasp the trunk. Looks like
an uncomfortable position but it makes his biceps bulge.
He's not completely naked. They almost never are. He's
wearing a jockstrap, except not like the jocks we wear for
gym. Just a pouch really, white as his teeth against his
golden skin. And just a little fringe of hair peeking out
over the top.

I gather up a *Time* and a *Saturday Review* and, putting the *Physique* on the bottom, walk over to the cash
register. The old man comes over, brushing salt from his
hands. I stand there while he reads the price on *Time* and
carefully punches a key on the register. I'm sure he can
hear me breathing. He inspects the *Saturday Review* and
punches it up. He picks up the *Physique* and stares at it
for a long time. Shit. He's never said anything before but
this time he's going to ask me for an ID, I just know it.
I'm thinking about leaving the magazines on the counter
and tearing out of the terminal when he says, "I don't
know where they hide the prices on these damn things." I
point out the little red sticker over the "i" in *Physique*.
He rings it up.

"I suppose you want a bag."

"Yes, please."

He rummages around under the counter, leaving the *Physique* faceup next to the register. Hurry up, hurry up. What if someone comes in? He comes up for air. "We're clean out of bags."

"That's okay." I grab the magazines, roll them into a tube and head for the door.

Sally and I are waiting above the turn in the front staircase for Father to give the signal that he's ready for us to come down. (There's still a big dark spot on the stair runner from Christmas, 1954, when Sally got so excited she lost all control.) When Father gives the word we're supposed to come bounding down so we can be blinded by the floodlights of his movie camera. Sally still does the whole bit except for peeing on the rug. She dashes across the room to the fireplace, white satin housecoat flapping open so the camera gets a good shot of her white lace baby dolls.

"Come on, Jared. Let's have a little more animation. This is the movies," Father says. I cross my eyes and stick out my tongue.

"Someday your face is going to freeze like that," Grandmother Fortman caws from beyond the floodlights. Her face already has frozen like that. She always sleeps over on Christmas Eve, dried-up old bitch.

For the record my take isn't bad. Four fifties in my stocking (from Father), along with a malacca fountain pen and a pair of jade cuff links (from mother, to go with my new suit) and Grandfather Fortman's intaglio ring. That's a surprise. Grandmother Fortman's kept it all these years in a small black velvet box in an inside drawer of her secretary along with a pink ball of Silly Putty.

When I was little she'd press the ring into the putty so I could see the impression of the Greek soldier's head. I put the ring on the third finger of my left hand and go over and kiss her fuzzy cheek. "Thank you, Grandmother. It's lovely." Sally makes a gagging sound at *lovely.*

"I was saving it for your graduation from high school," Grandmother says, eyes brimming, "but who knows if I'll be around that long." I know she wants me to say she'll be around a long time yet but I'm afraid if I do she'll take back the ring.

Mother's best present to me is a long paisley silk dressing gown. "Silk!" Grandmother Fortman cries as it slithers out of the box. "For a boy his age, Helene?" Mother says quietly that I know the value of nice things. I throw off my old blue corduroy robe and try it on.

"Looks pretty swishy to me," Father says.

He digs around behind the tree and comes out with a big brown paper shopping bag. "Didn't have time to have it wrapped." Never does. I open the bag and see he's joking. He's had lots of time. Must have bought it last summer in Chicago after I saw it in the Art Institute gift shop. The pale linen cover's stamped with thin gold letters: Frank Lloyd Wright.

I page through it slowly, looking at the pastel drawings of all my favorite buildings—Taliesin East and West, Unity Chapel, Robie House, Falling Water.

"I figured if you're really serious about being an architect, it's something you ought to have," Father says looking over my shoulder. I think about hugging him but I'm pretty sure he wouldn't like that. I'm pretty sure I wouldn't either so I keep turning pages. He stays, hovering over my shoulder until I reach the end. Then he gets up to change the film in his camera and that's that.

Sally sits in the middle of the floor surrounded by all her stuff and wearing her new white lapin chubby coat. Makes her look like a snowball. Mother sits in the wing chair and slowly unwraps each of her dresses. She holds them up for the camera and makes the proper noises. I can tell the royal purple cocktail dress is going back to the Bon Ton first thing tomorrow. Father ducks behind the tree again and emerges with a long box wrapped in red foil. Mother carefully peels off the tape and hands the foil to Grandmother, who smoothes it out across her knees.

"But the dresses were more than enough," mother says to Father as she lifts off the lid. She rustles back the pink tissue paper. I can see dark glowing fur. Looks like mink. I watch to see how she'll hide her disappointment. She hates mink stoles and won't have a mink coat because it would be "too much."

"Sable." She sighs, holding it up. A cape not a stole. She runs one hand down over the sleek fur and bursts into tears.

Grandma and Grandpa McCaverty arrive just after noon, their old blue Nash crunching up the gravel drive. Rex and Louis go wild, jumping up around the car and nearly knocking Grandma over when she gets out. First time they've shown any spirit since Lady Jane died. Grandpa's carrying a small pink paper bundle—the best of the week's bones from his butcher shop. He slowly unrolls it while Rex and Louis drool at his feet. Rex snarls at Louis, Louis nips Rex's neck and Grandma says, "Here, here, boys." They calm down right away. She opens her purse and takes out two little packets of aluminum foil. She uncrinkles them to reveal two pale balls of suet and makes Rex and Louis sit back on their haunches like polite dogs before she'll give it to them.

Everyone else arrives in short order—Uncle Fox and Aunt Lily in their new Sedan de Ville, Grand-aunt Hermione in her old Plymouth. She's brought along Mr. Popoff, the fluttery little fat man whose travel agency is next to Father's office. Aunt Lily and Grand-aunt Hermione go straight out to the kitchen where Grandmother Fortman and Grandma McCaverty are fussing over the food. Uncle Fox, Mr. Popoff and Grandpa McCaverty cluster around the bar in Father's den while he spikes their eggnogs and sprinkles the tops with nutmeg.

There's no way anyone can really enjoy Christmas dinner. For one thing it's lunch, not dinner. For another it's not even lunch since they don't manage to get it on the table till after three. (Mrs. Krapo gets Thanksgiving, Christmas and Easter Sunday off.) By then everyone's so hungry that hardly anyone says a word except "pass this," "pass that," as bowls, platters and tureens sail up one side of the long table and down the other.

As usual I get the left drumstick. I've forgotten how that became a tradition. Big tough old thing. After Father hoists it onto my plate and sends it down I saw on it a while, pushing slivers of dark meat under my yams. Everyone knows I won't touch yams but there they are on my plate year after year looking like something the dog left behind.

The oyster tradition bothers me more than anything else—who gets the most oysters in his helping of stuffing, who hardly gets any. For some reason it always gives everyone a big laugh. Uncle Fox always claims to find two big ones in every bite and makes loud smacking noises with his fat greasy lips to prove it. If I had my way he'd find ground glass.

I fill up on shoelace noodles and pocketbook rolls spread with apricot preserves. When they bring in the desserts I promise myself I won't eat all day tomorrow and have a sliver of pecan pie, a sliver of mincemeat and a narrow slab of Grandmother Fortman's date cake with burnt-sugar frosting, everything spread thick with whipped cream. And three Mexican wedding cookies. It sounds like a lot but not compared to Sally's plate.

By the time Grandma McCaverty and Grand-aunt Hermione bring in the coffee everyone's moving in slow motion. Uncle Fox undoes the bottom three buttons of his vest and belches loudly. Aunt Lily, sitting next to him, blushes. He produces a leather pouch from his breast pocket. "Mr. Popoff, will you have one of my last Havanas?"

"Oh, Fox, not if you're running low. With Mr. Castro so firmly in place you don't know when you'll see more." Mr. Popoff speaks perfect English but with a catch in his throat because he's a Displaced Person. He finally accepts a cigar after saying "I don't know if I should" three times. At the far end of the table Grandpa McCaverty looks like he knows he could and is about to say so when Father cuts him off at the pass. "Dad, you know what Dr. Barker says about cigars."

We all sit quietly for a time watching the blue cigar smoke curl around the candles in the poinsettia centerpiece and spiral up toward the chandelier's crystal pendants. Then the clocks start in. The grandfather clock in the corner bongs, nearly knocking Grand-aunt Hermione out of her chair. The banjo clock in the entry hall pings. The Belle Époque clock with the gilt statues and tiny tarnished mirrors whirs and chimes from the living room. The cuckoo clock in the kitchen chirps anemically. Grandma McCaverty looks like she's about to say something but evidently thinks better of it. Mother looks discreetly at her wristwatch. Mr. Popoff clears his throat.

"Un ange passe." Aunt Lily looks as surprised as anyone else that she's actually said something. Uncle Fox scowls at her the way he always does when she murmurs something in French. Aunt Lily taught French at Indiana State Normal until she married Uncle Fox and he made her give it up.

Grandmother Fortman looks like she missed the angel and the clocks. All through lunch she's been unusually quiet and everyone's been so grateful for that I don't think anyone noticed she's slipped into some kind of trance. Her long knotted fingers brush crumbs into interesting patterns on the damask cloth but her eyes are set and glazed. She hasn't touched her date cake or her pecan pie. I'm trying to think of something nice to say to her to jog her a little when she turns to me.

"Just look." She leans in close and whispers in my ear. "Just look what happens when you get old." One lizardy hand creeps up to the neck of her dress and starts undoing the tiny pearl buttons that run down the front. For a second it looks like she's going to bare her breast just like the Greek women we read about in *Masterpieces of World Literature.* But she stops six or seven pearls down and pulls back the cloth. A swath of liver-spotted flesh hangs from her protruding collarbones. Everybody's watching now but no one says a word. Everybody's waiting to see what she'll do next.

"This is what happens, Jared." She's stopped whispering now that she has the whole table's attention. "This is what happens when—"

"More coffee anyone?" Mother rises from her chair.

"I could stand half a cup, Helene." Grandma Mc-

Caverty says. Usually she doesn't drink coffee. Maybe today she sees the need.

"Mine could bear warming up," Grand-aunt Hermione puts in.

"I wouldn't say no to a bit more," Aunt Lily says, "but don't drain the pot on account of me."

"Must be about time for the game," Father says, getting up too. "What about it, Fox? I'll give you six points and you'll still lose."

Father and Uncle Fox head off for the den, Mr. Popoff rolling after them. Grandpa McCaverty, seeing his chance, slips into the living room. I can hear the front door softly shutting. He'll have his pipe out on the front porch with Rex and Louis at his feet, gnawing their Christmas bones.

Grand-aunt Hermione comes around the table and sits down on the other side of Grandmother Fortman. She lays one plump arm across Grandmother's sagging shoulders and says, "It's all right, Tressa. It's all right." She helps Grandmother with the tiny buttons.

The twin ponds are completely frozen over, dark as pewter. I've been thinking about getting my skates from the basement but the idea of even getting up from the window seat is too much for me.

I've got a piss hard-on but don't feel like going all the way down to the bathroom. Summer I just crank open the window and let 'er rip down the side of the sycamore trunk—that way there's no big splashing sound when it hits the ground, just a gentle hissing through the leaves. I feel under the cushion until my fingers graze the slick covers of my *Physique* collection. I've got six now but the new one's the only one I'm interested in. I slip the other five back under the cushion.

He's still smiling, still tan. Looks like a real athlete. Probably a student somewhere. California maybe. The tree he's leaning against doesn't look like any around here. Inside more of the same except the pictures are all black-and-white. Throwing a football, lying on the rim of a swimming pool, posed on the end of a diving board, hands forming a V above his head so his torso makes a V too.

I take the magazine over to my rolltop desk. In the recess behind the drawer I keep my cuff links in I find what I need. I sit on the edge of my bed and tear open the white foil packet. The smell always gets me—antiseptic and cheesy, like library paste. I unbuckle my new lizard belt. Slowly I ease the ring down. The milky white skin feels like someone else's. I run my fingers up and down its length. *Physique* on the bedspread at my side I stretch out my legs and pull the pillow over my face. I like to have something to hold on to. And kiss. Kissing's real important. I grip the satiny skin with a thumb and two fingers. Up, down, up, down—slowly, slowly until the tingling begins. I run my left hand over the sweat-beaded chest. His belly's ridged and plated as armor, the fringe of gold hair soft below. Slowly, slowly drawing down the white pouch. I grind the corner of the pillow between my teeth and run my fingers over him—the round plum of the head, the shaft's smooth length, the thick cord of the dorsal vein. The skin's warm to my fingers. I can feel the blood pulsing. His buttocks grind into the tree trunk. His breath comes fast and hard. A trickle of saliva traces down his chin. His head rolls from side to side. He's moaning deep in his throat, moaning like he's dying. Then his shoulders stiffen, his nails show white against the tree trunk. The ridges of his belly clench. His head jerks back—once, twice, three times as his pelvis bucks convulsively. Christ! I pull the pillow up over my eyes and lie back in darkness.

I'm falling. Not very far. My tailbone hits the bare wood floor. My whole spine feels like a foot that's gone to sleep.

"What is this filth? What *is* this filth?" Father's standing over me, waving the *Physique* in my face. I know he doesn't really want an answer. I lie there on the floor, knees up to my chin, the rubber clammy between my thighs.

"Get up. Get up and . . . clean yourself off. Then get your tail back downstairs. What a way to spend Christmas." He stomps down the stairs, taking the *Physique* with him.

I lie on the floor a while hoping I've broken something. I shift a little to the left. A new wave of prickling shoots up my spine. The bastard. His favorite sport: catching me at it. My room used to be the hayloft so the staircase comes up in the middle, right next to my bed. No door at the bottom and the stairs are carpeted. He can sneak right up and suddenly be standing next to my bed. All he had to do was grab my ankle and yank me to the floor.

I get up slowly and peel off the rubber. Using the sock from under the mattress I clean up as well as I can. Total paralysis of the spine would be better than what I'm feeling, the ache in the bottom of my stomach, worrying about what he'll do next. Is he going to come back later the way he usually does and use his belt? He really can't, not on Christmas with everybody here. He could wait till after everybody's gone. I wonder if he'll tell mother. Show her the *Physique*.

When I finally go downstairs it's like nothing's hap-

pened. They've taken the damask cloth off the dining
room table and replaced it with a bright red paper one.
Platters of turkey sandwiches flank the poinsettia centerpiece, which is looking kind of droopy.

Mother's passing Mr. Popoff an emerald glass bowl
of cranberries. "There you are, Jared," she says. "Did
you fall asleep?" So he hasn't said anything to her. That's
white of him. I wonder what he's done with the *Physique*.
Probably out in his workshop. He sits at the other end of
the table looking grim. Grandma McCaverty's gabbling
to him about the Christmas when he was seven, sneaking
downstairs at five A.M. to open all his presents. He
doesn't look like he's listening. Doesn't matter much. She
tells that story every Christmas along with the turkey
sandwiches.

Uncle Fox is murmuring to a round-eyed Mr. Popoff
about "native girls with breasts as big as melons." Uncle
Fox is just back from his annual African safari. Everyone
knows he goes more for the melons than the hunting,
although every year he does manage to bring back a new
animal head for his office and a new skin for the floor of
his den. Aunt Lily won't have them in the rest of the
house. Says they give her asthma. Uncle Fox kneads Mr.
Popoff's chubby shoulder and laughs. Aunt Lily, who's
been picking at a slice of mincemeat pie, gets up and
walks out of the room.

The projector clatters away throwing a blue funnel
of light across the darkened living room. I don't know
why he even bothers. Does he really think one Christmas
looks any different from another? Or one Easter, Thanksgiving, Fourth of July, birthday? Everyone doing the
same boring things year after year—running for the red
felt stockings, dyeing eggs purple and yellow and tur-

quoise-blue, eating homemade ice cream down by the twin ponds, willows swaying in the background like grass skirts.

The projector clacks, the image jumps and Sally and I come busting out the front door. Looks like Easter. Sally with a navy-blue ribbon trailing from her straw hat, me in a navy blazer, short pants and white knee socks. I must be about three. "Aren't they precious?" Grand-aunt Hermione calls from her chair by the hearth. I'm running down the steps, mugging at the camera and—*bam!*—down I go. The camera tilts down and there I am, bawling away, blood trickling from my nose. Sally's tugging at my arm. Lady Jane wags her way between Sally and me and with a long pink tongue licks the blood off my face.

"Poor Jared fall down and go boom!" Grandma Mc-Caverty says.

From the depths of her chair I can just hear mother. "How young Lady Jane looks. Almost a pup."

Once Father has the projector out he never knows when to quit, sorting through the flat tin cannisters and snapping another reel into place.

"Just one more," he says to the darkened room. "How about Yosemite, 1954?" No one answers. "Or Cuba, 1958? What do you say, Fox—our last trip together?" Uncle Fox snores away on the sofa. We get Cuba anyway.

Mother, very tan, standing in front of a chalk-white church. Little dark-skinned kids with flies on their mouths sleeping in doorways. Whole gangs of them running at the camera, dirty hands held out. Uncle Fox and Aunt Lily on a dock. Uncle Fox, hairy belly sagging over bright green trunks, sneaks up behind Aunt Lily. She's looking out at the dark water and has no idea. He makes like he's going to push her in but suddenly she turns

around—someone must have called out a warning—and
Uncle Fox throws his furry arms around her and gives
her a big kiss on the lips. She pulls away from him, blushing through her freckles and looking like she wishes he'd
pushed her off instead.

I'm lying in bed with the lights off staring at the
ceiling and wishing I hadn't eaten so much. Maybe I
should go down to the bathroom and stick two fingers
down my throat the way Sally does.

I must have fallen asleep instead. The cry that makes
me sit straight up in bed is weird and high, like a hurt
animal. I pull on my new silk dressing gown and run
down the stairs. My foot catches in the hem—I've never
had a full-length robe before—and I skid down the last
six steps.

The door to Sally's room opens and she peeks out,
hair up in big pink curlers, fat face white with Noxema.
"What's going on, Jared?"

The cry again. Louder this time. Higher too. I rush
past Sally and throw open the door to their room. The
bedspread's pulled back but the bed's empty. Another
cry. Their bathroom door's angled open a little way. I
can see the big round mirror over the sink, Father in his
striped pajama bottoms, triangle of black curly hair on
his chest. Where's mother?

I push the door all the way open. She's crouched on
the floor in the narrow space between the toilet and the
tub. All she has on is bra and panties. Pink satin. Her
hair droops down over her face like a big tear about to
fall. She arches her neck and screams again. Her eyes are
red and shiny in the bright light. Tears stream down her
face and neck and streak her breasts. The scream trails

off into sobs. Her head drops. She hasn't even noticed I'm standing here.

"Go away," Father whispers. "You've caused enough trouble today."

So that's it. He showed her the *Physique*. The interfering prick.

"What have you done to her?" I'm screaming now. My jaw's seized up and my head's quivering like mad. I want to shake him, hit him across the face, bang his head against the mirror until it splits open and the mirror runs with blood.

"It was only the movies, Jared," Father says, no longer whispering. "Only the movies. Seeing you and Sally so young. Now go on back to bed."

Mother presses her cheek against the side of the tub. She's stopped crying. Hair sticks to her wet cheeks like cobwebs. "It's all right, Jared. I'm sorry. I didn't mean to wake you."

I back out of the room. Only the movies. I guess. But not Sally. Not me. I'm pretty sure of that. Only the late Lady Jane, coat thick and sleek as sable, nose so long and fine, tongue pink and alive, licking away the blood.

Father wheels the Olds into the granite-paved courtyard, turning a tight arc around the big wrought-iron sundial at the courtyard's center. As I'm getting out he looks up at the big house. "Don't break anything. They might make you pay for it."

The first thing he's said straight at me since Christmas. I think I prefer the silent treatment. Now that he's talking again, sooner or later he's going to bring up the *Physique*.

The big wooden door swings open before I can lift the tail of the bronze mermaid knocker.

"Hey, Jared."

"Hey, Marc." At first it's hard to tell it's him. Going away to school sure has changed Marc Himmel. At least his hair has gotten a lot longer. Way down over his ears. And his acne's gotten worse, if that's possible.

"Nice hair."

"You like it?" He shakes his head from side to side so his hair flares out some, sprinkling dandruff onto the shoulders of his black turtleneck. "Betty hates it. Says it makes me look like Rasputin." He belches happily. I step back. Too late.

"Sorry. Too much garlic for dinner. Arab cuisine's Betty's latest thing. Ed hates it." Betty and Ed are Marc's parents. They're very modern. They even dropped the -*farb* from their name so they could buy a house in Allynvale. I'd do almost anything to live in Allynvale too. Father says it's pretentious. He thinks it's so neat to live in a remodeled pre-Civil War barn. Says it's more original. Except once he got finished fixing it up our barn looks like any other house. Inside at least. From the outside it's still a barn but with too many windows and no silo. I've always thought it would be a lot more original if it looked like a normal house outside and a barn inside. With everyone sleeping in stalls. Like animals.

"How do you like boarding school?" I ask, slipping out of my camel's-hair coat.

"It's all right." A fat Negro woman in a gray uniform appears out of nowhere. Marc hands my coat to her and she heads up the wide curving staircase with it draped across her outstretched arms. "Except it's all guys."

"Oh."

"Everyone's downstairs." He opens a door set into the entry hall paneling so it's hardly noticeable. Screams and the sound of splashing echo up the narrow spiral staircase. So does the throat-clenching smell of chlorine. Brass torches with flame-shaped electric bulbs are bolted to the curving stone walls. I follow Marc down.

Nobody's ever liked Marc Himmel much, not even before he went East to school, but everybody always comes to his annual New Year's Eve party. At the bottom of the stairs kids swarm all over the long low-ceilinged basement room. Not that it looks much like a basement anymore. Corinthian columns line the walls with hand-painted (by Betty) murals of Greece in between. It's hard to make out the Parthenon for all the kids crowded in front of the long snack table, which is loaded down with bowls and baskets of Kurly Karm-L Korn, Kurly Cheese Wheelies and Kurly Ridgies. Ed Himmel owns Kurly Potato Chips. They're sold throughout the tri-state area. At the far end of the pool kids are lining up at the bar for cherry phosphates and brown cows, or cannonballing and belly flopping into the pool so water splashes high into the air and slaps down on the white tile floor.

Marc and I are the only ones still in clothes. Guys run past us in flowered baggies. Girls in bikinis and ruffled one-piecers stand about in small groups. The colors look extra bright against their skin, which is fish-belly white.

"Looks like a circle in Dante's Hell, doesn't it," Marc says casually. That's probably the way they talk at boarding school all the time. I know who Dante is. They've got *La Divina Commedia* in the library at Slope's with these amazing engravings by Gustave Doré. But there sure isn't much opportunity to talk about Dante or anything else in this town. When he was still going to school with the rest of us Marc wanted to be my friend. He's really smart but he usually smells bad and he

belches and farts a lot and thinks the sounds his body
makes are absolutely hilarious. Besides, practically all he
ever wants to talk about is girls.

"Dressing room's through there. I better get back
upstairs."

A girl in a pink gingham bikini dashes past me
screaming. Half a dozen guys charge after her, wet feet
slapping against the ceramic tile like applause.

I stand in front of the wall-to-wall mirror over the
row of pink marble sinks. From the front it's hopeless.
Always is. The lumps at my waist look bigger than ever
even though I haven't had practically anything but tea
and toast since Christmas. From the side it's not too bad
if I stand real straight and try not to breathe much. I find
a stack of towels in the cupboard next to the steam room.
Huge towels, the same deep blue that's used on the Kurly
Potato Chip bags. I drape one of the towels around my
neck and let the ends hang down. Not bad. Hides the
lumps completely and doesn't go badly with my royal
purple baggies with the scarlet piping.

The door swings open behind me. He's in the mirror.

"You got a safety pin or something?"

"A what?"

"A safety pin. For my trunks. Look." Randy Sparks
pulls out the waistband of his khaki trunks. I can see
right down. Flat belly with its tight navel like a tiny bud.
Thickly curling honey-colored hair. The curve of brown
flesh sprouting out of it.

"My mom bought them for me. Today. I didn't even
have time to try them on. It's embarrassing. On account
of the girls I mean."

"Maybe in here." I yank open one of the drawers
beneath the sinks. Band-Aids in a blue-and-white tin box,

rubber bands, a stopwatch on a black cord. And a small disc-shaped plastic box. "Needles!"

"Great. Now all we need is someone who knows how to sew."

"I know how to sew."

"You do?"

"Yeah, they taught us how in Scouts." I wouldn't join the Scouts if they paid me—the uniforms are so ugly. He doesn't have to know that. Mrs. Krapo taught me how to embroider when I was real little.

"You're a Scout?"

"Not anymore. Didn't like it much."

"Me neither." He smiles a little, showing his tiny teeth. "So what are we waiting for?"

"Thread."

He grabs the box from my hand. "Shit! Every size needle and no thread. Maybe I should just get my pants and—"

"There must be something here." I start pulling open more drawers. Plastic combs, hair-clogged brushes, pink rubber noseplugs, gray wax ear stopples, a squeezed-out tube of Pepsodent, two rusty razor blades, a fraying roll of dental floss. "Floss!"

"Huh? Oh yeah, smooth idea."

"Stand still." I kneel before him and with a rusty razor blade slice the button off the waistband of his trunks.

"What'd you do that for?"

"Just hold still." I thread a yard or so of floss through the needle with the biggest eye. The floss keeps splitting and peeling off. I move the button an inch and a half to the left.

"You're not going to prick me are you?"

"Stand still, dammit." My hand's shaking more than

he's moving. I run the needle and floss back and forth through the four holes of the bone-colored button, my knuckles grazing the warm flesh of his belly. He's brown all over, even in December. The veins on my wrist stand out blue against my white skin like shadows across the moon.

"You really think this is going to work?"

"Why wouldn't it?" I give the button a tug. "Just let me knot the thread . . . floss." I bite off the ends, my bangs falling softly against his belly. "There." The word catches in my throat. I cough. Stand up.

"Hey, that's great." He buttons his trunks. "Thanks a lot, man. You saved my life."

"Any time." In clothes, in homeroom, in the principal's office, he looked small, kind of lost. In khaki trunks he looks just right. Like one of the Greek statues in the Sculpture section of the *Encyclopaedia Britannica*, every muscle right on the surface, perfectly outlined, perfectly curved, about to burst. Even his hair looks right, not too long but curling down over his forehead and down the brown column of his neck like a warrior's helmet.

"Let's go for a swim." He puts one hand on my shoulder and guides me toward the door. I flinch. Always do when people touch me. He takes his hand away.

"I didn't know you knew Marc."

He grins. "I don't. I came with some other guys. They don't know him either so I figured it would be cool. You a friend of his?"

"Not really." I follow him through the crowd to the pool edge, watching the muscles shifting across the broad triangle of his back. He jumps in feet first. I dive after him.

The water's warm. Randy bobs up next to me squirting water through his teeth so it sprays my face. "Race you to the other end." He pushes off the side of the pool, arms pinwheeling, legs thrashing wildly. Swims like a statue too. I dive beneath the surface and skim along the turquoise bottom. I can see his body frantically churning above me. I've been swimming since I was three when Father taught me how by throwing me into one of the twin ponds. What he called the sink-or-swim method. I swam. It's the only sport I'm good at. In water I'm sleek and weightless, capable of anything. Everything. Scissoring my legs three times I leave him far behind. Three more scissors and I'm hanging by my arms from the low diving board.

"What'd you do, take a taxi?" He's gasping for breath, chest pumping up and down as he holds on to the pool rim. "You're really fast, man."

"I've got my Senior Lifesaving."

"Really? Already?"

"It's not that big a deal."

"That's not what I heard."

I let go of the diving board and slowly scull water at his side. "So how do you like it here?"

"*Here?*" He looks up at the blue ceiling.

"Living here."

He pushes a clump of wet curls off his forehead. "It's okay, I guess. Kind of quiet."

"Yeah, *quiet*'s the word. How's your mom like her new job?"

"I don't know. All right, I guess. Why?"

"I don't know. I was just wondering, you know, her teaching music and all—does she give private lessons?"

"Sure. Anything to make money, right? You know someone who's looking for lessons?"

"Me."

"You got a harp?"

"Piano."

"Any good?"

"I can read music."

"That's a start."

"And I've always wanted to take piano."

He shakes water out of his ear. "I don't know if she takes beginners. I could ask."

"Really?" My voice cracks a little.

"Sure. Why not?"

He hoists himself out of the pool, biceps rounding big as oranges. "I'm starved. Let's get something to eat."

I pull myself up onto the slippery rim feeling my stomach sag. Where did I leave my towel? Too late to worry about that now. I pad after him, arms crossed over my stomach.

"It'd be nice to be rich," he says shoving a fistful of Karm-L Korn into his mouth.

"Yeah, I wouldn't mind having a pool in my basement." I take three Ridgies and a Wheelie and promise myself that's it.

"Where do you live?"

"Out near Creve Coeur Park."

"That in the country?"

"Sort of. Where do you live?"

"Just off The Boulevard. On Cherry. It's temporary."

"You're not moving again?"

"We're only renting. My mom bought a lot on a lake out near Diamond. We're going to build there if her contract's renewed. A real log cabin."

"Neat."

"It's a beautiful lake. We've got more than an acre. And no one else has built on it yet. Real wilderness."

"Sounds great. You want to get something to drink?"

"Sure."

We head back to the other end of the pool threading our way through knots of dripping screaming kids. Half hidden behind a Corinthian column Jimmy Stripling spikes his cherry phosphate from a silver flask.

"I could go for some of that," Randy says.

"Me too."

"You got anything?"

"I wish."

"I don't know anybody here to buy for me."

"If I'd thought, I'd have stolen something from my father's liquor cabinet."

"My mom doesn't drink much."

"Too bad."

"I'll say."

He asks the white-jacketed Negro bartender for an Orange Crush. I order a brown cow without the ice cream. "You on a diet?" The Negro chuckles showing his white teeth. I don't think he means that smile at all.

The girl in the pink bikini comes shrieking by again. "Save me! Save me!"

Four big guys—they have high school written all over them—come pounding after her swinging soaked blue towels over their heads like soggy propellers.

She grabs onto Randy's bare shoulder and screams in his face, "Don't let them get me!"

They run straight for her.

She ducks under Randy's arm, knocking his bottle of orange crush to the floor. It shatters, orange fizzing across the shiny white tiles.

"Get her!" one of the towel-spinning guys shouts. They dive for her.

Randy steps to one side and says, "Ouch."

"Watch out," I say, which sounds pretty silly since he's already stepped on it.

"Stand still," I say, crouching down. It doesn't look like it's gone that deep.

He looks down at me. He lifts his foot and stares at the long splinter of glass sticking out of his heel.

"You want me to pull it out?"

"Sure. It doesn't hurt at all."

I take hold of his ankle with my right hand. I touch the splinter carefully with my left. It doesn't give. I pull on it and my hand slides right off. A thin red line opens along my index finger. I lick off the blood and tug at the splinter again. Randy bites his lower lip. I ease it out as slowly as I can. It's in deeper than I thought. At last it slides free. For a moment I can see inside him—a small white vein, pale and smooth as an albino nightcrawler within the split dark skin. Then the blood spurts out hot across the palm of my hand.

The girl in the pink bikini bursts into tears. The four guys say *"Hey!"* in unison, lift Randy up and carry him over to a chaise longue. Marc Himmel comes rushing up. He's changed out of his black turtleneck and black cords into—it's not exactly like the pouch on the guy in my *Physique* but it's close.

"What's happening?" he says and I get a whiff of garlic. The guys move out of the way so he can see. Marc looks at Randy's foot and the pool of blood soaking into the blue canvas cushion. "Oh, my God," he says and throws up all over the white tiles.

One of the four guys knots a towel around Randy's foot and carefully elevates it on a stack of blue cushions. Somebody else goes upstairs and finds Betty Himmel. She comes downstairs with the doctor who lives next door and in twenty minutes Randy Sparks is all bandaged up but still a little green around the mouth. Betty Himmel tells the bartender to take care of the mess and she and the doctor help Randy hobble up the winding stair.

The party doesn't amount to much after that. Marc Himmel recovers enough to do jackknives off the low board and a little while later two guys and the girl in the pink bikini go skinny-dipping in the deep end. I wait a while and call home.

"That was one short party," Father says as I get into the Olds. "What happened—somebody steal the silver?"

"A guy got cut."

"Badly?"

"I don't think so. It was an accident."

"That's what happens when you horse around."

I keep my left hand in the pocket of my camel's-hair coat. Don't plan on washing it till I absolutely have to.

JANUARY

When he said they lived just off The Boulevard I assumed Randy meant one of the little crescents where the houses are all connected but nice anyway, with green shutters and window boxes. I hadn't realized how close to downtown Cherry Street is. It doesn't even curve.

The house is tiny and flat-roofed, about the size of a Dairy Queen, set way back on a narrow lot. Whoever built it was aiming for Spanish. Gray stucco walls, greenish tiles over the little bay window and a brown wooden porch about as big as a closet set in under a green tile awning.

I press the doorbell and wait. I lean my head against the door to listen for the chime. Nothing. I press again. Maybe she forgot I was coming. A dirty white Corvair stands in the cinder drive looking like a washing machine on wheels.

I knock hard. I roll my sheet music into a tight tube. Something rattles on the other side of the door.

"Just a sec," a faint voice calls. The sound of scraping wood. The door opens an inch. I can see red hair, lots of it. "I'll stand back and you give it a big shove. On three. One. Two. Three!"

I hit the door with my shoulder and fall into the house. My sheet music goes all over.

"I'll get it." The red hair swoops down toward the flagstone floor. A wide mouth comes up smiling. "Jared?"

"Dr. Sparks?"

She laughs, shaking the hair back off her face. Small teeth for such a large mouth. "Mrs. Sparks. I'm just an instructor. Most people call me Bobbie-Anne. Sorry about the door. Humidity."

"I'm glad you brought your own music." She leads me into the front room. It looks like it's supposed to be a living room except there's no sofa or armchairs or tables or anything. Just a big piano, a real grand, stretched out in front of the bay window. The front half's painted robin's-egg blue, the rest is pale unstained wood.

"Wow!"

"You like my piano? It used to be Liberace's. At least that's what they told me at the auction house. Who else would have a Steinway that color? Anyway, it's the only way I could afford a real grand. Randy's stripping it for me, *poco a poco.*"

She's even shorter than Randy. Her pale green dress looks like something a medieval princess would wear, floor-length and kind of gauzy with a scooped neck that shows pretty much of her freckled breasts. The black horn-rimmed glasses sort of spoil the princess effect though.

"Sit down, sit down." She pats the black tufted leather bench. "We're just going to play around today so I can get an idea of where you are and where you ought to be heading. You want to start with what you brought?" She opens out the music on the stand. " 'Stormy Weather'! My, I haven't heard that one in years."

She folds back the keyboard cover. "You go ahead and warm up. Take your time."

Warm up? I move the music slightly to the left and cough. I put my hands on the keys. She looks down at them. God I wish I could stop biting my nails. The Band-Aid on my left thumb pretty much hides the worst of the damage but the nail on the little finger is so stripped away there's hardly any nail left, just raw red flesh.

"Am I making you nervous, Jared?" She jumps up from the bench. "I'll stand over here and you forget all about me. Pretend you're at home practicing on your own."

Practicing's practically all I've been doing since New Year's Eve. I don't even need the music now. I've played it so much Mrs. Krapo whistles along from the kitchen if I forget to close the den door. She even repeats the right notes when I get stuck.

Fuck warming up. I give the left hand everything I've got. What sounded tinny and flat on the Fischer upright at home comes out like thunder on the big baby-blue Steinway. When the right hand comes in, pianissimo, it's like rain. The bare room resounds like a big echo chamber.

In places I know I'm going too fast. I hit the sustaining pedal a lot to smooth out the tricky stuff. Once I get completely lost and she says very softly, "That's okay. Start again whenever you feel sure of yourself."

By the last page I'm really tearing along, left hand not seesawing so much but really rolling along, right hand almost singing. I know I'm swaying on the bench like a real idiot. The bench creaks along with my swaying but I don't care. I let the music carry me through to the last crashing chords. They seem to pound on and on even after I lift my fingers from the keys. A drop of blood glistens on one of the keys. I quickly wipe it away.

Mrs. Sparks walks back to the piano very slowly. "How long did you say you'd been taking?"

I thought I made that clear on the phone. "I haven't. They taught us to read music at Gifted Children's Summer School when I was in sixth grade. We had a recorder ensemble. But the music's my mother's. She used to play. I picked it out a little at a time."

"You picked it out?" She laughs an ascending scale. "But you must have worked for weeks."

I don't know what to say. I know I'm awful. She doesn't have to laugh at me. I don't care what she thinks anyway. I know why I'm here. Who I'm here for. She can make fun of me as much as she wants as long as she doesn't tell me it's hopeless. As long as she doesn't say she can't take me on.

She sits down next to me again. "Jared, this is truly amazing. To work all that out on your own. Of course you don't have any technique at all but that's what makes it all the more unusual. Such gutsy playing. And you did it all through sheer will, didn't you?"

I nod.

"You really do have a passion to learn. Anyone can see that."

She wasn't making fun of me. Isn't. She bought it.

"You understand it's probably too late for you to become a serious pianist? To be really good you have to start very early."

"I don't care about that. It's just something I've always wanted to do."

"But why haven't you had lessons before?" She looks straight into my eyes. I hate it when people do that but I make myself look right back. Just like his, narrow with gold-flecked irises, except her right eye is green, pale as her dress, while her left is the same soft brown as Randy's.

"My older sister took when she was little." It took old Mr. Buhasz three weeks to teach Sally the difference between the black keys and the white ones. "But she never practiced or anything so after five years or so Father let her quit. When I said I wanted to take he said he wasn't going to shell out five dollars a week so I could learn 'The Spinning Song' too."

"That's a real shame, Jared. To punish you for your sister's lack of . . . interest. You have such a good ear. You know exactly how it should sound even if you can't quite figure out how to make it sound that way."

"You don't think I'm wasting my time?" This time I look into her eyes.

"If you truly love music"—she leans in close to me so I can smell her spicy perfume—"it's never a waste. A lot of hard work certainly. I expect you to practice at least an hour a day, weekends included. And not just 'Stormy Weather.'" She props a thin yellow book up on the stand. "This is how we begin." Dark blue gothic letters spell out *Hanon's Chromatic Exercises, Book One*. "But first let me see your stretch."

I look at her blankly.

"Place your right hand on the keyboard, thumb on

middle C. Now stretch your pinky out as far as it will go." I press down. It sounds terrible.

"That's wonderful! Three notes over an octave. I'd give anything for a hand like that." She puts her hands on the keyboard. Her fingers are short and blunt, barely stretching one note over an octave. She lifts her hand off the keyboard and waves it in front of my face. "These are what stopped me. As a serious pianist I mean. No amount of practice can make your fingers longer." Her eyes look sad behind her horn-rimmed glasses but only for a moment. Her smile unfurls again. "Let's begin. Exercise one, page one. Legato. You know what that means?"

I don't.

"Liquid, Jared. Smooth, flowing. Like there are no separate notes, just one long uninterrupted one." She reaches up and turns on the little wooden metronome. It starts ticking, very slowly. "Begin."

I get halfway up the first scale and she stops me. "No pedal. Not for months and months, not even at home. You think I won't know but I will. Only your hands. And your back." She touches the small of my back. I shiver. People should warn you when they're going to touch. "You feel that? Good. Put your back into it. The swaying's fine too if it helps you to feel the music."

I sway up and down scale after scale, major, minor, right hand only. She shows me how to arch my right hand instead of just laying it on the keys. "And keep that spine straight, even as you sway. No slumping."

After a while I've got a cramp in my right hand and my lower back's starting to feel numb. But I keep at it. Nothing's going to stop me now that I'm so close. Up down up down, sway sway sway. Pretty boring after crashing through "Stormy Weather" but even scales sound nice pouring out of a Steinway grand.

At some point I become aware of another sound, a muted rhythmic clanking like somebody somewhere's playing with a giant Erector Set. Maybe it's the furnace. Mrs. Sparks doesn't seem to notice anything but my mistakes.

I'm on scales a good forty-five minutes when there's a heavy thudding at the door. Mrs. Sparks springs up from the bench. "That must be my five o'clock. Is someone picking you up?"

I tell her my father's coming for me on his way home from the office and that I can wait for him out on the porch.

"Don't be a goose," she says. "You go on into the dining room. I'll let you know when he comes."

The dining room's almost as bare as the living room —no rug on the floor, no drapes at the window. A huge wooden table's shoved up against the window, the clothless surface dotted with glass-rings and streaked with layers of old polish. I sit down in the ladder-backed chair nearest the window. The cane seat sags and creaks.

Three doors lead off the dining room. One goes to the entry hall. Through a second I can see the corner of a bed. Actually just a mattress set right on the floor. It's covered with a purple-and-pink patterned cloth that's too flimsy-looking to be a real bedspread. A low table next to the mattress holds so many different colored candles it looks like a fairy castle crowded with towers. Wax—pink, red, purple, green, blue—has run down over the side of the table and pooled on the floor like a frozen moat.

The third door goes to the kitchen. White metal cabinets and red brick-pattern linoleum worn down to nothing in front of the old round-shouldered fridge.

A door I can't see opens somewhere near. Randy walks into the kitchen and opens the fridge. Gray sweatpants riding low on his buttocks, gray T-shirt dark with sweat between his shoulder blades and under the arms. He takes out a red plastic pitcher and drinks noisily from the beak. He puts the pitcher back and slowly turns around, wiping his mouth on the back of his hand. His T-shirt says PROPERTY OF U-MICH ATHLETIC DEPARTMENT.

I sit up in my chair. The cane seat squeaks like a frightened bird.

"You waiting for your lesson?" He's breathing hard. Sweat streams down his flushed face. Wet curls dangle down over his forehead.

"Had it. I'm waiting for my father."

"Oh." He stares down at his bare feet. His toenails look thick and hard. They need cutting. "So how'd it go?"

"Okay, I guess. How's your foot?"

"Okay." He comes over to my chair and lifts his foot so his heel's right under my nose. An oval purplish bruise surrounds a short pale scar.

"Healed fast."

"Yeah." He runs a hand across his forehead, wiping away the sweat. "I was working out."

"Exercising?"

"What else?"

"What do you do?"

"Usual stuff." He folds his arms across his chest. The veins in his forearms stand out.

"Like what?"

"You know, weights and stuff."

"You lift weights?"

"Nothing serious. Just enough to keep me in shape."

"Yeah. Where do you work out?"

"Down in the basement." He hitches up his sweatpants. "I ought to get back to it. See you."

"See you."

Father smells of mint. Cepacol antiseptic spray. For the filthiest orifice of the body.

"How'd it go?" He turns the Olds onto The Boulevard. "Can you tell the difference between the white keys and the black ones yet?"

"It was okay. She's real nice."

"She's a professor?"

"Yeah."

"She know her stuff?"

"Seems to."

The Boulevard ends at Creve Coeur Park. Instead of turning south on Appleseed Road he eases the Olds through the park's stone gateposts. Shit. This is where he always brings me when he wants to have A Talk.

He slows the Olds to a crawl. The duck pond drifts past, oily gray in the twilight. The worst part is waiting for him to say something. We ease up the hill past the Fred J. Swinney Municipal Pool. A black tarp stretches across the pool, sagging in the middle where sodden leaves and beer cans have accumulated.

"I've been thinking," he says at last as we cruise past the empty monkey house, "about what we're going to do with you." He looks off to the left like he's suddenly spotted a rare monkey. "And I have to tell you I'm really stymied.

"It doesn't do any good to hit you anymore. I know that. You're getting too big for the belt. But something has to be done. Your mother and I are very worried about you."

Christ, he showed her the *Physique.*

"No, I didn't show her that . . . *filth."* He spits the word out so hard the car swerves a little. "But we both know there's something wrong, Jared. Seriously wrong. You must know it too. You don't seem to have any friends. You spend all your time alone in your room or you go off to the movies or to that museum by yourself. You can't tell me that's normal."

I know what's normal in his book. And I don't like it. If everyone would just leave me alone I'd be fine. If *he'd* just leave me alone.

"And that . . . magazine." There, he got it out without driving us into the ditch. "That's not healthy. You can't tell me it is. I know boys your age sometimes have crushes on other boys or sometimes even on teachers. That's natural, I guess. Just a phase. But actually buying something like that." He shakes his head slowly.

The road curves past the tennis court. Pools of dirty water stand on the gray asphalt.

"You've got to help me a little, Jared, if I'm going to help you. We can't let you go on like this. Your mother and I just don't know how to reach you anymore.

"I know this is a difficult time for you, but you're not the first person in the world to be a teenager, you know. You've grown so much over the past year or so—sometimes I hardly recognize you." His eyes go all watery. "Don't you see that we've got to nip this in the bud? Don't turn away from me like that. We've got to face this together."

He reaches over and squeezes my shoulder. I'm not about to look at him.

"Please, Jared. I'm your father and I want to help. If we don't deal with this now, just what kind of a fruit do you think you're going to turn out to be?"

It just comes right out. "A kumquat?"

I see his hand coming but I don't feel it. Not really. Just my head snapping back and the ringing in my ears. The Olds tilts off the road, eating up the culvert. A tree stops us. The dash is in my mouth.

His hands are pulling at my shoulder. "Jared, Jared, are you all right?" I pull away from him and curl up next to the door. I put my hand to my mouth. It comes away red.

He cuts the engine and pulls me to him, putting a hammerlock on my neck. "Open up. Open up, goddammit!" Like I have much choice. His forefinger forces its way between my lips, pries open my teeth, probes the roof of my mouth.

"You're all right." He lets me go. "Just a cut lip." He hands me his handkerchief. It smells of mint too. I dab at my mouth. The handkerchief's dark red.

The car's tilted so much his face is right up next to mine even when I try to get away. "You see what happens when you mouth off?" He opens his door as far as he can and eases himself out into the culvert. The skinny silver birch that stopped us angles across the hood.

"You stay here," he shouts through the windshield. "I'll go to the groundskeeper's place and call a tow truck."

The whole side of my face tingles. I roll the handkerchief into a ball and press it between my lip and gum to stop the bleeding. Nothing I can do about the ringing in my ears.

FEBRUARY

Eugene pulls up at the back door while we're still eating breakfast, the tires of his '37 Plymouth spraying gravel against the side of the garage. Eugene is Sally's new boyfriend. I'd rather have no boyfriend at all than one named Eugene but he's actually not so bad, especially for someone as ugly and fat as Sally. He wears a white T-shirt, jeans and a black nylon blast jacket no matter what it's like out. Doesn't even bother honking for her. Just pulls this wire under the dash that makes the car give off this huge wolf whistle. Drives Rex and Louis wild.

Father looks up from his *Tribune-Star* like he's thinking about exploding but then he looks back down. Since the accident he's been real quiet.

"Can I get a ride with you guys?" They're still work-

ing on the Olds down at Tippecanoe Olds and Cadillac so
Father's using mother's Buick.

"We don't want you tagging along," Sally says, gulp-
ing down her orange juice.

"I don't want to tag along. I just need a ride downtown."

"You're still in your bathrobe. We can't wait." She
slams the door behind her.

"Fat bitch."

"What was that?" Father says from behind the *Tribune-Star.*

I leave the room. I hate him so much it makes my
head ache.

Mother's on the second-floor landing kneeling before
the open doors of the linen cupboard. All the inner drawers are pulled out like steps leading nowhere.

"What're you doing?"

She sits back on her haunches, embroidered sheets in
neat piles all around her. "They get musty, like everything else in this old barn." She lifts a stack of pillowcases to my nose.

"They smell nice. Lavender."

"That's the sachet. Can't you smell the sourness?
It's underneath everything."

"It is?"

"Of course it is. The only way to get at it is to make
sure everything's as clean as humanly possible. Even then
you're fighting a losing battle. Rot just creeps into everything."

"Couldn't Mrs. Krapo do it?"

"Mrs. Krapo has more than enough to do. Besides, I
like keeping busy." She pulls the bottom drawer open
wide, lugs out a stack of patchwork quilts and buries her

face in them. She comes up for air. "Terrible. And look at these stains."

All they look is yellowish to me. They always look like that. They're so old we never use them anyway so how could they be stained? No point in asking. She looks almost happy, quilts, sheets and pillowcases piled all around her.

Takes half an hour to walk to the nearest bus stop but anything's better than staying home on Saturday, *his* day off. The big green-and-yellow city buses don't run on any kind of schedule—they just run. I wait in front of the Brown Avenue Beauty Salon twenty minutes, stamping me feet to keep warm.

When the bus finally rattles up I drop my dime in the box. The red-faced driver looks at me and laughs. "Big date in town, son?" He must think my camel's hair is a little dressy for the bus.

Practically nobody from our part of town takes the bus except Negro maids going to and from work. I sway down the aisle past a big group of them and take one of the single seats across from the back door. They're all real quiet as I pass by but then they burst out talking— low mumbling sounds mixed in with rumbly laughter. I know it's all about me and my coat.

The Orpheum's packed. Little kids swarm around the refreshment stand. The birthmark that runs down the counter girl's neck is bright purple. I go up to the Royal Box in the first balcony. It's full of little boys in St. Pancreas blazers, their feet propped up on the brass rail. I end up in the third balcony—what Grandmother Fortman always calls "nigger heaven."

The Birds is a real disappointment. Very slow at the start with lots of talking. Everytime something terrible's about to happen it never does. Tippi Hedren is very beautiful with her blond hair up in a French roll. She looks kind of stiff though, like she's worried it's going to fall down. The St. Pancreas crowd gets restless real fast, running up and down the aisles and shooting Good & Plenties at one another. The first big attack quietens them down some. Neat part where the crows chase the schoolkids and this one really big bird gets caught in a little girl's hair. She's pretty homely, with glasses and everything, so it looks like the bird will peck her to death but it doesn't. Instead the crows end up getting Suzanne Pleshette, which is really sick because she's one of my favorite actresses. Besides she's the only person in the movie who isn't a pain.

The end's a real bust. Tippi Hedren and Rod Taylor and his daughter and the prune-faced grandmother crowded into that little car, just driving away. And taking those two lovebirds with them. Any normal person would have wrung their fluffy necks.

I push open the heavy brass doors and trip over a coil of black extension cord. Two-by-fours are stacked against one wall of the narrow entry hall. Sawdust films the steep black marble stairs. I can hear hammering from above.

Mrs. Mandle's at the sales desk, wall-eyed with panic. A yellow velvet ribbon dangles from her bangs. The postcard rack, print bins and glass display cases are all draped in muslin.

"Jared, Jared, Jared." *Click-click-click.* Her false teeth are going like Mrs. Sparks's metronome doing double time. "You can't imagine what it's been like."

"What's going on? What's all the banging?"

"Renovations!" Her lips pucker through all four syllables like each one tastes bad in a different way. A nerve jumps along her jawline.

"The whole place?"

"The South Galleries this week. The north ones next week although they're already *far* behind schedule." She looks hopeful for a second as she sticks her bow back into place, more or less. "You must go and see what he's doing. You know it's not my place to criticize, but . . . oh, just go and see what he's up to!"

Gray plastic sheets cover the doorway to the South Galleries. I push my way through. The Oval Gallery's empty and dark. Orange and black cables curl across the floor. A sheet of canvas covers the Long Gallery doorway. The hammering's growing louder, accompanied by sharp clacking sounds. I duck under the canvas.

A big-bellied man in bib overalls stands holding the bottom of a ladder. On the top step a wiry old guy uses a big silver staple gun to fasten acoustical tiles to a wooden frame suspended from the ceiling. At the far end of the room another pair of workmen are fitting a wallboard panel over a tall glass-brick window. Mr. Clay directs them. They look like they'd like to seal him up with the window.

"Careful. A little more to the left. No, no, not *that* far!" His voice is muffled by the white surgical mask covering his mouth. Sawdust is sprinkled through his blond hair. His gray coverall bristles with zippers, loops and pouches. Looks like something paratroopers wear in those old war films on *The Late Show*.

The men finally ease the panel into place. Mr. Clay looks over at me. "Out, out! This part of the gallery is closed to visitors."

"But Mrs. Mandle said . . ."

"Jared! I'm so sorry. I thought . . ." He pushes the

surgical mask down around his neck and fumbles with several zippers and pouches on his coverall until he finds his Dunhills and his red-and-gold lighter.

"Welcome to the new Slope Museum." He exhales a cloud of smoke right into my face.

"What have you done with the 'Pietà'?"

"That hunk of plaster was the first thing to go. I called a piano mover and had them haul it up to the storeroom. I'm afraid Christ lost his right big toe in the process. He may never tapdance again."

He's so neat. Nobody else around here talks the way he does.

"Tell me truthfully"—he waves his Dunhill toward the workmen—"what do you think?"

I look the room over slowly. What ceiling the old guy on the ladder has managed to staple into place is a good three feet lower than the original one. With the glass-brick windows sealed off the only light comes from the bare fluorescent tubes running along the perimeter of the new ceiling.

"It's quite a change."

"Yes, isn't it?" He flicks ash onto the sawdust-smeared marble floor. "We're going to drag the Slope Museum screaming and kicking into the twentieth century." He rests his Dunhill hand lightly on my shoulder, not like a jock, more like a friend. I hardly even flinch. The smoke goes right up my nose.

I smile at him through the smoke. "Are you going to do this to all the galleries?"

"Come with me." Pushing aside a canvas sheet he leads me into the Flower Gallery, a perfect cube of a room that has always been used for displaying still lifes of flowers. With the new acoustical ceiling the Flower Gallery's more a rectangle now than a cube. It smells of fresh paint. The beige walls are grooved just above and below eye level so paintings can be hung more easily. Nubby oatmeal-colored carpet covers the floor. Fluorescent lights glow behind translucent panels set into the ceiling.

"This is what we're aiming for. The ideal museum of the sixties. Pure, functional, nondistracting. A perfect machine for displaying art. No glaring slippery hard-to-keep-clean marble, no dusty old potted palms. In short, nothing to prevent the visitor from focusing all his attention on the works of art themselves."

He's so enthusiastic I don't have the heart to point out that without the distractions there isn't all that much to look at at Slope's.

I wish he'd put out his cigarette. I don't know if it's the smoke or the paint fumes but my head's starting to ache again. Not exactly my head, but my cheek, in the hollow to the left of my nose. Not ache really, more a throbbing emptiness, like the bone is being hollowed out beneath the skin.

"What's the matter, Jared? You look so pale." Mr. Clay's face is right next to mine. I can smell his hot nicotine breath but his voice sounds like it's coming from a long way off.

I'm staring at my penny loafers. They look very big and shiny and maroon. A streak of dried mud runs along the instep of the left one. Must be from my walk to the bus stop. Looks terrible. I ought to wipe it off. Something's pressing down hard on my back.

"Do you feel better?"

I try to lift my head.

"No, stay like that a minute or so."

Sure. It feels good, my head hanging down heavy between my knees, his hands massaging my shoulders.

"I feel fine," I say to my penny loafers. "Really I do."

"All right. Sit up. Slowly." I raise my head and bright pinpoints of light swirl around me. We're sitting on a wide wooden staircase, Mr. Clay one step above me.

"Where are we?"

"Service stairs. Up to the storeroom. You're sure you feel better?"

"Yeah, I'm fine." I *fainted.* So humiliating. And in front of him. He must think I'm a real sissy.

"The fumes *were* awful. I must see about proper ventilation." Mr. Clay reaches into a pocket and lights another Dunhill. "Do you want to try standing?"

"Sure." He helps me stand up. He's so nice.

"There. You've got a little color back. You really gave me a scare, my boy." He softly pats my cheeks with both hands. His palms are soft and cool. "Have you ever been up to the storeroom?"

I shake my head.

"Come on, then. You have to see it to believe it. But let's take it slow, all right?"

The wooden stairs are as long and steep as the black marble ones downstairs. By the time we reach the top I feel fine. Headache completely gone. In fact my whole head feels light, like it's filled with helium or something. The air around me looks so sharp and clear I feel like I could break off a piece of it. Mr. Clay is puffing a little from the climb.

"Et voilà!" He waves his Dunhill toward the ceiling, which is thirty or forty feet above us. Large-paned windows big as billboards stretch upward along two facing walls. The floorspace must be equal to that of the galleries downstairs except here there are no dividing walls

so it's like being in some high-roofed barn smack in the middle of the city.

"Amazing."

"Isn't it?" Mr. Clay leads me to the center of the room, the pale plank floor creaking and popping under our feet. Sunlight streaks in through the dirty windows.

"This is where Slope's should be."

Mr. Clay smiles, tobacco-stained teeth catching the the sunlight. "My sentiments exactly. I see the current renovations as merely an interim measure. Someday I'm literally going to turn this place upside down. Use those pokey galleries downstairs for storage and all this up here for display. Can't you just see it? Plain white walls, a new floor. Stained blond, I think. Interior walls on casters so we could arrange and rearrange the display areas. We'd have to do something about all this light though, otherwise the paintings would fade right out. Tinted glass perhaps. Or louvered blinds. And of course we'd have to figure out what to do with all this dreck."

So many things. Piles and piles of things. The "Pietà" 's standing over in one corner looking smaller than I remember, like a blow-up pool toy that's slowly losing its air. Big wine-colored horsehair sofas are pushed up against the walls, strewn with hatboxes, mailing tubes, shawls, rolled-up carpets. Between the sofas fat life-sized bronze gods and goddesses hold up beaded lampshades. Chinese vases that come up to my waist sprout spears and peacock feathers. Elaborately carved cabinets, cupboards and sideboards in dark glossy woods cluster in clumps. Gold-framed smoky mirrors large enough to reflect whole families lean against big army-green brassbound trunks. A long flat piano stands on curving dragon legs, looking like it could stalk around the room at night when no one's there. A black fountain in the shape of a clamshell is pushed up against a twelve-foot-tall Indian totem pole.

It's kind of sad, so many things that people owned once. Things they probably really loved. Somebody buying that piano or maybe even the totem pole and thinking, *This is absolutely the last thing I need to be complete. I'm finished.* And now that person's dead but the piano and the totem pole are still here.

Mr. Clay taps his ash into the waterless clamshell. "The kitsch of a thousand households is assembled here. If I had my way I'd bring in a bulldozer and clear it all out, but the tireless Mrs. Mandle has properly acquisitioned every stick of it so we can neither sell nor give it away."

"But where are all the paintings?"

Mr. Clay's inspecting the arrows sticking out of a bronze statue of a man writhing against a bronze tree trunk. "They're detachable you know. For easier transport. The Victorians thought of everything." He unscrews one of the arrows and hands it to me. "A souvenir of your stay at Slope's." The shaft's about six inches long, the bronze pitted and grained to look like real wood. The head isn't an arrowhead at all, just a threaded tapering screw.

"The paintings are kept downstairs in a proper storeroom off that den of knickknacks Mrs. Mandle calls the Glass Gallery. Temperature- and humidity-controlled. We wouldn't want a single Sunday painter's fruit to wither on the vine."

He looks at me from under his shaggy blond eyebrows. Half the time I think he's deliberately trying to shock me.

He smiles. "Actually the basic collection isn't that bad. Not for a gallery of this size. And in this part of the country, God knows. Old Mr. Slope knew exactly what he was doing. He couldn't afford to go after the big boys —Impressionists, Cubists and so on—so he set about buying up good examples of American work from the twenties and thirties. I haven't had time to scout around much yet, but we do have a Burchfield and a lovely Reginald Marsh, a pretty good Ben Shahn and a Tom Benton, a flashy Grant Wood and a horribly bland Hopper. I don't suppose any of these names mean that much to you."

Sometimes he can be just like any other grown-up. He's been here a couple of months, I've been coming every Saturday since I was nine. "The Burchfield's a couple of old run-down houses with an old witch walking between them. The Reginald Marsh shows two girls on a pier, wind blowing their skirts up and a bunch of sailors whistling at them. I've never seen the Shahn. Mrs. Mandle says the old director was afraid to hang him because he said Shahn was a Communist. The Grant Wood's a guy with his shirt off digging his garden. The colors are kind of glazed on, like lacquer. In the Benton a big combine's threshing wheat, with the clouds making the same curves as the furrows. The Hopper's a white farmhouse and lots of telephone wires."

I stop, feeling like an awful show-off. Nobody likes a show-off. Mr. Clay doesn't say anything for a moment, just exhales and watches the smoke drift upward. Then he laughs, throwing his head back so far I can see the gold crowns on his molars. "But that's marvelous. You know them all."

"I don't know who they all are but I know their stuff. It isn't that big a collection. And I look them up in the library sometimes except there isn't much on a lot of them."

"But you've digested so much. And you really see what you're looking at. That's obvious. How old did you say you were?"

"Fifteen." He asked me before, at the reception, and I told him the truth. If he can't remember that's his problem. Anyway I'll be fifteen in June.

"You're a funny kid, Jared." He looks at his watch. "Maybe I'd better get back downstairs and see how the work's coming along. You have to stay at them all the time."

I follow him down the long wooden stairs. He pauses at the bottom before opening the service doors to the Flower Gallery. "Would you be interested in giving me a hand here this summer? Help me sort things out? Mrs. Mandle has everything on those infernal cards of hers but there's no real catalogue, with descriptions and provenance and all that. And there are so many other things you could help me with.

"There might even be some weekend work before summer. That is, if you think it wouldn't be too much, what with your schoolwork and all. I'm afraid we can't offer to pay you very much. Minimum wage and maybe a little more."

Doesn't he realize I'd do it for free?

"I know it wouldn't be the most exciting job in the world. You'd be spending most of your time deciphering Mrs. Mandle's copperplate and running errands and helping me hang shows but . . ."

I'm so excited I drop the bronze arrow. It clatters across the floor. We both stoop down to pick it up. Our heads bang together. Mr. Clay sits down fast on the bottom step.

"Are you all right, Mr. Clay?" I give him my hand and pull him to his feet.

"Christ but you've got a hard head." He hands me the bronze arrow. "So what do you think?"

"I'm ready to start right now." I shove the arrow into the pocket of my camel's hair.

I wake up at five. The ache's back. Not just my cheek but the whole left side of my face. Feels *wrong* more than it hurts—a tingling like termites are burrowing under my skin, nibbling away at my cheekbones, building little nests behind my eye. I stumble down to the bathroom to look into the mirror. The left side of my face looks like a negative of the right. The skin's blue as skimmed milk across the hollow of my cheek but dead white around my nose and along the jawbone. A purple vein in my forehead squirms under the bright fluorescent light. I get the hot-water bottle from the cupboard and run the tap till the mirror steams over. I wrap the bottle in a bath towel and take it back upstairs.

With the bottle over my face I feel a little better. The hot rubbery smell makes me feel like I'm a little kid with an earache. The water sloshing back and forth helps block out the ringing in my ear.

"Jared, get up! We're going to be late for church."

I jerk upright in bed, then lie right back down, pressing the water bottle against my cheek with one hand, pulling the covers and a pillow over my head with the other. The bottle's lukewarm now, the towel damp against my cheek.

"Jared, come on!"

"I don't feel well," I shout from under the covers. My jaw pops from the effort.

Thud-thud-thud on the stairs. He's standing over me. "Jared, I'm warning you."

"I'm sick."

"I bet you are." He yanks off the covers.

I lie there naked and shivering, holding the water bottle tight against my cheek, the corner of the pillow clenched between my teeth. "Go away."

"Come on, Jared." He grabs at the pillow. I clamp down hard with my teeth. The termites are going crazy, gnawing away. He yanks again. I grind my teeth together and there's a bright flash of pain behind my left eye. I feel like I'm going to throw up.

He tosses the pillow aside. The hot-water bottle slows him down a little. "What's wrong?"

I hold on tight to the water bottle. "Nothing."

"Is your ear acting up again?"

"Leave me alone." I'm so cold my teeth are chattering. I rub my naked legs together trying to get warm.

"Let me see." His voice is low and gentle now. And real close.

"I'm all right. Leave me alone." He grabs a corner of the hot-water bottle. We can play tug-of-war or I can let him see. I'm too cold to play anything. I let go. He must have let go at the same time. The water bottle falls to the floor with a sloshy plop.

His finger runs lightly down my cheek. "Jesus Christ!"

I hate to say it but his office is nice—soothing. Kind of colonial, with old brick on the outside, white pediments over the windows and doors and split cedar shakes, just like the bank across the street.

Inside it's even nicer. Williamsburg-blue walls, creamy white trim. Blue tweed wall-to-wall. He has four chairs in four separate rooms with everything arranged so efficiently he can work on four patients at one time, an oral assembly line. Since it's Sunday there's only me. He puts me in the front chair, a new white leather contour job he ordered from New York.

"Here we go." He flicks a switch on a panel set into the chair back. The chair hums, slowly tilting until I'm lying flat on my back. "Not bad, huh?" He glides up beside me on a white leather stool. "This way I can work sitting down. Saves my back."

He hooks the saliva sucker onto my lower lip and takes a long look with his little silver mirror on a stick. He prods the roof of my mouth with his forefinger. "Feel that?"

I practically levitate.

"I don't know how you kept from noticing that this long. Run your tongue over it."

I carefully touch the roof of my mouth with the tip on my tongue. A bump nearly as big and corrugated as a peach pit. I poke at it gently with my tongue. It gives like a sponge and a rotten taste floods my mouth. Then a worse smell, like wet decaying leaves.

He removes the spit sucker. "I want to get some pictures of this."

"What is it?"

"Don't know yet. That's why I want to get some pictures." He maneuvers the cone of the powder-blue X-ray machine until it's pointing at my cheek. "Open." He slips the cardboard wings between my teeth. "Bite down. Gently." Clutching the remote contol he ducks behind the oak-paneled wall, which has a lead sheet underneath to protect him from the rays. "Hold still," he calls. The cone buzzes a second or two.

I offer him the cardboard wings on the tip of my tongue.

"You just relax while I run these through the developer." He flicks another switch on the chair back. The chair starts vibrating. "You want the headphones?"

I nod.

He slips the black leather earmuffs into place and leaves the room. At first nothing, only a windy sound in my left ear. At least the ringing seems to have stopped. The needle falls into place like it was dropped from way high up. It pops and fizzes as it rides the staticky grooves. *Ta-dum.* Ferrante and Teicher pounding through "Slaughter on Tenth Avenue." It could be worse. When I came in for my fall checkup it was "Ruth Wellcome and her Romantic Zither: The Great Movie Themes."

I drift along in the purring chair, watching the spinning silver balls of the mobile suspended from the ceiling. Father thinks of everything for the patients' comfort.

He comes back carrying a small metal rack of X rays. He removes the earmuffs, turns on the lightboard and lays out the tiny round-cornered negatives.

He points to one of them. "What we've got here is a large pouch of infection. Probably an incipient cyst. You see that dark shaded area over the bicuspid? The trauma of the accident may have caused it, although it could have been there before. There's an outside possibility the bone got chipped when you hit the dash. Anything—even a tiny particle of food lodged between tooth and gum—could have acted as a breeding ground for bacteria."

I brace myself. I know what's coming. Needles and novocaine, lots of cutting and scraping and blood in the cuspidor. Well, let's get it over with so I can go home.

He rearranges the X rays on the lightboard like that's going to make a difference. "The problem is, that pouch of infection has spread so deep into the upper jaw area that I can't reach it."

I'm stretched out on the recliner chair, paper bib snapped around my neck and he can't reach it?

"This is something for a surgeon to handle, Jared. They're going to have to lay open the gum and clean out the area."

"They?" A whole platoon of dental surgeons advances on my mouth, scalpels flashing.

"I called Dr. Lancet at home while I was waiting for your pictures to develop. He's making room for you on Tuesday. He would have taken you today, even on a Sunday—he's that kind of a guy—only we have to get that swelling down first. A good jolt of tetracycline should take care of it."

I squirm in the chair. "Couldn't you do it?"

"Dr. Lancet's much better at this kind of thing. You know I'm not a surgeon. People come all the way from Chicago to see him."

"I can't do it Tuesday."

"Why not?"

"My piano lesson's on Tuesday."

"I think you'd better forget about piano until we get this cleared up. In fact there's no point in you going to school this week at all."

Great. Just great.

Today I don't feel that bad. A little headachy and kind of boneless from the tetracycline but nothing serious. I read all morning. *The Fountainhead* by Ayn Rand. For the third time. Not as good as I remembered it, maybe because between the second time I read it and this one I saw the movie on *The Late Show*. Now whenever I read about Howard Roark, in my mind I see Gary Cooper. He's a big guy, just the way Howard Roark should be, but he seems kind of slow. Everybody knows

Howard Roark's a genius, an architectural genius. In the beginning though, when he's working in the quarry, it's hard to tell Gary Cooper from the rocks. Finally I throw the book aside without bothering to mark my place.

Mrs. Krapo fixes me toasted cheese and tomato soup for lunch. Afterward I go out to the den to practice my scales. After twenty minutes or so I give up. The notes sound muffled, maybe because my left ear's ringing again.

I wander around the house a while, working on my nails. Pretty soon I've got them all peeled right down to the quick. I bite away at the skin too, until the little finger on my right hand has a jaggedy red line running along- side the nail. I have to stop because it makes my teeth hurt.

I go into the morning room and leaf through old issues of *Life, Look* and *American Heritage.* The clocks are striking three when mother wanders past the window, Rex and Louis trailing after her. I start to tap on the window but she doesn't look like she wants to be both- ered. She walks on down toward the twin ponds and stands looking at the leaden water a long time. The sky starts to spit sleet but she doesn't seem to notice. She has on an old green duffel coat I don't remember seeing be- fore and an ugly flowered scarf tied under her chin. I hope she doesn't go downtown dressed like that. She looks like somebody's cleaning lady.

Tuesday morning I'm dressed and down in the kitchen before Mrs. Krapo has had time to get breakfast on the table. I didn't sleep much. The kitchen looks extra bright and unreal in the white morning light. When Mrs. Krapo scrapes the spatula across the frying pan it makes my teeth ache.

I decided to hell with my diet and am starting to slice into a big stack of flapjacks when Father comes in.

"I wouldn't do that if I were you. Dr. Lancet will be giving you a sedative, so you'd better not have anything."

Mrs. Krapok loudly sucks her gums and carries my plate over to the garbage can.

The old Rose Dispensary looks like a cross between a castle and a prison. It's eight stories high and made of rough gray stone blocks that have gone black around the turrets and arches which are scattered across the building's front like the architect just threw them in whenever he got tired of flat stone wall.

The long main hall stinks of antiseptic, like a vet's office only worse. Old men in plaid shirts and baggy pants sit on wooden benches along the dirty green walls, mumbling and hacking and spitting into tarnished brass spittoons.

An old hunchback in suspenders slides open the gate of the elevator's cast-iron cage. He has to climb up on a little wooden stool to press the button for the eighth floor. His white shirt's yellow under the arms and across the hump that bulges out right above where his suspenders cross.

"Here you go." His voice is high and cracked. He rattles open the cage door. Father doesn't say anything so I smile politely. Cripples make me so nervous.

The door at the end of the hall has DR. LANCET printed in gold letters on the frosted glass. Father presses the buzzer. "Dr. Lancet doesn't go in much for show." He's almost whispering. "He's a real old-school practitioner."

A squat woman in a pink nylon uniform lets us in.

She smiles broadly at father. "Why Dr. McCaverty, it's been a coon's age."

"Hello, Maggie. How have you been keeping?"

"Could be worse." She pats the bangs of her pageboy. Her hair's black as Shinola but her skin's almost as creased and liver-spotted as Grandmother Fortman's. "And this must be young Jared. My, what a handsome fellow you are. Take after your father, don't you? Come in and take a pew. Doctor won't be a minute." She opens the door to the inner office and disappears.

Same hardwood benches as downstairs. No magazines except an old *Field and Stream* with the cover half off. No pictures on the walls, which are pea-green to about shoulder-height and then mint-green the rest of the way up. No drapes on the big dirty windows. Dark green linoleum on the floor. An ugly little cactus with a bright red head pokes up out of a green plastic pot on Maggie's desk. No one else is waiting.

We sit up very straight on the bench. The back ends at the middle of my spine.

"You sure this guy is painless?"

Father looks ticked off. "Jared, you'll have a sedative *and* novocaine. What more do you want—egg in your beer?" He angrily crosses his legs and nearly slides off the bench.

A shadow comes up on the frosted panel of the inner-office door. The door opens. A small man comes in taking small precise steps. His freshly starched beige dental gown crackles a little as he reaches out to shake Father's hand.

"Dr. McCaverty, a pleasure, as always." His round rimless glasses catch the light from the rack of bare fluorescent tubes dangling by chains from the ceiling. His

perfectly bald head shines too. "And you, young man"—
his glasses flash at me—"I know you don't remember me
but I met you at the Dental Association Fourth of July
picnic out at Indian Mounds State Park when you were
just a wee fellow. But aren't you a strapping young man
now! Just look at the shoulders on you." His small fingers
clamp onto my arm, groping for a bicep. "Football?"

I jerk my arm away and mumble something about
swimming.

"Well, that must account for those broad shoulders." He claps his hands soundlessly together. "What
say we get started, gentlemen?" We follow him into a
narrow room, taller than it is wide. "Jared, you sit down
and make yourself as comfortable as you can while your
father and I take one last look at these X rays."

The chair looks like it's made from the same silver-
painted cast iron as the elevator cage. More like a bar-
ber's chair than a dentist's, the seat and headrest covered
with dark green plastic veined to look like marble. The
edge of the seat has worn away and bits of stuffing stick
out. I sit down. Maggie leans over me and clips the paper
bib into place. I grip the plastic-padded arms tight.

"So, a little nervous?" Dr. Lancet smiles down into
my face. "Let's crank you up a little, shall we?" He
treads down several times on a bar set in the chair base
and I rise up into the air. He tilts his work lamp this way
and that until it beams right into my eyes. Maggie wheels
up a cast-iron stand topped with a porcelain tray and
positions it right next to my jaw. A long steel syringe lies
on a white paper doily in the middle of the tray.

The silver-painted radiator under the sooty window
gurgles and hisses. It's real hot in here, maybe because
four people are crammed into a space hardly big enough
for two. I can feel sweat trickling down my spine. As Dr.

Lancet picks up the syringe I can hear Father's voice somewhere behind me. "Don't you want to give him a sedative first? I mean, there's no hurry, is there?"

"A sedative for such a small job, Dr. McCaverty? I'm just going to cut and run. We'll have Jared patched up and out of here before he knows what hit him. Right, young man?"

I open my mouth to answer but he's already swabbing my gum with a sour-tasting Q-tip. Father does that too—a little raw novocaine painted directly onto the gum eases the needle's sting.

His thumb pushes up my lip. "A little prick now." The prick isn't what I mind—it's what comes after. The needle probes deeper and deeper into the gum. Then the sudden foul taste at the back of my mouth, like I've been sucking pennies. Dr. Lancet massages my upper lip with two fingers, murmuring, "Good, good. Now one in the roof of your mouth. This one's going to sting a bit. It has to go in right where the infection has puffed out your palate."

I can feel Father's breath evaporating the sweat on the back of my neck. "Don't you think it would be better to . . ."

Dr. Lancet locks his arm under my chin. "Hold tight." The needle plunges in. I scream. Maggie jumps. Something clatters to the floor.

"I'm sorry, Jared." Dr. Lancet lays one small hand on my shoulder. He sounds like he really means it. "That was the worst, I promise you." He turns to Maggie and whispers, "No, that one's blunted now. No time to sterilize it. We'll have to go with a number three. Larger than I need but it will do in a pinch."

He massages my lip again and prods my nose with

his forefinger. My lip and nose together feel like a foot that's fallen asleep in the middle of my face.

I don't see the blade coming or feel it cut into the gum but the impact bangs my head back against the headrest. This guy works fast. I can see his elbow sawing the air as he cuts back and forth. A warm rusty taste fills my throat. The air smells salty and a little rotten. Something wet runs down my chin. "Sponge, Maggie," Dr. Lancet orders. She dabs at my chin, then my neck. The sponge comes away crimson.

His elbow goes way high again. My head bangs back against the headrest. The sponge comes cool against my chin, across my cheek, along my neck. I feel like I'm going to choke on the hot liquid in my throat. I try to concentrate on the fluorescent tubes hanging from the ceiling. One, two, three. The fourth one's dead.

His elbow angles high for another slash. I shut my eyes and brace my feet against the footrest.

He's panting now. His forehead gleams with sweat. "Never had one that squirmed so much. Give me a hand here, Dr. McCaverty. Make yourself useful." Father's hands are on my shoulders, holding me down. Dr. Lancet's voice is hoarse. "Can't you hold him still?"

I'm looking at the insides of my eyelids. They're so beautiful—delicate and translucent. Orange-and-gold veins marble them, throbbing with light. The smell of ammonia hollows out my nose. What a time for Mrs. Krapo to be doing the windows. Small hands slap my cheeks. I hear it more than I feel it. I'm not going to open my eyes. This is all too pretty to leave behind. A hand slaps my left cheek. Hard. My ear pops. My eyes spring open. Dr. Lancet stands high above me. "Lost you for a moment there. You all right?"

My tongue feels like a big dead animal. I try to answer him but my throat's caked and dry.

"He's all right. Let's crank him up again." Dr. Lancet stomps on the foot pedal half a dozen times and I rise back into the air. Father's hands press down on my shoulders until I can feel his nails. He whispers into my ear, "It's nearly over."

Dr. Lancet's arm cranes up again. My head snaps back. Maggie's given up on the sponge and is mopping me up with an icy towel. She can't keep up with the flow. The swooping blade sprays drops of blood across my forehead and into my burning eyes.

Father's whispering, "Almost over, almost over." My shoulders ache from his nails.

I'm on the floor again, voices high above me coming through blackness.

"You ought to have warned me he was such a sensitive plant."

"I still think a sedative would have lessened—"

"I didn't give my own mother anything stronger than novocaine when I—"

"Doctor, you want me to try the salts again?"

My chest feels clammy. I open my eyes.

The bib's brown with blood at the center, bright red around the edges. It's soaked right through my shirt. My favorite Oxford-cloth blue-and-pink pinstripe. Will Mrs. Krapo be able to get it out?

Dr. Lancet smiles down into my face. "So, Fainting Beauty. We've finished. Just have to sew you up and you can go home."

He cranks me up again and I don't care. I lie back in the chair staring at the fluorescent tubes.

"Cut off the ends"—*snip, snip, snip*—"and you're done."

Father puts his arms around me to help me out of the chair. I'd like to push him away but I have to concentrate on keeping my knees from buckling.

"Just look at your pretty shirt," Maggie says as she closes the door behind us.

When I open my eyes I'm lying in the backseat of the Olds. I can see bare branches of trees drifting by, gray clouds against a gray sky, black telephone wires thin as pencil lines. Most of the time I keep my eyes shut. Father folded his overcoat and put it under my head. It rubs rough against my cheek. We're going very slowly, like we're in some kind of procession. I can hear the steady breathing of the heater but I'm shaking all over. The worst is when my teeth chatter. It's like concrete blocks knocking together inside my head. I try to clench them so they won't but that hurts too.

Next thing I know the door's wide open. Cold air's rushing in one ear and out the other.

"We home?"

Father's face is right above mine. There's a little smear of blood across his chin. He holds his open palm under my mouth. "Can you get these down without water?" I open as far as I can and he lays two white pills on my tongue.

"Where are we?"

"Muller's Pharmacy."

"Oh."

He shuts the door very softly and climbs in front.

I don't remember it being day or night, just these unbelievable dreams. Sometimes even with my eyes open, lying there in the dark. Mostly red roses over and over, petals like skin. Budding, blooming, fading, then starting all over again.

People come into my room. I remember that. Sometimes Father to give me two more pills. Sometimes I feel like I'm falling and then my head is flat against the mattress. A cracking sound, like wind snapping a sail, and my head is on the pillows again, sharp with the smell of bleach.

I wake up feeling incredibly thirsty. Head almost clear, jaws locked together tight. Have to pick away the crust to get my eyes open. I switch on the lamp. So bright I have to shut my eyes again. I slowly open them again. The first thing I see is the stain on my pillow, kidney-colored at the center, pink at the edges, like a rose in the rotogravure section of the Sunday *Tribune-Star.*

On the stairs I feel weightless, like I'm skimming along an inch or two above the steps. I turn on the bathroom light and look in the mirror. The left side of my face is puffed out to here. My left eye's just a black slit with a purple ring around it. My cheek's gray as old meat, upper lip so swollen out it looks like part of my nose. I slowly pull the lip back off my blood-encrusted teeth. The gum's dead white. Black stitches stick out like thorns. I fill the toothglass with warm water and rinse again and again, watching the brown water swirl down the drain.

By the time I get back upstairs the whole side of my face is pounding. I lie in bed and press my cheek against the cool wall. My tongue won't stay away from the stitches. They seem to be getting bigger, like wire knots under my lip.

After a while I sit up. Look at the alarm clock. Almost four-thirty. The small plastic vial's partly hidden by the alarm clock. I read the label: McCaverty, Jared, 36 XDOL 30 mg. Take two tablets every four hours or as needed for pain. DR. LANCET. I shake out four tablets and swallow them dry. The dreams start up again the second my head hits the pillow. Roses and more roses, smelling salty as a dark red sea.

Hungry. I probe the stitches with my tongue. Smaller. My face hardly throbs at all. Just to be safe I swallow three pills.

Mrs. Krapo's down on her knees in front of the big black range, her head stuck way inside the oven. The kitchen reeks of ammonia. I say good morning except I can't move my lips much so it comes out 'Gub mobbin.'

Mrs. Krapo pulls her head out of the oven. "Goodness you gave me a scare!" Her sparse white hair is tied up in rags. She's got a Brillo pad in one hand, a white soup bowl full of blue ammonia in the other.

She stands on her toes to get a better look at my face. "You look like you've come back from the dead."

I nod.

"Feeling better?"

I nod again.

"It's what I always said. No good ever came of having a full set of teeth. One of them's always going to be acting up. I haven't been to see a dentist in thirty years and I'm here to tell you I don't feel the worse for it." She bares her gums to show me her three stubby gray teeth— one upper, two lowers. "I expect you're hungry enough to eat a horse."

"Yub."

"Your father laid it on the line for me. No hard foods, no chewing."

Fine with me.

"There's a gallon of ice cream in the deep freeze. He said to start with that. I'll whip you up a floating island for supper if that sounds good to you. Just let me wash my hands and I'll dish you up some ice cream."

Too hungry to wait. I open the freezer. A full gallon of Howard Johnson's Burgundy Cherry.

Mrs. Krapo hands me a bowl and the scoop. "Your father drove all the way to the Interstate to get that for you so it better be good."

It is. Cold, creamy and a little soft. I can't do much with the chunks of bing cherry so I just suck on them till they're pulpy enough to slide right down. I scoop the bowl full a second time and take it out to the morning room. I switch on the TV. Usually I don't care much for soap operas. They're always so slow and mainly full of people sitting around talking about what other people did. But today the first one's over before I know it. Even the commercials are neat—dancing Tide boxes and a pretty one full of huge quivery bowls of Jell-O. The ice cream makes me shiver so I wrap up in mother's afghan.

Sometime later mother comes in. I think I may have fallen asleep. She's all dressed up for a change. One of my favorites—a gray wool suit with silver fox at the collar and cuffs. I'd like to tell her how nice she looks but my mouth hurts too much. Her hair looks nice too, puffed up on top and kind of swirled around the ears, a little like Mrs. Kennedy's.

"Hello, stranger." She rests a stack of books on top of the TV. "Are you feeling any better?"

I nod and the room goes up and down too. Weird. Tiny bright stars streak past my eyes.

"Your color's better." She sits down on the edge of the daybed. "You're not in a lot of pain?"

I shake my head and the room slides sideways a little. The stars jump up and down.

"I stopped off at school on my way home from the beauty parlor." Her fingers pluck at the edge of the afghan. "I don't think you should even consider going back until next week and then only if you feel up to it. I talked to most of your teachers and they seemed to think you wouldn't be missing all that much."

No kidding. I could be out the rest of the year and I wouldn't be missing much.

"Mr. Sibley said to work through to the end of the chapter on congruency. Mr. Thornkill said not to worry at all about Advanced World Issues. He'll help you catch up when you get back. Oh, he did say you should be sure to read the newspaper every day. Miss Ohm is the only one who sent along a lot. She said you should try to get through the Edwardians and the War Poets because they're going to be on the test, which is a week from Friday. I said I thought she might let you take it late, under the circumstances, but she didn't seem to think that would be a very good idea."

She wouldn't. Took her three months to drag us through the Victorians. I bet we spent six weeks on Tennyson alone. Now all of a sudden it's rush, rush.

Without the least bit of warning she reaches out and touches my hand. "You look tired."

I feel tired. Too tired to nod. My head's throbbing again. The little stars are keeping time.

She takes her hand away and stands up, smoothing down her skirt. "Miss Ohm told me Miss Tilley went back into the hospital on Tuesday. And just when she seemed to be doing so well. Isn't that a shame?"

"Yub."

The sound of the Olds crunching up the drive wakes me. I throw the afghan over my shoulders like a cloak, grab my books and stumble up the back stairs.

Up in bed my mouth feels raw. The stitches are too tight—they're biting into the gum. I open the plastic vial and shake out three pills. They seem to work faster chewed up dry than taken with water. They taste chalky and bitter. I lie in bed a long time, counting knots in the pine paneling.

At suppertime Mrs. Krapo brings up a tray. Chicken noodle soup. Homemade. The noodles slide right down. The floating island's even better, lemony and sweet.

I open *Masterpieces of English Literature* to "Introduction to the Twentieth Century." "The First World War was widely known as the War to End War. Initial optimism and high spirits, however, quickly gave way to . . ." We had all that in American history. Although there are some interesting new details. Like why they're called trenchcoats. Puts a whole new light on my Burberry.

I stare at Rupert Brooke's picture a while. If I could look like that I wouldn't mind dying young. His poems are beautiful too, especially the one about things he loved:

Then, the cool kindness of sheets, that soon
Smooth away trouble, and the rough male kiss
Of blankets; grainy wood; live hair that is
    Shining and free.

No picture of Wilfred Owen. His poems are hard. The only one I can get all the way through has a Latin title. The poem's real short but it takes a while to figure out. For instance, the soldiers returning from battle are "bloodshod." At first I thought that was a misprint. Then it suddenly made sense and I wished it hadn't.

The best one though is by somebody who sounds like he fought for the other side. Siegfried Sassoon. The footnote says he was English though. Such a beautiful poem, so simple and sad:

> Why do you lie with your legs so ungainly
>   huddled,
> And one arm bent across your sullen, cold,
> Exhausted face? It hurts my heart to watch
>   you,
> Deep-shadowed from the candle's guttering
>   gold;
> And you wonder why I shake you by the
>   shoulder;
> Drowsy, you mumble and sigh and turn your
>   head . . .
> *You are too young to fall asleep forever;*
> And when you sleep you remind me of the
>   dead.

I read it through half a dozen times and each time it gives me the chills. I've almost got it by heart when I hear him creeping up the stairs. I let the book slide off my stomach and roll over on my side. I concentrate on breathing deeply.

He stands over me a long time. Finally he switches off the light and goes back down the stairs. Real slow.

My pills are gone. And I know I haven't taken them all. There were at least a dozen left last night when I went to bed. But this morning I felt for them before I even opened my eyes—I was hurting that much—and the vial wasn't there. I stripped the blankets off my bed, thinking I might have knocked them off the shelf during the night. I pulled the bed away from the wall. Nothing.

I throw on my dressing gown and run downstairs. Mother's in Sally's and my bathroom folding towels.

"Have you seen my pills?"

"What?" She doubles a thick white bath towel.

"My pills. For my teeth."

"I haven't seen them, Jared. Did you look in your room?"

"Of course I looked in my room."

"Then I don't know. Maybe . . ." She scans the neat piles of towels and facecloths laid out on the counter.

"Mother, I need those pills. My mouth's killing me."

"Have you asked your father? I really don't know a thing about it."

"Where is he?"

She pats a stack of pale yellow towels. "I believe he's out in his workshop."

I tear down the back stairs and into the kitchen. Mrs. Krapo's laying my place at the table.

"I thought I heard you stirring. You want breakfast or lunch?"

I run right past her, through the laundry room and into the garage. The concrete floor's cold and gritty under my bare feet. I charge up the rickety stairs to the old workshop.

He's bent over the sawhorses sanding away at a big old clock case, red bandana tied over his mouth to keep the sawdust out. The pot-bellied stove in the corner glows orange.

I kick one of the sawhorses to get his attention. He

looks up, surprised, and pushes the bandana down around his neck. "So, you look like a new man."

"Have you got my pills?"

"What?"

"My pills."

"Oh, those."

"My mouth hurts. I need them."

"You don't need them, Jared. Forty-eight hours is all that's indicated for the kind of surgery you had. I let you stay on them for seventy-two. They're very addictive, you know."

"I don't care. My mouth still hurts."

"Well, a little pain's inevitable. Let me see." He grabs my chin and tilts my head toward the light. "The swelling's way down. The gum's still a little inflamed though. A.S.A. should do the trick."

"But it hurts!" I can't believe how much. Not the gum itself but deep down inside like the scalpel's still there carving away.

"Don't be so dramatic. A little pain never hurt anyone."

"It's not *your* mouth. You don't know how it feels. You don't care."

He sighs and picks up a sandpaper block. "Getting excited will only make it worse. It makes the blood rush to your head. That's what causes the pain."

I try to stop shouting but I can't. "I'm not excited. It hurt before I got excited."

He studies the grain of the clock case. "Try soaking it in salt water. A teaspoon of salt in water as hot as you can stand it. That should ease the inflammation. Take a couple of A.S.A."

"And call you in the morning, you prick." I run down the stairs.

"What was that?"
Fuck you. Fuck you. Fuck you.

Mother's still in my bathroom. I creep past the door
and into their bedroom. Their bathroom door's open.
The bottles in the medicine cabinet are neatly ranged by
size. She's been straightening up in here too. The vial
isn't there. I'm about to leave when I notice the tall bottle
at the back of the top shelf. Cheracol. Large economy
size. Nearly half full, the liquid so deep red it's nearly
black until I hold it up to the light. I check the label just
to make sure. Caution: contains codeine. Use only as di-
rected. May cause drowsiness. Dosage: 2 tbsp. every 4
hrs. Not to exceed 8 tbsp. over a 24-hr. period. If cough
persists, consult your physician. I hide the bottle under
my dressing gown and climb back up to my room.

I don't have a tablespoon. A good swig probably
equals one. I take three swigs. Then a fourth just to be
safe. Dark, rich, sweet, it bites at the back of my throat.

By the time I go back downstairs he's having lunch.

"Salt water help?"

"You bet."

"I knew it would. Pain's a funny thing. It's usually
not as bad as you think it is. Mind over matter you know.
You'll feel fine in a day or so. Of course you'll get twinges
every now and then for quite a while. The nerves growing
back."

Orange juice tastes real bitter after Cheracol.

"Dr. Lancet wants to see you again first thing Monday morning."

"*No.*"

"Just so he can take out the stitches."

"I'm not going back to him."

"Jared, he did what had to be done. Otherwise your

whole mouth could have become infected. You didn't want that, did you?"

"I'm not going back to him."

"I've got some tapioca pudding made up, Jared." Mrs. Krapo hates it when we fight.

"All he's going to do is look you over and remove the stitches."

"He's a fucking Nazi."

Mrs. Krapo heads for the kitchen.

"Jared, I'm warning you."

"What are you going to do—hit me again?"

I get up from the table and walk out of the room. I feel real calm. Up in my room I take two more swigs of Cheracol just to make sure I stay that way.

After everyone has gone to bed I finish off the Cheracol. There's enough left to tide me over for another few days but I'm pretty sure I'm going to need it all tonight.

I lie down for a while until my mouth feels cottony and I can see roses when I close my eyes. I slip down to the bathroom and lock myself in. I find Sally's manicure scissors and eyebrow tweezers in her makeup drawer. Nothing to cutting the stitches. *Snip, snip, snip, snip.* I stand for a long time looking in the mirror. My face looks better—still a little lumpy on the left side and a pale bruise runs from my eye down to the corner of my mouth, but I look nearly human.

I pick up the tweezers and count to three. Then I count right up to twenty-five. And yank. The first piece of black thread comes out clean. No problem. Easy. It leaves two indentations in my gum like a tiny snake had sunk its fangs in.

The second thread's in tight. I tug with the tweezers. Feels like it's anchored to the jawbone. I jiggle the thread up and down. Doesn't give at all. I grit my teeth and yank hard. The thread slices through the gum. Feels a yard long at least, like flossing with razor blades. The inside of my head flashes red with pain. Then black. When I open my eyes two tears ooze out.

I hold the tweezers up to the mirror. Half an inch of glistening black thread.

The bleeding takes a long time to stop. I press a cold facecloth to my gum until it does. Then I wash all the blood out and hang it back on the rack.

I go back up to bed and lie there in the dark running my tongue over the gum. Doesn't help. Neither did the Cheracol really. The pain's outside and in, snakebites on the surface and something worse underneath. Something my tongue can't get to, opening deeper inside me. The shining blade flashes through the dark, laying me open, cleaning me out.

MARCH

*M*other wasn't sure I should go because she didn't know how the family would feel about having a lot of kids there. Turned out not to matter because there isn't any family, only Miss Tilley's sister standing at the door looking a lot like Miss Tilley, only older and thinner and faded, like Miss Tilley had been run through the wash and hung out to dry too long in the sun.

Practically the whole class is here. I get in line behind Suzie Beagleman, who's already sniffing into her hankie. We can't even see the coffin from here, just Miss Tilley's sister shaking kids' hands and then scooting them on into the Viewing Chapel. Bobby Meckles and Howard Lenowitz get in line behind me, giggling and nudging each other until Suzie Beagleman turns around and shushes them. They both look like such hicks—Bobby's wearing white socks with his suit, black Scotty dogs romp up and down Howard's red tie. I felt strange about wearing my heather-green suit but my black pinstripe from last year is too small and anyway mother says a tasteful green is perfectly suitable for a funeral.

I'm at the front of the line before I know it. Miss Tilley's sister smiles and holds out her hand. It's dry and weightless, like a dead bird. "I'm Jared McCaverty. I'm in Miss Tilley's homeroom. I mean I *was* in—"

"Hello, Jared. Good of you to come. I know my sister thought an awful lot of you. There are so many young people here. Marjorie would have liked that."

Miss Tilley's sister lets go of my hand and gives me a little push into the Viewing Chapel.

The Viewing Chapel looks like a big living room in a nice house—thick gold carpeting, dark wood paneling, long low sofas and low tables with big lamps made from amber glass vases. And way down at one end, what everybody's here for.

From across the room she looks pretty good. I get this flash of her suddenly sitting up and calling the roll to see if anyone skipped—it almost starts me laughing. Banks of flowers cover the wall on either side of the casket—orange, pink and yellow glads, white mums big as snowballs, carnations and daisies clumped together to make hearts, crosses or just plain old wreaths. An enormous bunch of red roses sprawls across the bottom half of the casket lid. A wide red ribbon's draped across them like the sash Miss America wears. The gold lettering says IN LOVING MEMORY, THE 9B3'S. We all chipped in.

I stand next to Suzie Beagleman and stare down at Miss Tilley. Up close she doesn't look so hot. She has on her steel-rimmed glasses but somebody's taken them off their chain. Her white hair's combed back off her face in little ripples, neater than I've ever seen it. Her face is sherbet-orange all over with a bright pink circle on each cheek. Some of the pink has melted under the floodlights and runs down over her jaw like syrup on a sundae.

I turn to walk away so Bobby Meckles can have a chance to gawk and I bump right into Suzie Beagleman.

"Oh, Jared, isn't it sad?" Then she hugs me.

If people hadn't been watching I'd have shoved her right across the room.

After everyone gets a good gander we sit down in rows of wooden chairs that squeak every time anyone breathes. The organist doodles away a while and then the minister talks a while. A real old guy, he sprays a lot of spit. You can see the front row ducking for cover whenever he gets worked up, and he gets worked up a lot, swaying and shouting and pounding the lectern. "I am the *resurrection* and the *life!*"

When he gets to "ashes to ashes, dust to dust," I finished it off for him in my head: *You're a pretty good team but you can't beat us.*

The newsreel's pretty gross. "The New First Family at Home." They're so disgusting. Grandmother Fortman says she never thought she'd live to see the day when there were crackers in the White House. And the names —Luci Baines and Lynda Bird and Lady Bird. If they had a son they could call him Tweety. I don't think I'd mind the names so much if they weren't all so ugly with those big floppy hound-dog jowls. When I think of what they replaced it makes me sick. Why couldn't they have shot *him* instead?

The maroon velvet curtains whir shut and then creak open again. The ad in the *Tribune-Star* said "Terror Beyond Your Wildest Nightmares" but I don't know.

The Innocents looks pretty tame to me. Two little kids run around like something's after them and the music gets all creepy but I can't see a thing. In black-and-white too, although I don't mind so much since it's a horror movie.

Anyway, I'll go see anything that has Deborah Kerr in it, even if this does make the second time she's played a governess. The first was in *The King and I,* which I saw way back when I was six or seven. She was so beautiful in that, so calm and kind and loving, like the mother the little princes and princesses never had. I know nobody's like that in real life, at least nobody I've ever met, but it's still kind of a nice dream.

Maybe the best thing about Deborah Kerr is that when she's a governess she always does everything she can to protect the children she cares for, no matter who tries to hurt them. Even when it's their father, the King of Siam, with his bare oiled chest, she still stands up to him, although he's the man she secretly loves.

In *The Innocents* she tries to protect the kids too but it's harder because she can't see who's after them. After the first half hour it's pretty clear she's got her work cut out for her because the kids themselves turn out to be evil —they act like they *want* to be bothered by the ghosts.

The end, when the ghosts and the little boy are out in the garden in the dark, is really scary. The ghosts are still invisible, lurking behind the statues and bushes, but Deborah Kerr fights them with everything she's got. It's kind of sad because by trying to save the little boy from the ghosts she ends up killing him. Accidentally. I guess the important thing is that she tried—she really tried to protect him. Anyone can see that.

*   *   *

I hold the last note, a whole one, four beats and then one more because it's the last note. I lift my fingers off the keys and instead of flopping them down in my lap I let them hover half an inch above the keyboard the way I've seen Artur Rubinstein do on *The Ed Sullivan Show*. Except Mrs. Sparks isn't looking at my hands. She's staring at the rain streaming down the panes of the bay window.

"Was that okay?"

She jumps at the sound of my voice. Then she smiles, showing both rows of tiny perfect teeth. "Lovely, Jared. Just lovely. So grave and stately. Handel's 'Sarabande' isn't a piece I often give to beginning students. They usually find it so gloomy."

I find it just right. Slow and sad. The rain only makes it better. She explained last week that a sarabande is a very formal eighteenth-century dance usually performed at the court of Spain. To me it sounds like something that should be played at a funeral—left hand the heavy steps of the black-veiled mourners, right hand the clicking of the plumed horses' hooves on the black-draped rain-slick street.

"I don't know what else to say. You could sharpen your attack a little at the beginning of each new phrase. And you can try adding the sustaining pedal. But sparingly, where you think it's needed to draw out the majesty. You're really making such progress. For next week I'd concentrate more on the two pieces from *The Well-Tempered Clavier*. Work on really making them sing. And your scales of course."

I go into the dining room to wait. The side yard looks like a big mud pie.

Three minutes later the basement door bangs open. Randy Sparks goes straight to the fridge and yanks the door open so hard it bangs against the edge of the sink.

He takes a long drink from the red pitcher's beak. Water spills down over his sweat-stained gray T-shirt. He turns around real slow, like he's all alone, and then jerks his head back to show he's surprised to see me sitting here. Like I haven't been sitting here every Tuesday for the past month when he's come up from doing his exercises at five past five.

"How you doing?"

"Okay."

He nods toward the window. "Still pouring."

"Yeah. Good workout?"

"All right. Harder when it's humid. You feel like coming down, see what kind of stuff I do?"

"Sure."

At the bottom of the steps he tugs his damp T-shirt over his head and throws it across the room. "Like a fucking hothouse down here."

The room's long, low and narrow and smells of sweat and lots of Right Guard. A single window, a half one, is set high into one cinder-block wall. Under it stands a narrow bed covered with a red-and-brown striped blanket. Pipes and beams crisscross the ceiling so I can't stand up straight. Randy's short enough he doesn't have to worry. He goes over to the low bench at the foot of the bed. At the head of the bench a metal stand supports a barbell loaded with eight discs, four on either end, covered in sparkly gold plastic. The bench itself is covered with brown spongy plastic grained to look like leather.

"You can lift all that?"

"It's not that much."

"Looks like tons." A poster taped to the wall over the bench shows twenty or thirty small black-and-white photographs of a muscular man in a tiny black bathing suit holding weights in different positions. His skin gleams like he's been basted. I study the pictures closely. "You can do all that?"

"Yeah."

"Even that one?" I point to a picture showing the guy spread-eagled on a bench, dumbbells in his out-stretched hands. He looks like a really meaty Christ wait-ing for the nails.

"Easy." He takes a pair of dumbbells and places them on the concrete floor on either side of the bench. He lies back on the bench and wraps his hands around the dumbbell bars.

He arcs them up until they crack together directly over his head. "One!" He eases them back down to the floor. "Two!" His chest swells, the veins in his neck jump and squirm. "Three!"

"Neat."

He gets up from the bench, rubbing his palms to-gether. "It's really no big deal. You feel like a beer?"

"You got one?"

"It's warm."

"That's okay."

He reaches under his bed and pulls out a sixpack. Schlitz Malt Liquor.

"Where'd you get it?"

"A friend."

"Nice of him."

"Her."

"Oh yeah?"

"Lives across the alley. She's a senior at Tech but she looks twenty-one at least. Has a fake ID, but she says they hardly ever ask."

"That's great."

"She says she'll buy for me anytime I want." He pops open his can. "Drink up."

It's warm and fizzy. He chugs his and bends the can double. With one hand.

"Feel like another?"

"I'm still working on this one."

"Why don't you sit down?"

Not much room on the narrow bed. I sit down next to him. He leans back against the cinder-block wall.

"Feels good."

"What?"

"The wall's cool."

I lean back too.

We look up at the bare beams and pipes a while. He belches.

"Who's that?" I point to a big picture of a soldier taped to the opposite wall. Olive T-shirt and a helmet with olive netting over it. Green tropical-looking leaves brush the guy's shoulders.

"I found it in *Life*. Pretty cool, huh? Vietnam."

"Oh yeah?

"Wish I was there." He crushes his second Schlitz can.

"In Vietnam?"

"Why not? Anything's better than here."

"I guess so. You want to be a soldier?"

"I'm going to enlist as soon as I graduate."

"That's a long way off."

"Hope it's not over before I'm out."

"It's not a real war anyway. Our guys are only there as advisors."

He nods toward the picture from *Life*. "He look like an advisor to you?"

"I guess not."

"Hey, don't say anything about this to my mom, okay?"

"She doesn't want you to be a soldier?"

"You kidding? She goes crazy when I talk about it. Sometimes I do it just to set her off. That's how my dad died."

"Really? In the war?"

"Korea."

"God."

His face is red and he's breathing fast. Not like just after weights but shallow, like he's afraid there isn't going to be enough air to go around.

"Think of it, man. Out there in the jungle, fighting for your life. Just you and your buddies."

"I'd be scared to death."

He puts his face real close to mine. "No, you wouldn't. No time to be scared. Besides, they train the fear right out of you so you're a killing machine." He pounds the pillow with his fist.

"It'd take a long time to train the fear out of me."

"Nah. They can teach anyone to kill. I've read a lot about it. It's all just discipline. Like sports. When I first went out for football at Ann Arbor I was a real chicken-shit. Nobody thought I'd be able to hack it." His face crinkles up so that for a moment he looks like a scared little kid. "They said I was too small. But you train and train and train and by the time you're ready for the game it's automatic."

"And size doesn't matter?"

"Fuck no. Speed matters, guts matter. That's what I love—diving right into the action, plowing into guys twice my size. By the end of the season you know what they were calling me at Ann Arbor?"

Crazy. "What?"

"Kamikaze. They knew I'd do anything just to be able to play. It was only Pee-Wee football but we suited up and everything. That's the main reason I didn't want to come here. No real football till high school. Really fucked."

"I've never been too big on sports."

"You're a demon swimmer."

"That's different."

"You've got the body for football."

"I do?"

"Sure. Broad shoulders, long legs, narrow hips. You just need some building up is all. You're a little skinny."

Skinny! What a nice thing to say. "I think I'd need a lot of building up."

"I bet you're stronger than you think." He jumps up from the bed. His eyes look kind of wild and unfocused. A vein's pulsing in his neck. "How many push-ups can you do?"

"I don't know."

He falls to the floor. Really falls, like he's going to drive his chin straight into the concrete. But he catches himself on stiffened arms and slowly lowers his chin to the floor. Then he pumps up and down. Fast.

". . . eight . . . nine . . . ten. Come on, show me what you've got."

I get off the bed and lie facedown on the cold concrete. I raise myself up on my arms, swaying a little.

He crouches down next to me. "Head up. Chin out. Don't let your back sag. Stiff as a board. Okay, down slow."

I lower myself by degrees until my nose touches the gritty concrete. I push back up. My arms are trembling like plucked rubber bands.

"Again. And keep that chest off the floor." He

reaches his hand under my chest and keeps it there, not really holding me up but almost.

"Again. Good. Again."

I make it up to five and sag to the floor.

He slaps my shoulder. "See, you can do anything if you put your mind to it. You want to try the weights?"

"Sure."

I lie down on the plastic-covered bench and scoot under the weight bar. I look at the four big gold discs on either end of it. "I can't do that much."

"Don't worry." He unbolts both ends of the bar and takes off two discs from each end.

"You don't think that's still too heavy for me?"

"Relax. I'll spot you." He moves around to the head of the bench so he's standing right over me. He places his hands on the bar on either side of mine. "Now we'll lift it off the support and just hold it in the air a second so you can get the feel of it. Ready?"

I nod. My hands feel slick with sweat, my mouth's dry. I brace my arms. They still feel weak from the push-ups.

"Okay. I'm going to take my hands away."

I hold my breath.

"You've got it." The bar sways over my head. My shoulders dig into the bench.

"Steady, steady." He's whispering now, bending his face to mine. I've never seen his eyes so close. The bar stops swaying.

"Okay. Bring it down. Slow."

I lower the bar until it's under my chin.

"Good stuff. Take another deep breath and push up hard."

I jerk the bar up off my chest. And exhale. Nearly into his open mouth. I close my eyes and push. The bar rises slowly into the air until my arms are completely straight.

"That's it. You got it. Way to go. Now exhale and take it down."

It's hot in here. I can feel the sweat breaking out on my forehead.

"Two more times," he says. I watch his lips move. So close. "Down. Breathe. Up. Hold it. Down." He wraps his hands lightly around the bar. "Last time."

My shoulders ache. My arms feel like the bones have fallen right out. "I don't think I can."

"Sure you can. Even when you're beat the important thing is to do one more. That's the way it works."

I roll my head from side to side. "I'm pretty sure I can't."

The door at the top of the stairs opens. Mrs. Sparks calls down, "Jared, your father's here."

I push up hard. Hold. Bring the bar down quick and thrust it right back up into the air again.

Randy shakes his head and smiles down at me. "Not bad."

APRIL

Working for Mr. Clay's like not working at all. And it gets easier every week. The first Saturday Mrs. Mandle met me at the top of the stairs all businesslike with six rubber-banded stacks of index cards clutched to her bosom. She had on a severe black suit I'd never seen before. And no bow in her hair for a change but a man's striped tie around her neck, a little dark stain about three quarters of the way down. Must have borrowed it from Charles.

She'd cleared a space for me at the long refectory table in the library. It was my job to sort the catalogue cards according to type—Glassware or Pottery, Furniture, Sculpture, Prints, Paintings and Miscellaneous—and then chronologically according to date of acquisition. I was hard at it from nine until ten-twenty, when Mr.

Clay came rushing in to say he needed me—"urgently"—in his office.

I'd never seen his office before. It's about the only part of Slope's that hasn't been remodeled yet, a small room that seems larger than it is because the ceiling's so high and a glass-brick window fills one whole wall.

I stood in the middle of the room waiting for Mr. Clay to tell me what he needed me for. He closed the door with a muffled thud. The back of the door was covered with black tufted leather crisscrossed with brass tacks.

He walked over to his desk. "This is my predecessor's idea of elegance."

The desk takes up about a third of the room, the smooth dark wood carved into arches, columns, scrolls. The desk lamp looks like a real Tiffany, ruby-and-violet glass lozenges arranged like bunches of grapes with tarnished brass twisting around them like vines. Mr. Clay sat down behind the desk in a carved wooden chair with a high back covered in burgundy velvet.

"Sit down, sit down. I'm afraid they're about as comfortable as they look." I sat down in one of the twin low-backed chairs in front of the desk. They look sort of Oriental, with lion-paw feet and dragon-head arms. The carving on the back of the chair dug into my spine.

He lit a Dunhill. "So how do you like your first day on the job, young man?"

"I love it."

"You do? You really and truly do?"

"Yeah, it's so . . ."

Mr. Clay pushed a shock of strawy hair off his forehead. "Well, perhaps you should be sitting in my chair, and I'll take over Mrs. Mandle's inexhaustible supply of index cards. Christ, Jared, this place! I tell you it's going to be the death of me."

He slung one leg across the corner of the desktop. He has such beautiful shoes. He was wearing oxblood loafers, almost the same shade as his burgundy silk tie, with little leather tassels. I've always wanted tasseled loafers but mother always says she doesn't think Father would like them.

With such excellent taste in footwear it's strange that Mr. Clay doesn't know about Executive-Length socks. The cuff of his gray flannel trousers had ridden up, exposing a good three inches of calf covered with thickly curling reddish-gold hair. I tried not to stare at it.

"You don't like it here?"

He moved the pink marble inkstand half an inch to the left. "Slope's is fine. Slope's excites me. Given time and proper community support, I think I could turn this place around. But you tell me what I'm to make of this." He handed a manila folder across the desk to me.

I opened it and studied the single sheet of paper. It was all in Mrs. Mandle's scrolly handwriting: "Attendance Figures for Nineteen Hundred Sixty-three." I scanned the list. "January: Forty-three, June: Thirty-one, August: Twenty-seven, November: Sixty-eight, December: Two hundred ninety-three." (Mrs. Mandle never uses numerals if she can help it.)

"It looks about right to me." I handed the folder back. "I don't think Mrs. Mandle would cheat on the figures."

Mr. Clay pounded the desk so hard the sphinx-shaped ashtray jumped. It was just like Khrushchev at the UN. "My God, man, we're not talking about dishonesty here. We're discussing the lifeblood of any museum: People, Jared. Where are all the people?"

I didn't know what to say to that. It didn't matter because he charged on. "You've lived here all your life. You know this town. You've been coming to Slope's ever since you were in short pants. You and half a dozen others from the look of things. But what about the rest? The sign out on the highway clearly reads Terre Haute, population 72,500. Where are all the people? Why don't the other 72,490 come to Slope's?"

"Because they're philistines, Mr. Clay?"

"Philistines!" he shouted, the long ash falling off his Dunhill and onto the gold-and-scarlet Persian rug. He doubled over in his chair, nose right down on the burgundy blotter. At first I thought he was crying—he was making high squeaky sounds, just like a balloon when the air's let out in little pinches. He lifted his head and he *was* crying but only because he was laughing so hard. The high squeaks were giggles.

He wagged a finger at me. "You, young man, are very wicked. Very wicked indeed. Wherever did you learn a word like that?"

"*Masterpieces of English Literature.* Matthew Arnold? He wrote this beautiful poem called 'Dover Beach'? There was an essay by him too called 'Culture and Anarchy.' It wasn't assigned but I always try to read everything by authors I like."

"And did you agree with Mr. Arnold?"

"I didn't read the whole thing. It was kind of dry."

"Good Lord, yes. I haven't read him since my university days. A bit of an elitist as I recall. The opposite of the image we want to cultivate for Slope's. People around here may be philistines. From the ones I've had the pleasure of meeting I'd say they are, by and large. But it's our job as custodians of culture to change all that. A good museum must be educative. Challenging. Eye-opening.

But before we can open their little piglike eyes, we've got to be able to bring them in. And precisely how do we bring them in?"

"The renovations?"

He waved a hand dismissively. "I've already thought of that. The *Tribune-Star* is sending over a reporter and a photographer on Monday. They've promised me a big spread. And we're going to have another god-awful reception to unveil the galleries. But after that?"

Mr. Clay talked on till well past lunchtime. And I was beginning to get the hang of my new job. He likes to think aloud and there's not much point in that unless somebody's there to listen.

So now every Saturday morning I come in and get out the index cards and shuffle through them a while. Then Mr. Clay comes out of his office and says he needs my assistance, and that takes care of the rest of the day.

I'm learning so much from him. Last week he explained all about fund-raising. How it boils down to having tea with every rich old lady in town and bourbon on the rocks with lawyers and bank presidents. With the old ladies he has to praise all the dreck in their big old houses, always keeping an eye out for something Slope's genuinely could use. For instance, Mr. Clay found a real Fabergé Easter egg out at Wilhelmina Laudermilk's place. She owns the Tastee Shoppe Cafeteria and is so fat her Lincoln Continental has to have special springs. Mr. Clay's working on her to donate the egg before she dies. He's worried she's going to eat it first.

This morning I'm finally getting the Glassware and Pottery cards into chronological order. It's the biggest collection of all—four hundred sixty-three cards, some of them for full sets of goblets or matching paperweights. One card alone lists two dozen Venetian thimbles. At ten thirty-two Mr. Clay storms in. He's wearing a long gray lab coat.

"Your hands clean?"

"I guess so."

"No guessing. Go into my bathroom and give them a three-minute scrub. Then come on up to the storeroom."

I go into the little bathroom off his office. It's all black—black ceramic tiles on the floor and walls, black toilet, black marble sink. Kind of claustrophobic. I carefully wash my hands. Even Mrs. Mandle isn't allowed to use Mr. Clay's bathroom.

He's in a dim corner of the storeroom back behind the "Pietà." He stands next to a flat wooden box set up on sawhorses, leafing through an oversized book. The shiny white cover has fingerprints all over it.

"Just look what I found stuck away in one of the steamer trunks! Can you imagine?" He puts the book down on the wooden box. Somebody had scrawled across the cover in black ink, *Les Enfants Terribles*. It's not really a book at all—more like a big folder tied together with black ribbon.

Mr. Clay unties the ribbons and lays the cover aside. Inside, a stack of large cream-colored sheets of paper, most of them covered with printing half an inch high.

"Do you know what this is?"

"It looks like a play."

"It's more than that. Look." He pushes some sheets aside to reveal a drawing. Nothing fancy. No color. Just a squiggly profile that looks like it was done by somebody who didn't once lift his pen off the page. A young man's profile. The nose looks like it slid down from the bulging forehead, the mouth's a perfect bow. Hair curls down over the back of his neck and the single eye is a star. Three more stars dot the lower right-hand corner of the sheet. The signature's big enough you can't miss it: Jean Cocteau.

"He's . . . it's beautiful."

"Isn't he? One of eighteen drawings. This is a hand-pulled limited edition of Cocteau's greatest play. The printing was so superbly inked they look like actual drawings, but they're not. Just forty copies were pulled. The only other one I've seen was at the Library of Congress." He claps his hands together. "Jared, this is *such* a find. And it's going to inaugurate my new project: Art Object of the Week. Each week I'll select a painting or print or whatever, and the *Tribune-Star* will run a photo of it in that god-awful rotogravure section along with a short paragraph. Which I of course will write. I wouldn't trust them to write my obituary after the dog's breakfast they made of that piece about our renovations. Anyway, the beauty of it is, every single week of the year we'll be getting fresh publicity. Free publicity. And every week new people will come pouring into Slope's to see the week's treasure. What do you think?"

"It's a great—"

"Of course these need a little work before they can be exhibited." He pulls out a second drawing, a profile of a girl. At least it looks like a girl. The hair's a little longer than in the other drawing, although her lips aren't quite so full and she has long curling lashes instead of a star-eye. "See those brown specks next to her ear? Mold. Fungus. That's where this contraption comes in." He pats the wooden box. "You simply set the timer like this and slip the sheet into this slot here. The mold gets cooked away. You got it?"

Not much to get. I nod.

"Good. It will be your job to run Cocteau through the cooker. The timer will buzz when each sheet's done. All you have to do is keep feeding the cooker. I'm meeting Mrs. Laudermilk at the Tastee Shoppe for lunch. To discuss her egg. Actually, the cornbread's quite nice there, but I find the lady playing popular favorites on the pipe organ a bit much, don't you think?" He makes a face and dashes off.

He forgot to say anything about when I can take lunch, but that's okay. I don't eat lunch anymore. This means I get a little lightheaded around three but it also means I keep off the weight I lost after my surgery. I think I may have lost a couple of more pounds. It's hard to tell because Sally's always setting back the scales whenever she's gained a ton or two. I also do sit-ups every morning now. I'm up to forty-five. And fifteen push-ups every night before I go to bed.

This is the first time I've ever had the storeroom all to myself. I slip a drawing into the cooker and start rummaging around, pulling open drawers, wardrobes and trunks. Totally amazing stuff—beaded purses and rhinestone tiaras for fancy-dress balls, rows of ivory elephants ranked by size, a man's beaver hat with a silk label inside saying it was made in Montreal, lots of inlaid snuffboxes and pillboxes, a pair of mother-of-pearl opera glasses, monogrammed silver napkin rings, a teakwood Chinese junk, three bronze Buddhas, a foot-high model of the Chrysler Building in New York, half a dozen feather fans, trays and trays of butterflies and lace doilies under glass, filigree hatpins stuck into velvet pincushions, a Turkish hookah on a carved sandalwood stand.

In one of the big wardrobes I find a long hooded cloak, black velvet with an ivory satin lining. I drape it over my shoulders. It falls almost to my ankles. Standing in front of one of the big spotty mirrors I put up the hood and pretend I'm Dracula, lurking and turning suddenly so the cloak swirls about me.

The big windows darken fast and soon rain's pinging against the dirty glass. Thunder rumbles, and the big panes rattle. Spooky being up here all alone. The rain comes on hard, slick sheets of it peeling down the windows. Lightning turns the room silver for an instant. The headless and armless statues vibrate like bowling pins after every thunder roll.

I slide another drawing into the cooker, set the timer and wrapping the cloak about me, curl up on the big horsehair settee on the other side of the "Pietà."

The buzzer wakes me. Rain's still sliding down the windows. Thunder grumbles far away. The big room's nearly dark. I creep around the "Pietà." Mr. Clay's easing a drawing out of the cooker. I pull up the cloak hood. Dracula lives. A floorboard creaks under my feet. Mr. Clay spins around. Lightning flashes the room negative-bright.

"Good Lord—*la dame aux camélias.*" One eyebrow's frozen in the up position. Does that mean he's scared or just startled? He laughs a little. "Wherever did you find that?"

"Did I scare you?"

"Let's just say you took me by surprise, Mr. Mc-Caverty. You look very glamorous you know. Like something out of an old film."

I push back the hood. "I didn't hear you come up."

He fumbles for a cigarette. "And I assumed you'd gone home. It's well after five." His lighter flashes, the flame flutters. He cups his hand to shield it. His hand's shaking like crazy. Maybe I did scare him.

"I fell asleep." I ease off the cloak and drape it across Christ's feet.

"You've been up here ever since I left?" He keeps looking at me funny, like he's not sure it's me. "Didn't you go out for lunch?"

"Wasn't hungry."

"Well, you must be starved by now. Listen, why don't you come and have supper with us? I know Dorcas would be delighted to see you again. A friend of hers is staying with us. Come on, you'll make the table even."

Supper with Mr. and Mrs. Clay. I think I'd be too nervous to eat. "I don't know. I'd have to check with my parents."

"Then hurry on down and phone them. I'll finish up here and meet you in the lobby."

From the outside their house is kind of disappointing. It's on one of those short dark streets that run off Debs Avenue. Looks like all the other houses on the street—old, except not old enough to be interesting. Small, boxy, and brick, with neat shrubs clustered around the narrow front windows. A brick walkway runs up to a little semicircle of brick steps and the front door. Mr. Clay turns the key in the lock and ushers me in.

What a difference. He's been remodeling here too. No inside walls are left, just one big room with the floor built up here and sunk down there.

Mrs. Clay and her friend are lounging on large black cushions over by the fireplace, which doesn't have a mantelpiece or firescreen or anything, just a big square hole in the wall surrounded by shiny black tiles.

"I've brought company, Dorcas." He slips off his tasseled loafers. "You can leave your shoes here, Jared."

Mrs. Clay gets up and sort of floats over to us, her

green silk kimono rippling in the soft light of the floor lanterns scattered around the room like miniature paper houses.

"How nice to see you again, Jared." Like everything else she says, it's hard to tell if she means it. Her black hair's even shorter than before. When she turns her head I can see the pale glow of her scalp. "Julian's been threatening to bring you home."

Mr. Clay laughs loudly and walks away, leaving me alone with her. As he ducks behind a long wood-and-paper screen, she calls after him, "Julie, you want to get Jared a drink?

"Come and meet my friend." She takes my hand and leads me across the room, the hem of her kimono whispering against the panels that cover the floor. They're spongy and look like they're made of straw or grass. Weird. They crackle a little under my stocking feet.

"Bronwyn, this is Jared Mc . . . Mc . . ."

"McCaverty."

"He's Julian's man Friday down at the gallery. Bronwyn and I were at Vassar together."

Vassar. Bronwyn's brown hair is very long. So's her face, especially the nose. One arm glides out of the long loose sleeve of her dress like a snake out of a sewer pipe and snatches my hand. "Excuse me if I don't get up, Jared. I'm afraid Dorcas has got me absolutely pissed."

They both burst into laughter and then just as suddenly get quiet again. Dorcas takes a sip of her drink. I stand there looking down at the top of Bronwyn's head trying to think of something to say.

"Sit down," Dorcas says at last. "I'd better go and give Julie a hand." She drifts away, softly rustling.

I sit down on one of the black cushions. It looks soft

but it doesn't give much. Bronwyn studies me through her long eyelashes. "So, you must be in high school."

"Junior high."

"Middle school? How dreary for you." She laughs way down in her throat like she's too lazy to bring it up. "I won't ask you what that's like because I remember. Perfectly." She smooths her hair back over one shoulder. And waits.

My turn to say something. "Are you here for long?"

"God, I hope not. Just passing through really. On my way to Berkeley."

"That's nice."

"Yes, isn't it." She puts her drink aside and uncoils to a standing position, like she doesn't have any bones at all. Her long brown dress looks like it's made of burlap, cinched at the waist with a belt made of copper coins and some kind of animal teeth. "I think I'll go and see if I can be of any help to Dorcas. You stay here and tend the fire."

There isn't any fire to tend. Inside the fireplace small pillow-shaped coals glow on a low iron grill. Muffled laughter comes from behind the long wood-and-paper screen. A toilet flushes somewhere.

Mr. Clay comes back in. He's put on a short blue kimono over his flannel trousers and carries a black lacquer tray set with four red saucers and a small white vase. He tilts the vase over one of the saucers and hands it to me.

"Have you ever had sake before?"

I shake my head and take a sip. It tastes like warm plywood broth.

He sits down next to me and looks over the room like he's seeing it for the first time. "So. Do you like what we've done?"

"It's very Oriental."

"Japanese, actually. Although dinner's going to be Mongol. A slight clash of decor and cuisine."

Pretty soon Mrs. Clay and Bronwyn come back in, Mrs. Clay carrying a big gold lacquer tray loaded down with black plates and bowls, Bronwyn holding at arm's length what looks like an Oriental temple made of brass. About two feet high, it has a smokestack sticking up in the middle with a little brass moat encircling it.

"This," Mr. Clay says, "is a Mongolian hot pot." Bronwyn carefully lowers it onto the grille in the fireplace. "When the broth gets hot"—he points to the clear liquid in the moat—"we're ready to go."

Mrs. Clay hands out these long-handled tea-strainers while Mr. Clay shows me how to hold my chopsticks. Then Bronwyn passes around a platter of raw meat cut into thin strips.

"You go first, Jared," Mrs. Clay says, neatly scooping up a slice of meat with her chopsticks and dropping it into the basket of my tea strainer. "Now dip it in the broth and count to ten."

The broth in the moat's bubbling and spitting a little. I dunk the tea strainer basket into the moat and count. When I pull it out the meat's lightly browned. I dump it out onto my plate. Now comes the hard part. The meat keeps squirming off my chopsticks and they're all watching like it's the funniest thing in the world except no one's about to laugh because that would be impolite. Finally I get the meat up to my mouth. Seems like a lot of work for one little sliver but it tastes great.

"Neat," I say and they all laugh and applaud.

The rest of the meal's easy. I don't have to say much because everyone's so busy loading and unloading the tea strainers. I dunk red meat and pink chicken and something gray and slimy that tastes like real chewy fish. And Mr. Clay keeps filling my saucer. Before long even the sake tastes good.

When all the platters are empty Mrs. Clay ladles the broth out of the moat and into lacquer soup bowls. We drink it down. Delicious. Like Mrs. Krapo's oxtail soup only fishier.

"Dorcas, that was so scrummy," Bronwyn says, lying back on her cushions. "I don't know how you do it."

Mrs. Clay blushes and hurries away. Mr. Clay fills my saucer again. "Drink up, young man. You know I've never seen anyone get the hang of chopsticks so fast. We'll make an old Asian hand out of you in no time."

"Better than an old Asian foot." I start giggling so much I nearly roll off my cushion. Mr. Clay starts up too. His face gets all red and shiny. Bronwyn sits looking at us like she thinks we're being very silly.

Mrs. Clay comes back carrying a red lacquer tray. Bronwyn groans. "Not another bite."

Mr. Clay is trying to stop giggling. Tears are streaming down his cheeks.

"Did I miss something?" Mrs. Clay says, handing around bowls of sherbet the same pale green as her kimono. Mr. Clay wipes his face with his napkin. The sherbet's nice and cold but not very sweet. It makes my lips pucker. I wash it down with sake and Mr. Clay pours me some more. After the sherbet it tastes almost sweet.

"I nearly forgot," Mrs. Clay says and rushes away again. She comes back carrying a small brass bowl. "Fortune cookies!"

"Oh, Dorcas, how corny," Bronwyn says.

Mrs. Clay looks like someone slapped her. She's standing right over me, the bright brass bowl shining like a sun in my eyes. "I'm sure Jared would like one, wouldn't you, Jared?"

I reach up into the bowl. She holds it so high I can't see the cookies. My fingers graze a crispy edge. I pluck a cookie out of the bowl and hold it above my head a moment. It looks so pretty—pale gold, like a sand dollar folded over on itself. So pretty I put it on top of my head. And giggle. It feels so funny balancing there. I giggle some more, but carefully. Don't want it to slide off. Mrs. Clay stands looking down at me and the cookie on top of my head like I'm some kind of retardo.

Mr. Clay, smiling, reaches over and takes the cookie off my head. "My boy, I think it's time I took you home."

MAY

I'm standing in line trying to decide whether I want Sloppy Joes or Tuna Delight when Randy Sparks bounces up next to me, T-shirt ultrawhite under the fluorescent light. He's not even pushing a tray. Come to think of it, I've never seen him in the caf during B-block.

"Hey, you don't want to eat that shit."

One of the caf Negro ladies, hair in a pincushion bun under a gold net, gives him a real dirty look as she scoops up a Sloppy Joe for the girl in front of me. He doesn't notice. He's practically dancing right here in line, bouncing from one ratty Ked to the other and pushing down hard on the chrome tray runners like he's about to do a handstand.

"You got any better ideas?"

"I got a car."

"Where'd you get a car?"

"What'll it be?" The Negro lady's spatula hovers over the Tuna Delight.

"Come on." He tugs at my arm.

I leave my tray right there on the rail and follow him to the center of the caf where the tables are close together and crowded with yelling kids. We sit down at a two-seater behind a pillar.

"Here's what we do." He leans so close I can see the pale down on his cheek. "You go ask Mr. Strunk if you can go to the bathroom. While he's talking to you I'll duck out the window."

"But where are we going? Where'd you get a car?"

"I've got my permit. I'm fifteen."

"But you have to have an adult with you."

"Who's going to know unless we crash and burn? Then it's too late anyhow."

"I don't know." I've never skipped school, unless staying home when I wasn't really sick counts. I've never just walked out in the middle of the day.

"Come on, man. It's summer." The lawn stretches beyond the half-opened windows, green and perfect as grass in a movie.

"But where will we go?"

"I don't know. We'll just go. Out to our lake. It's warm enough to go swimming."

He jumps up from the table. "You coming or not? I've got a six-pack."

"But how do I get out once I'm out of the caf?"

"Don't you know anything? Through the auditorium and out the fire door. I'll be in the alley behind the power plant."

"But the alarm will go off when I open the door."

"So? You'll be long gone."

I want to ask, But what will happen when I miss homeroom? And Latin and biology afterward? Will they call mother right away? But he's already sidling toward the windows.

Mr. Strunk's standing over by a big table of giggling girls. He's grabbed an orange from one of them and is tossing it high in the air. The girl keeps reaching for it but he keeps stepping back. He has a hungry smile on his face.

"Mr. Strunk?"

He glances over his shoulder at me and forgets to catch the orange. The girl scoops it up just before it hits the floor.

"What is it, McCaverty?" The smile's completely gone.

"May I be excused?"

"What for?"

"I have to go to the bathroom."

"Make it quick."

"Yes, sir."

With its windows all rolled down the little white Corvair rides like a bathtub on wheels, jolting along Route 46, shimmying with every strong breeze. Randy has kicked off his Keds and is driving barefoot, dark lines of grit under his thick toenails.

"Open me up a Malt, will you?"

I reach into the backseat for two cans. "They're cold."

"Only the best. Went home and got them."

"Your mom lets you keep your beer in the fridge now?"

"Stuck them in after she went to school." He holds

the beer in one hand and steers with the other. "See if you can find some music."

I fiddle with the radio knob. Country music, *twang, twang*. Static. "Hogs are up . . ." Static. "Wipe Out!" The Surfaris. Surfer music. Fine for California but kind of silly here in the Midwest. I start to look for something better but Randy yells, "Turn it up! Up!" So I do, just in time for the last throbbing run down the scale and the maniac at the end screaming "Wipe-out!"

Randy screams it too, presses the gas pedal to the floor and pulls out to pass two cars. On a hill.

Just before we reach the Plainville Bridge he jerks the steering wheel hard to the left and suddenly we're careening along a deep-rutted dirt road cut between two low hills covered with knee-high pines and yellow scrub. The road dips and we split a crater of muddy water like a speedboat, brown water splatting across the windshield. He punches on the wipers and we're looking through twin muddy rainbows.

The ruts angle upward. He downshifts, the car bucks and rattles. At the top of the ridge we skid out of the ruts and barrel straight into the woods. I can't make out any track at all. Randy spins us past stands of taller pines. Rabbits dart for safety. Red-winged blackbirds burst out of the brush, chevrons flashing. We come over a low rise flying, pine branches screeching against the side of the car. When we thud back to earth my head hits the roof.

"Slow down!"

I feel silly the minute I scream. He's already cut the engine and is leaping out of the car. A dozen yards ahead of us an old yellow school bus, axles up on cinder blocks, pokes its snub nose out of a tangle of lilac bushes.

"Grab the beer," he calls and plunges into the woods.

Sloppily stenciled black letters spell out NEW HAR-
MONY SCHOOL DIST. on the side of the bus. Little green
café curtains hang in the windows. This must be where
he and his mom stay until they're ready to build.

I get the beer from the backseat and head into the
woods. The pine trees are so evenly spaced it doesn't
seem like a real woods at all. I try to keep an eye out for
poison ivy but after a while it's hard enough keeping
track of my feet in the thick undergrowth. I stumble over
a branch hidden by vines and grab for the nearest tree
trunk. My hand comes away sticky with resin, smelling
like Christmas.

A little farther along the ground tilts down at a
scary angle. The pines march steeply down, hairy roots
threading the loose sandy soil. I crouch like a skier and
half slide, half fall down the hill, trying to steady myself
with one hand, holding the beer aloft with the other.
Halfway down I'm bumping along on my ass. I grab onto
a sapling to slow down. It bends right down to the
ground but doesn't break off or uproot. I dangle against
the hillside, feet treading dirt. I find a foothold on a narrow ridge. The pines are taller here and more closely
planted. Sunlight angles down between them in thin
golden shafts. Twenty or thirty feet below I can see water
green and smooth as Coke-bottle glass. A narrow dock
juts out into the water. Randy stands on the end of the
dock, waving his T-shirt.

"Next time take the path."

"Where is it?"

"You're on it."

He slides his jeans down over his knees. They're so
tightly pegged he has to hop from one foot to the other to
pull them down over his bare feet.

I follow the narrow ledge as it zigzags down to the dock.

Randy silently watches my descent, fists on hips. His white boxer shorts are dotted with diagonal rows of red and blue stars.

"At least you didn't drop the beer."

The lake's long and narrow, like a tiny fjord, pines climbing the steep hills.

"Like it?"

"It's great." I set the beer down on the dock.

"Used to be a strip mine. It's all divided up into lots now. But we're the only ones who have bought so far."

It's so isolated and quiet. Can't hear anything—people, cars—except birds tweeting and the occasional plop of a frog dropping into the water.

"Skinny-dip?" He hooks his thumbs under the elastic band of his shorts.

I nod. They drop to the dock.

"What are you waiting for?"

I kick off my penny loafers and strip off my socks. That's the easy part. Pants or shirt first? Unbuckling my belt I pull down my khakis, wishing he'd go ahead and dive in but he stands there waiting. I'm thinner now than I've ever been since I was a kid, when Father used to say my rib cage looked like a xylophone, but the lumps are still there on either side of my waist. I line up the creases and fold my khakis on the dock.

"Come on already."

I unbutton my shirt but leave it on, tails hanging down. I can't look at him. If I did I wouldn't be able to take off my underpants. I slide them down around my ankles and step out of them. He's still watching like I'm the only show in town. I shrug off my shirt. I feel white and fat. The breeze is cold on my ass. My teeth start chattering.

"You cold?"

"A little."

"The water's worse."

"Really?"

"Like fucking ice water, man, but you get used to it pretty fast. Or you die."

I dangle one foot off the dock.

He pulls me back. "No fair. All or nothing."

"I don't know, Randy. If it's too cold and you jump in, it can give you a heart attack."

"Fuck that. Race you to the raft." The raft floats on oil drums close to the opposite shore, maybe a hundred yards away.

"Okay."

He leans forward and falls more than dives into the water.

I leap straight out into the air, arching my body so I barely break the smooth green surface when I land. The water's so cold it gives me an ice-cream headache all over my body. I cut across the lake so fast I'm belly down and panting on the rocking raft when Randy comes paddling up. He hoists himself onto the raft, muscles knotting in his forearms.

He sprawls next to me and lays his cheek against the rough planking. "Told you it was freezing."

"The air feels warm now."

"Ummm." He rolls a little from side to side like he wants to sink right into the wood. The raft tilts gently and beads of water run across the planks, hitting my skin like electric shocks.

We lie there a long time not moving at all, his wet thigh just grazing mine.

Then he rolls lazily over on one side, propping his head up on one arm.

"Wish I could swim like you."

I take a deep breath and turn over on my side too. "Just a question of practice. Like anything else."

He looks down. "You're really hairy."

I look down. Compared to him I am. A copper-colored halo of curls surrounds the base of his cock but his belly and thighs are smooth and hairless.

I feel the warmth rising up inside me and roll back over onto my stomach.

"You want to teach me?"

"Teach you what?"

"Life-saving."

"Sure, why not? Not much to it. A couple of basic carries. What to do if the victim panics. That kind of thing."

"Carries?"

"How you hold the victim to tow him back to shore. Easiest one's the cross-chest carry."

"How's it work?"

"I can't show you here." Not in the state I'm in.

"Why not?"

"I mean I can't show you on the raft."

"Oh."

"Swim out a little and start drowning."

He rolls off the raft and paddles out to the center of the lake.

"This okay?"

"You don't look like you're drowning."

He bobs up and down, thrashing his arms about in the water.

"Help. Help."

I crawl off the raft, cock scraping against the rough planks. Ten strokes and I'm swimming past him.

"Where you going?"

I tread water a yard or so behind him.

"That's the first rule. Never approach the victim head-on. He could grab onto you and drag you down with him."

"I got it."

I dog-paddle up close behind him. He starts to turn around.

"Keep looking straight ahead." I slide my left arm across his chest and crook it around his neck. "Now lie back against me and I'll float you back to safety." I stroke the water with my right arm and lazily churn my legs. No need to hurry.

We glide along, spoon-fashion, his body now bobbing above, now resting against mine. He feels so warm, even in the freezing water. I'm sure he can feel me pressing against him.

I grab onto the raft. He doesn't try to break free, just lies there in my arms.

"Not bad."

"I told you there was nothing to it." My voice sounds like it isn't coming from me at all. He's breathing fast, like he did all the work.

"My turn," he says.

I swim out to the center and wave my arms.

"Help. Help."

He takes forever but eventually he swims up behind me and grabs me around the neck so hard my head goes under water.

"Hey!"

"Sorry, man."

I lie back against him, praying he won't sink under

my weight. He doesn't. He drags me along, flailing the water so hard with his free arm that we travel in wayward arcs back to the raft. My cock bobs up and down in the water like a long white fish pulled along on a line.

He clings to the raft, panting a little, one arm keeping my head above the water, his belly pressed against my back. A woodpecker starts up somewhere across the lake. It echoes over the water like someone hammering. Randy jerks away from me.

"It's only a woodpecker."

He grins sheepishly. "One more time?"

I nod.

I wait until he gets into position and then slowly dog-paddle out to him. My teeth start chattering again. Not cold. Nervous.

I swim up behind him and start to tuck my arm under his chin. He starts struggling like he's really drowning, swinging his arms and kicking at me. I've never really fought with anyone on land—I don't like getting hurt. Water-fights are just my style though because water acts as kind of a cushion. It's hard to hit really hard under water and impossible to fall down. I jump on top of him, pushing him under. We roll over and over in the clear green water, twisting about, intertwining arms and legs like slow-motion wrestlers. He has to come up for air first. I pull him back down, lever my arm under his chin and drag him back to the surface.

He's gasping for breath. "Okay, okay. I give."

Instead of heading back to the raft I tow him along the length of the lake.

"Where we going?" He tries to turn around to look at me but I tighten my lock on his neck.

"Scenic tour."

"You're choking me, man."

"If I ease up you'll just start fighting again."

"No, I won't."

"Promise?"

"Hope to die."

I loosen my grip and in one quick movement he flips over so we're lying face-to-face. It surprises me so much I forget to scull and go right under. He comes with me, arms around me, body against mine. We float back up to the surface, still clinging together.

I run my hands over his shoulders and down his back. I pull him to me tight. I try to press my cheek against his but he jerks his head away.

He opens his eyes wide. "What are you trying to do?"

"I don't know."

"Well, cut it out."

I don't get it at all. He's the one who started. I push away from him.

He pulls me back so our cocks rub together. "This is cool, man. I'm so fucking horny."

"Me too."

"But I'm only doing this because there are no girls around."

"Me too."

"So none of that lovey-dovey shit."

"I didn't mean—"

"Forget it. The important thing's getting your rocks off, right?"

"Right."

Somehow we're back at the dock, water up to our thighs, cocks bobbing in the cool air.

I reach out and touch him. It leaps up. I run my fingers along the shaft, tracing the bulge of the vein. I cup his balls. They play loose and low in the silky sac.

He slowly reaches out and touches me. I don't know who moved first but suddenly we're together again, pushing into each other. My tongue darts out to lick the beads of moisture from his shoulder.

"I'm warning you, man."

"Sorry."

I kneel down before him.

"What are you doing?"

"What do you think?"

I run my tongue over the pink head and take him into my mouth. For a moment it feels like he's going to pull away but he buries his fingers in my hair and arches his back. I can feel him against the back of my throat.

"Stop!"

I look up. His eyes are shut, teeth clenched like I've hurt him.

"What's wrong?"

"I'm about to shoot."

We stand there just looking at each other, not touching, swaying a little like the light breeze is moving us.

He leans back against the dock. I crouch between his legs. His hands are tangled in my hair. Almost right away the rushing along the shaft, thickness in the back of my throat, his hips bucking like mad. He slips out of my mouth trailing a silvery strand that hangs between us an instant, snaps.

I look down in time to see my cock pouring out onto his thigh. He swirls a finger in the shiny liquid, brings the finger slowly to his mouth and licks it.

On the way back to town he's real quiet. He even drives quiet. Doesn't go over seventy even on the straightaway.

I reach over and touch his arm.

He downshifts to third for no good reason. "Might as well finish the beer."

I reach into the backseat, unpop a can and hand it to him. He drinks it down fast.

"You don't want the last one?"

I shake my head.

"Then give it to me."

He drops me off at Meadowlark Shopping Center. Says he has to pick up his mom at the university. My lesson's at four. Says he doesn't want her to know we've been out at the lake. Says she doesn't mind him driving by himself as long as he doesn't give anyone else a ride. Says he doesn't want her to know he skipped school. I get the point.

I close the car door. "Thanks."

"Okay, man." He peels away from the curb.

Feels funny sitting on the bench next to her. She's chattering away, correcting my fingering, suggesting I try a difficult phrase a slightly different way, telling me to go easy on the pedal or she'll have to ban it entirely again. I know it's silly but I'm worried that somehow she knows, she's found out. I can't concentrate. My left hand keeps clomping off in the wrong direction, the right sounds tinny and fast.

Finally she stops me, laying her hand over mine. "Too much spring? No time to practice?"

I've been practicing at least an hour every day, like I always do, but I agree with her.

"Well, that happens to the best of us. These early Bach preludes look easy enough but you really do have to work them out a phrase at a time. You can't expect to ripple through them."

I feel bad, like I've let her down. She's taught me so

much and how have I repaid her? What would she think of me if she knew what I'd done to her son?

"Tell you what. Let's go back to something you know. That always helps to restore confidence."

She places "Sarabande" on the stand.

I'm wobbly at first but the long slow chords steady me. The right pace comes and I start rocking to it. I can see the blue sky and the faint streaks of white cloud above the pines. Paddling lazily through the clear green water, pulling him along. He stands before me, hands in my hair. I hit the final chords—*pum, pum, pummmm*—and shudder all over. At the back of my throat the taste of him.

"Wonderful!" Mrs. Sparks cries.

I knew he wouldn't call. No reason why he should. He's never called me before. Doesn't even know my number. I only know his because I called about piano lessons that time. He could look mine up in the book. That's how I got his: 555-6944.

I lift the receiver, depress the button and dial. Just to see what it feels like. Then I take my finger off the button, cup my hand over the mouthpiece and dial for real. *Brrr, brrr, brrr, brrr—click.* The receiver lifts at the other end. I hang up before I can hear who answered. If it was him did he know it was me?

I call Time and Temperature.

"At the tone the time will be . . ."

"Jared, get off the phone."

". . . five-seventeen. The temperature . . ."

"I'm using it."

". . . seventy-two degrees Fahrenheit."

"To call Time? Why don't you look at your watch?"

"Why don't you sit on it, Sally?"

"If you don't get off this instant I'm going to tell."

"So tell. I was on first. I'll tell you were listening in, you fat pig." She slams down her extension. I can hear her shrieking down the front stairs, "Jared won't let me use the phone."

I replace the receiver and go back to *Masterpieces of English Literature*. Test tomorrow. How the fuck am I supposed to study for a poetry test? You read it and either you feel it or you don't. I feel it: "The night when joy began/Our narrowest veins to flush . . ." Miss Ohm thinks she's going to test me on that. Stupid old bitch. I bet she's never felt anything. Ever. Not anything like what I've felt. Am feeling. I didn't know it would be like this. I've never felt anything like this. Way down inside. Like I'm sick. *Really* sick. I can't stop thinking about him. Only it's not really thinking. I can see him inside my head. Not just him but the whole afternoon, every detail of it, like a private movie looping endlessly through my mind. I can do anything I want with it too—run it forward, backward, in slow motion. The only thing I can't do is stop it. Not even when I sleep.

Sometimes I think it didn't happen at all. I must have made it all up. Otherwise he'd be feeling the same thing I am and would call. He'd have to call. But he hasn't called, so it must not have happened.

It did. And he hates me. That's why he hasn't called. He knows what I am now and he hates me. I know why I feel this way about him—he's so beautiful, more beautiful than anyone I've ever known. And I'm so ugly. Ugly and fat and dirty.

Not dirty. That's silly. I just got out of the shower.

Showers really help. One in the morning when I get up and another when I get home from school. One before going to bed too if I can pry Sally out of the bathroom.

Not to get clean. I'm not dirty. I know I'm not. But for the water. It rushes over me and I feel all right for a while.

I bet he thinks I'm dirty. I know he does. That's why he hasn't called. Probably out with some girl. That one who buys him beer. She's older.

I can't study so I sit at my desk trimming my thumbnail with my teeth. I can't get the nail any farther down—it hurts too much—but I can peel the skin away in little strips. My thumb bleeds and tingles until I have to shake my hand to ease the pain. It doesn't work very well. Not really.

JUNE

"*I*sn't she just the cutest thing?"

Sally squats on the rug at the foot of my bed. She tips the puppy over on its back, holds its front paws together and rolls it to one side and then the other. The puppy—Sally's already named it Lady Jane Too—yaps twice.

"Cut it out, Sally. Everyone will hear."

"Don't be crazy, Jared. You couldn't hear her as far as the bottom of the stairs, she's such a tiny thing."

Occasionally Sally comes up with a good idea, like driving out to Hopetown Kennels this morning to buy a puppy for mother's birthday. It would never have occurred to me because I don't like kennels and I'm not very big on dogs for that matter. They never take much notice of me either. I can come home and Rex and Louis won't even stir from their rug in front of the fireplace, won't even bother wagging their tails, but if it's mother or Sally they leap up and run, barking and shimmying with joy. It was like that today at Hopetown Kennels. This lady in a big bouffant blond wig let us into one of the pens and half a dozen pups tumbled and rolled straight for Sally. And she got right down on her knees with them in God knows what, letting them crawl all over her. I stayed pretty close to the chain-link gate, letting her do the choosing even though I was putting up half of the hundred and twenty-five dollars.

Sally was rolling them all over on their backs to check out which ones were girls. The mother, a long-nosed bitch with a dark ruff, lay back in the far corner of the pen looking like she was too exhausted to move. Then I saw she was nursing a seventh pup. Sally noticed too and rushed over to drag the puppy away from its teat. Just like her. She held the puppy up in the air and crowed, "It's a girl!" It was smaller than the others but fatter too, bulging tummy almost dragging the ground when Sally finally put it down. It waddled around in sloppy circles looking forlorn and sniffing the concrete runway with a stubby snout. Then it headed right back for the bitch's teat. Sally scooped it up and held it close to her white calypso blouse. "This is the one, Jared."

Mother was out for her lunchtime tramp with Rex and Louis when we brought Lady Jane Too home so no one knows except Mrs. Krapo, who just showed a lot of gum and said, "You kids."

Now all we have to do is keep Lady Jane Too quiet until it's time for the big presentation. I worry that if she pees on the floor one more time mother will smell something rotten and come up and clean my room "from stem to stern" the way she's always threatening.

Lady Jane Too wanders over toward my desk. For once Sally lets her go her own way without trying to hug her or pet her or shake her little forepaws.

"Don't you think mother will just die?"

I haven't seen Sally this worked up since the night she came home from a study date with Eugene and she had three major hickeys on the back of her neck.

"One of us had better get back downstairs and act normal. Mother's bound to be suspicious if we both stay up here all afternoon."

"You go, Jared."

Lady Jane zigzags toward the newspapers Sally spread out in front of the window seat. She sniffs them over good and then carefully squats, hind legs quivering. She misses the paper but only by a little.

Mother's in the kitchen arranging deviled eggs in concentric rings on an oval crystal platter. She's wearing a white silk shift with big purple irises painted on it. I've never seen it before.

"Can I have one?"

"Not now, Jared. You'll spoil the pattern."

"If I take one from the outer rim all you have to do is shift them around some."

She doesn't say anything. She almost smiles. I grab an egg. She never has cooked much—Mrs. Krapo doesn't tolerate anyone in her kitchen long—but her deviled eggs are amazing, the yellow whipped up into little paprika-sprinkled waves.

"Excellent. One more?"

She licks her index finger. "All right, but that's got to be the end of it. I can't be rearranging them all afternoon."

The pantry door swings open and Mrs. Krapo backs

into the kitchen carrying a big-domed carnival-glass cake dish.

"Need a hand, Mrs. K.?"

She starts and the big dome rattles. "Don't creep up on me like that."

"Can I see?" I reach for the knob on the dome but she turns away and carefully sets the dish on the counter.

"You get on out of here. Your mother and I have enough to do without you pussyfooting around."

"Can't I even see what kind?"

"Go on." She picks up a checkered tea towel and flicks it at me. "Scoot."

Father and Uncle Fox are out in the driveway cranking the ice cream. Actually Father's cranking. Uncle Fox sits back in a lawn chair, chewing on the stub of a Havana, a bottle of Pabst Blue Ribbon countersunk in the gravel next to his chair.

"Just in time to crank," Father says flashing his big jokey smile that never seems real, maybe because he only uses it when other people are around.

"With shoulders like yours you should just about be able to finish it off," Uncle Fox says, leaning forward to pour rock salt over the ice.

Father gets out of his chair with an exaggerated groan. I sit down. The yellow plastic runners are warm from his body. Makes me feel like getting right up again except there's no place else to sit. I grasp the wooden handle and give it a turn. Still pretty loose. The aluminum cylinder spins around, gray water trickling out of the drainage hole at the bottom of the wooden barrel. The briny water mixes with the chalky smell of the gravel.

Once I'm cranking Father and Uncle Fox go on talking like I'm not even there.

Uncle Fox clears his throat and spits a brownish gob off into the pansy bed that edges the drive. "So a Jew and a Catholic and a colored boy are waiting at the bus stop . . ."

I start counting turns of the handle to drown them out. With my head down close to the barrel all I can see are Uncle Fox's pink knees poking out of his madras bermuda shorts like two fat piglets.

". . . and so the colored boy sniffs his whole arm and yells, 'Sapphire!' "

Uncle Fox's laugh is like a cement mixer. *Rurr, rurr, rurr.*

Father's face goes red and then he laughs too, starting out low but then it cracks and goes high, a little like a kid whose voice is changing.

Uncle Fox slaps a fat thigh and one piglet jumps. "Old Nate Purdue told me that one the other night down at Masonic Temple. That Nate's a real card. Always has a new one too . . ."

Rex and Louis come bounding around the corner of the garage barking away. A couple of seconds later Grandma and Grandpa McCaverty's old Nash noses between the two stands of blue spruce just beyond the twin ponds. Grandpa honks the horn three times. Rex and Louis prance alongside the car.

Grandpa gets out holding a pink-wrapped bundle of bones high above his head as Rex and Louis leap about him. He rests the bundle on the car roof and opens the back door.

"Here, Tressa, let me give you a hand."

"Thank you kindly, McCaverty. I don't know why they make cars so low." Grandmother Fortman grasps his arm with one white eyelet-gloved hand and struggles out of the backseat.

"You took your sweet time getting here, Ma," Uncle Fox calls to her from his lawn chair. "We've already had our cake and our ice cream."

"You just hush up, Fox," Grandmother Fortman says, straightening her white straw picture hat. "Jared, there's a tray of cloverleaf rolls in the trunk. Bring the presents too and don't you go peeking."

Grandma McCaverty comes around from the passenger side of the Nash carrying two flat boxes wrapped in yellow tissue. Rex and Louis leap up on either side of her. "Down, boys, down. McCaverty's got your bones. I didn't think to bring you a doggone thing." She giggles at her pun like a little white-haired girl.

Grandpa McCaverty hugs me close, Sunday stubble grazing my cheek. "Happy birthday, Bud." He calls everybody Bud, even Sally. My birthday isn't till Thursday but it falls so close to mother's we always celebrate them together.

"Happy birthday, hon." Grandma McCaverty gets up on her tiptoes and kisses my cheek. "There, I've left lipstick all over." She wags a finger at me. "Don't let your girlfriend see that. Isn't he getting to be a fine young man, Tressa?"

"You'd best get those rolls, Jared," Grandmother Fortman says. "They won't get browned sitting in the trunk. I suppose your poor mother's inside doing all the work. And on her birthday too. Fox, you get fatter every time I see you. I don't know where you get it. Certainly not from me. Is Lily inside too?"

"She couldn't make it, Mother. One of her bad migraines." Uncle Fox massages his temples like he's got one coming on too.

"I shouldn't wonder," Grandmother Fortman says and heads for the back porch, big black old-lady shoes crunching across the drive.

Grandma McCaverty's trying to talk Uncle Fox into the last helping of three–Jell-O carrot-celery-and-cottage-cheese salad when Mrs. Krapo comes wobbling across the lawn in her cloudy plastic overshoes. The cake slides from side to side on the plate, the candle flames burning sideways in the early evening breeze.

"Lady Baltimore!" Sally squeals like somebody's shot her. Mrs. Krapo bakes a Lady Baltimore only once a year, for mother's and my birthday, because it takes forever. Six layers of lemon sponge cake held together by six alternating layers of lemon and vanilla frosting. From the side it looks like velvet corduroy, thin stripes of white and yellow between wide bands of soft gold. She sets it down in front of mother and we can see the top, a big lemon-yellow disc of frosting ringed with yellow-and-white striped candles. Everybody sings.

"You'd better blow them out fast." Mrs. Krapo wipes her hands on her pink ruffled "company" apron. "With this wind there's going to be wax all over creation."

"Jared, are you going to help me?" Mother looks down the long trestle table at me. The breeze picks up, rustling the leaves of the big sycamore above us. I go and stand next to her.

"Make a wish, Helene. Make a wish, Jared," Grandma McCaverty says, clapping her hands like a birthday cake's the most exciting thing she's ever seen.

"That's right, Bud. Make a wish," Grandpa McCaverty says.

Mother blows out three of the candles. I get the rest. Everybody claps. Without any warning she puts her arms around me and kisses my cheek. And holds on. I can smell face powder, hairspray and Arpège.

The usual stuff for presents. Mother gets a linen blouse and an old pewter teapot from Grandmother Fortman, a box of pale blue stationery from Grandma and Grandpa McCaverty, a thick ivory bracelet from Africa from Uncle Fox and a tiny diamond wristwatch from Father. I get an alligator wallet with a fifty inside from Grandmother Fortman, a card with a smiling waving bear on it and a twenty inside from Grandma and Grandpa McCaverty ("We never know what to get you kids") and beautiful royal blue satiny swim trunks and matching beach jacket from mother, ordered from Saks in Chicago. Father reaches across a platter of chicken bones and sticks four fifties in my shirt pocket. "Don't spend it all in one place, son."

I'm about to ask Mrs. Krapo for a second slice of Lady Baltimore when Sally staggers out the back door carrying a big cardboard box. I can hear Lady Jane Too sliding back and forth inside, claws scrabbling frantically on the slick cardboard. A dark stain's growing at one corner of the box.

Just as Sally gets to mother the bottom caves in and Lady Jane Too tumbles to the grass, paws batting the air. Sally scoops her up and plops her down in mother's lap. Mother looks down, forehead wrinkling, mouth going tight. Lady Jane Too looks up and licks mother's chin.

"Isn't that just what you need, Helene?" Grandmother Fortman says. "Another animal to worry over."

"It's from me and Jared," Sally says.

Lady Jane Too licks mother's chin again and mother smiles a little, tongue pressed between lips the way she always does when she's concentrating real hard. With one finger she lightly strokes Lady Jane Too's muzzle.

"We named her Lady Jane Too," Sally says.

Mother laughs a little at that. But not much. Her eyes are shiny in the fading light.

An awful clatter comes from beyond the garage. Backfire, a car door slamming like a washing-machine lid crashing down. Sally forgets all about Lady Jane Too and races around the corner of the garage so fast one of her sandals goes flying. Eugene hasn't been by lately.

She comes back, walking. "Jared, somebody . . ."

He comes around the corner like he wishes he didn't have to. Bare feet, bare everything except for an unraveling pair of washed-out cut-off jeans. He's reddish-brown all over, like polished teak, curly hair golden on top as the last slanting sun catches it.

He stops a good way from the table and looks down at his bare feet. Everyone sits looking at him except Father, who glances over at me.

"Hi." I stand up, knowing I should introduce him round but really just wanting to get out of there fast.

Mrs. Krapo picks up the paper plate with the piece of Lady Baltimore she cut for me and holds it out to him. "You'd better have yourself some birthday cake and ice cream while there's still some left to be had."

Randy comes over to the table, arms folded across his naked chest.

"Come and sit down, Bud," Grandpa McCaverty says. "There's plenty of room."

Randy squeezes in between Grandpa McCaverty and Uncle Fox and everyone starts talking at once.

"Didn't mean to crash your party, man." Randy quickly looks both ways and without bothering to stop spins out of the driveway spraying gravel and laying a short strip of rubber along Appleseed Road.

"It's okay. Really." The sun's down and the crickets are cranking up. The cool earth-smelling air rushes against my face.

"Your family's kind of neat."

I look over to see if he's joking. Even in the dark I can tell he's not. "Yeah, I guess so." Between the trunks of the overhanging maples that turn the road into a tunnel I can see fields streaking past, long rows of short corn fanning out, leaves silvery blue in the late light.

"Your dad's a funny guy."

Well, he sure was *acting* funny. Teasing Randy and grinning over at me, hopping up to get Randy more ice cream and coming back with a bowl piled so high it looked like an iceberg drifting through the dark. Later he went indoors and brought out beers for both of us, winking at us when Grandmother Fortman snorted her disapproval.

Sometimes he can be so nice. It's just that I can never tell when that's going to be. That's why I usually don't bring friends home. Not like I've ever had that many to bring. But even when I have he's always found something wrong with them. Paul Herzog from Gifted Children's Summer School for instance. He didn't like him even before he caught us together. Always saying things like, "He's so pretty I bet he squats when he pees." And after he caught me with Paul he wouldn't let me have anyone over for a long time, not even in the afternoon. "You can't be trusted," he said, and I guess he was right. I wasn't allowed to go to anybody else's house either. For so long that people stopped asking.

Tonight though when Randy asked in front of everyone if I wanted to spend the night out at his lake Father didn't say a word. I can never figure him out.

Randy slows down for the light and instead of hang-

ing a right onto 46, he barrels on past Creve Coeur Park
and turns onto The Boulevard, heading into town.

"I thought we were going out to your lake."

"My mom's out there with a bunch of her professor
friends."

"Oh." I feel kind of silly holding my new trunks
rolled up in a brown towel like a big Tootsie Roll.

"They're going to stay out there tonight so we've got
the house all to ourselves."

"Oh."

"Reach under your seat. Got a surprise."

A small brown paper bag. I pull out the flat pint
bottle, dark as Cheracol.

"Ballard's cherry brandy. We used to drink it all the
time in Ann Arbor. Happy birthday."

I break the seal and take a sip. It tastes a lot like
Cheracol too except it burns more going down. A lot
more. I try not to cough.

"You going to hog it all?"

The thing about cherry brandy is it has to go down
real fast, otherwise the taste is horrible. The sick sweet
smell burns my nostrils. Before long we're halfway down
Mrs. Sparks's bottle of cooking sherry. Doesn't taste better but at least it doesn't bite. Randy weaves about the
kitchen banging open cabinet doors. He's decided to
make popcorn. I don't know how he can be so hungry
after all he put away back at my house.

"The secret is," he says, plopping a whole stick of
butter into a big iron skillet and turning the flame on
high, "don't put in the corn until your butter's really
hot." He wipes his buttery fingers across his bare chest.

The butter's sizzling away and turning kind of cara-
mel-color when I suggest it's about time to add the corn.

He puts down the sherry bottle, almost missing the counter, and pulls on a pair of quilted silver oven mitts. "Out. Out of my kitchen." He pushes me into the dining room. "Go play me something."

"On the piano?"

"No, on your skin flute, asshole. Play the slow one. It's cool."

Funny to think of him down in the basement all those Tuesday afternoons, listening to me play the piano while I listened to him lifting weights.

I've got "Sarabande" by heart now, but it isn't easy. Not tonight. My right hand feels light and all rubbery. It keeps bouncing off on its own. The left clumps along, slipping off the keys altogether when I forget to concentrate real hard. Sometimes the purple-and-green aura around the piano lamp is so pretty I forget to play at all. I hold my breath and count to a hundred. That's supposed to be good for sobering up because it rushes oxygen to the brain. I exhale and sit up really straight. No pedal. I try to keep it slow and stately, the way Mrs. Sparks says. Ten or twelve bars and something clicks. Right and left hands start to merge and there's a new sound, like a third hand binding the other two together. I'm near the end when he comes in and sits down beside me with the oven mitts still on. His shoulders glow in the lamplight. I press the last chords home and lift my fingers half an inch off the keys.

He leans against me. His warm breath smells sickly sweet. "I'm so fucking drunk, man." His eyes look sleepy. He falls over, laying his head in my lap.

We sit like that a while. I'm barely breathing. I take one hand off the keyboard and touch his hair. He doesn't move. I can hear him breathing, shallow and regular. Asleep? I smooth down the soft curls. They spring right back up. I run my fingers over the back of his neck. He shivers. Not asleep. He presses his face into my crotch and rubs back and forth. The oven mitts knead the inside of my thighs.

I notice it first. "What's that smell?"

"Shit! The popcorn."

He opens the basement door. I start to follow him down.

"My bed's too small for both of us. We can use my mom's room. I'll be back in a second."

Kind of weird being in her room. I flick on the overhead light. Looks like she left in a hurry. Clothes hang from the closet doorknob and drape the chair in the corner. Shoes and nylons straggle out of the closet.

I sit down on the edge of the mattress. There are at least a dozen candles on the low table but no matches. Sheaves of sheet music and old paperbacks are wedged between the candles. More paperbacks litter the floor next to the mattress, covers splattered with wax. One of them has a drawing of a dark-skinned man in a white shirt and tight pants on the cover. *Giovanni's Room* by James Baldwin. I've heard his name someplace but I can't remember where. I shift a stack of books and find a box of kitchen matches. I light three candles—purple, green, red. I get up and switch off the light. I blow out the purple and green candles. The room smells like raspberries.

I lie back on the mattress and stare at the ceiling. The candle strobes some. Light washes back and forth across the ceiling. Makes me dizzy. I sit up and pull my blue Ban-Lon over my head. I wrap it carefully around *Giovanni's Room* and place it on the bare floor. I take off my khakis and socks, make a neat pile of them and slip under the flimsy bedspread. I feel so sleepy. Wish he'd

hurry up. Pressing thumb to neck I count my pulse. Have
to count fast.

I close my eyes only a second but when I open them
he's standing at the foot of the mattress wearing blue-
and-white striped pajamas. Tops and bottoms.

I can't help laughing.

"What's your problem?"

"Pajamas."

He looks at me like I'm crazy and with finger and
thumb snuffs out the red candle. He lifts the bedspread
and slides in next to me. We lie there looking at the ceiling.

"I'm so blasted."

"Me too." Except suddenly I'm not anymore. My
head feels real clear. The raspberry smell's gone now.
Strange.

"So drunk." He rolls over on his side and holds the
sheet up like a tent over our bodies. "You always sleep in
underpants?"

"Yeah." Even in the dark he can see the white ridge
of my hard-on.

He reaches down and inserts one finger in the slit of
my underpants, running it along the back of my cock.

The pearly buttons on his pajama jacket are big as
quarters. I undo them slowly, looking at his face after
each one to see if he wants me to keep going. His eyes are
closed so I guess it's okay. His whole hand has worked its
way into the pouch of my underpants. His fingers encir-
cle my cock, cup my balls.

I reach into the gap of his pajama bottoms and take
hold of him. The tip of his cock is wet.

"Oh." His lips part.

As though asleep he rolls over on top of me, nuz-
zling his chin against my neck.

He wrestles my underpants down over my knees and presses into me. I push his pajama top back off his shoulders and wrap my arms around him.

His cock slides back and forth against mine. He holds on to me like I'm not me but somebody bigger and stronger. Like he's drowning and I'm a log. So tight my shoulders ache and it's hard to breathe.

He's panting in my ear. Sweat pours off his face like tears. With the tip of my tongue I touch the wetness of his cheek. His parted lips are right there, half an inch from mine. He's gasping for air now, his breath rushes into my mouth. I raise my head and press my lips against his. He pulls away.

"Would you stop the fairy shit, for God's sake."

"Sorry."

"Sometimes I think you really get off on this."

"You don't?"

"Only because I pretend you're a girl."

"Oh."

He starts up again, pushing into me. I don't care what he pretends. I don't care, I don't care, I don't care. Suddenly he bucks and freezes, a diver angled across the air. He's stopped breathing. Then he gasps three times. His head jerks to one side. My shoulder gets his wet lips, my belly the gush of his cock.

He's dead weight, beached and gasping.

When he finally moves I feel a cold trickle down the side of one thigh. He rolls off me and onto his back, chest still rising and falling fast. One hand flops over and lands on my cock. I push it away.

His voice comes from the other side of the ocean. "Hey, man, don't you want to come?"

"I guess I already did."

*   *   *

"Goodness, Mr. McCaverty, you look like you passed a sleepless night. Or several."

Mr. Clay's unlocking the big brass doors as Randy drops me off. He pulls away without saying good-bye.

Mr. Clay watches as the Corvair putts off. "Your chauffeur, Mr. McCaverty?"

Today's my first day working summer schedule—five days a week, nine-to-five. First off, because it's Monday, we choose the Art Object of the Week for next Sunday's rotogravure section. Or rather, Mr. Clay's already chosen it and he shows it to me—a small whitish painting of a skinny man sitting on a skinny speckled horse. By Marino Marini. Nice name.

It turns out I'm going to write the Art Object of the Week articles for the *Tribune-Star* so Mr. Clay is free to handle more important things. I was a little scared at first, but Mr. Clay sat me down in his office, horse and rider propped up against one wall, and explained Marini and his work while I took notes. Then Mr. Clay went off for lunch with the chancellor of Indiana Normal and I spent the rest of the day pounding on the big Underwood in the library, trying to turn the notes I took into five hundred words that would read like a real newspaper article. That's not as easy as it sounds. I used Mr. Clay's piece on the Cocteau portfolio as a model and threw in words he used a lot when he was explaining the Marini to me—*stark, alienation, impasto, patina.* And I looked up Marini in *The Encyclopedia of Twentieth-Century Artists,* which used pretty much the same words. By four-thirty it sounded pretty good but I want to give it another shot before showing it to Mr. Clay.

I climb the stairs to my room, completely exhausted, thinking I'll get a quick nap before supper.

Father's sitting in the window seat. He's stretching a tape measure along the bottom edge of the window frame. He's got on his favorite hot-weather work clothes —his old Indian moccasins, a paint-stained pair of army shorts and no shirt. Likes to show off his tan. God I hate it when he comes up to my room when I'm not around. Almost as bad as when I'm there. Always snooping. I bet he'd just love to find another *Physique.*

"Hard day at the office, son?" He lets the tape snap back into its metal case and turns around, grinning at his stupid joke.

"What are you doing?"

"Just measuring the screen so I can get a new one made. Keep the flies off you." That screen never has fit right. Why's he worrying about it now? Why doesn't he take his tape and leave? He stretches real big, faking a yawn. It's not that hot but sweat glistens in the black hair that spreads across his chest like one of those ink blots shrinks use to test who's crazy. I go over to my desk and start emptying out my pockets so I won't have to look at him.

"You have a good time?"

"At work?" What does he care?

"Last night."

I won't turn around. He sounds like he's still smiling. Just making casual conversation. It's got to be more than that. I turn around, bracing myself against the desk. "It was all right."

He's fiddling with the tape, pulling it out an inch or two, letting it snap back.

"He seems like a nice kid." Interrogation time. I know he's working up to something. Always is.

"He's okay."

"Your mother tells me his mother's your piano teacher."

"Yeah."

"He's old enough to drive?" So that's it. I won't be allowed to ride with him anymore. But if that's it, why's he still grinning?

"He lost a year in school because they've moved around so much."

He pulls the tape out about six inches. "Was it cold?"

"What?"

Snap. "Out at his lake. It got pretty cool here last night. And it's always cooler on the water."

"We had sleeping bags."

"And a couple of beers to keep you warm?" He chuckles like he wants me to think he's just one of the boys. He's not going to catch me. I chuckle too and don't say anything.

"Just so long as he doesn't drink and drive."

"No."

He pulls the tape way out. "He seems like a real nice kid."

Come on, I feel like screaming, let's get it over with. What's on your mind? "He's all right."

The tape hisses back into the case. "A real chunky little guy."

Chunky. Makes him sound like peanut butter. "Yeah, I guess."

He lazily rubs one hand back and forth across his sweaty chest. "Looks like a real athlete."

"He's going out for football in the fall."

"Small for football." His eyes slit like he's remembering how Randy looked.

"I guess."

"But chunky as hell." He chuckles again.

"Yeah."

"Well." He stands up and looks around. "I'd better get back downstairs. See you at dinner."

"Okay." I sit down on the bed. I'm shaking all over.

Mrs. Krapo, dishtowel wrapped around one hand, pulls a pan of shortcake out of the oven. A glass bowl of strawberries sits in the center of the kitchen table. "Last I looked she was down by the big pond with the dogs."

I grab a handful of wet fat strawberries, their green caps still on.

Mrs. Krapo swats at my ass with the dishtowel. "Now you just get your fingers out of there. Barely enough to go around as it is."

Mother and Sally are sitting on the stone bench under the oldest willow tree, Lady Jane Too between them. Louis lies at mother's feet, nose between his paws. Rex sits up straight like he's waiting for someone to take his picture. The sun's getting low in the west. The big pond's so smooth they're all reflected in it.

Sally's holding Lady Jane Too's head up while mother checks her ruff for ticks and burrs.

"Hi. What're you doing?"

They're so busy with the dog they didn't even see me coming.

"Hello, Jared," mother says, smoothing down Lady Jane Too's ruff. "We almost came by Slope's today."

"You did?"

"But then we got so busy with shopping and all . . ."

"Oh."

"You should see all the stuff I got, Jared." Sally's

just like mother, always happiest when she's just bought something. Or fed her fat face.

"I can't wait."

Irony's completely lost on Sally. "If there's time before supper I'll show you. I got this incredible electric-pink swimsuit with a back down to here, and an ecru linen suit with bone pumps and purse to match—"

"I thought we'd better get started," mother says, "if we're going to get all the things Sally needs for college."

"—and the cutest little flowered cotton dress. Mother thinks it's too short but I think it's perfection."

"I didn't say it was too short, Sally." Mother's smoothing Lady Jane Too's ears and Lady Jane Too is leaning into her like she's in love. "I just think it emphasizes your hips, and that's surely the last thing you want to emphasize."

"I'll say."

"You shut your mouth, Jared McCaverty. I'm down to a size six."

"Make me. Don't you mean sixteen?"

"I wouldn't criticize anyone if I had a belly like yours."

I step toward her to swat her good. Rex snaps at my hand. Louis stands up. Lady Jane Too gives a high-pitched bark.

"Down, Rex. Down, Louis. It's all right, Lady Jane." Mother strokes Rex's flanks. Louis sits back down. "You're both getting too old to behave like this. It's so childish. And it upsets the dogs."

"He started it."

"You both started it. Now hush."

"I'm up to hundred sit-ups a day. I almost have ridges."

"Jared, I don't want to hear another word."

"You never want to hear another word unless it's about your precious dogs."

Mother stands up. "I think that's just about enough. Sally, will you bring Lady Jane Too? Rex, Louis." She heads across the grassy walkway between the twin ponds, Rex and Louis at her heels, tails pluming.

"Way to go, Jared. She was going to take you shopping next weekend."

"Fuck you, Sally. How's Eugene?"

It takes so little to make her cry—sometimes I wonder why I bother.

JULY

"Root beer?"

Randy swerves the Corvair across two lanes of oncoming traffic and jolts us into the parking lot of Dad's Root Beer, taking the first speedbump without slowing down. My teeth clack together.

He pulls into a slot and punches the button of the red metal speaker screwed to the post. "Two Supermugs."

The speaker roars and clicks.

Too hot to stay in the car so we get out and sit on the hood, which isn't much better. Practically all the other slots are empty but that doesn't mean our order comes any quicker.

The sun's white and high. The whole sky's white too. My red Ban-Lon sticks to my spine. Randy unbut-

tons his white rayon shirt all the way down and leans
back on his elbows. His belly gleams with sweat.

"How hot do you think it is?"

"I don't know. It was ninety-six when I got up."

"Must be way over a hundred by now."

The girl comes with the tray. Her brown ponytail
curls around her sweaty neck like a drowned rat.

"You'll have to get back in your car. I can't serve
you like this."

I start to slide off the hood but Randy just lazily
rubs his belly. "It's like an oven in there."

She looks down at him, squinting her eyes against
the glare from the hood. "Look, I don't make the rules.
My boss sees you, I get hell."

He doesn't even look at her. "Fine with me."

I slide off the hood. "Come on, Randy."

She smiles at me. Her left front tooth's missing.
"You can leave the doors open if you want. That way
you'll get the breeze."

"What breeze?" Randy eases off the hood and opens
the door. The girl clamps the tray onto the window. He
pays her and she goes away.

He hands me a big thick-bottomed mug, sides white
with frost. The head's two inches thick.

"Tastes great."

He sits holding his mug between his legs like it's
cooling him off. "I know what would taste even better."

I lick the foam from my lips. "What?"

He wraps his hands around his mug and slides them
slowly up and down, wiping away the frost.

Reaching over I dip my finger in the foamy head.
"Can we go out to your lake?"

"My mom's out there with her friends. As usual."

"Oh."

"What about your place?"

"Fourth of July. Everybody's there for ice cream."

"That all they ever do?"

"About."

He lifts his mug and chugs it. "Well, at least we can go swimming. Right? No one's going to object to that."

"I guess not."

We have to wade pretty far out in the big pond just to get to where it's deep enough to swim. Even close to shore the bottom's about a foot deep in green fuzzy weeds. At the center the water's dark and warm. With the weeds spiraling around just below the surface it's like swimming in a bowl of Mrs. Krapo's chicken-noodle soup.

Everyone's up at the house sitting under the sassafras tree in the back yard waiting for the ice cream to set. I hunted up an old pair of baggies for Randy. Even with the drawstrings pulled tight and double-knotted they still slide down over his ass when he dives.

I go after him, eyes open in the water. I can just make out the blur of his kicking feet a yard or so in front of me. Two hard kicks and I'm next to him, sliding my body against his. His hand runs over my crotch.

We come up and tread water, facing each other.

"Don't go away." I slip below the surface and tug the baggies down. His cock springs out. I take it into my mouth and suck until I think my lungs will burst. I bob back up to the surface.

"How'd you do that?"

"Easy. Just forget about trying to breathe through your nose."

He stops treading water and sinks like a stone. I can

feel his hands tugging at the waistband of my trunks and then the tight ring of his lips, the rushing deep inside.

He comes up sputtering.

"Not bad for a beginner."

This time we go down together, rolling over and over in the warm thick water, twisting, twining, bucking —corkscrewing through the dark.

We come up panting and coughing, his arms still around my neck.

"Jared. Jared!"

Father's standing on the bank, shouting through cupped hands. He's wearing a shiny plastic chef's apron over his army shorts. Even from the middle of the pond I can read the big red letters on the apron: ALL FIRED UP.

"What?"

"Hamburgers are ready anytime you guys are."

"Coming."

We're toweling down in my room. I rub his head hard. When I take the towel away his curls spring up gold in the light. He leans over and pushes my trunks down past my knees. They hit the bare floor with a splat.

"We don't have time. They'll . . ."

Too late. He's down on his knees, breathing through his nose. I count silently, telling myself I'll make him stop when I get to twenty. At forty-three I pull him up. He leans into me, rubbing his cock against mine.

"Randy . . ."

"Relax, will you?" He holds me close, breath hot against my cheek. I rub my cheek against his. He moans a little, eyes closed. His parted lips glow dark pink against his brown skin. I can see the wet tip of his tongue. I lick his chin and wait. He doesn't move at all. My lower lip brushes his. He opens his eyes and stares right into mine. Flecks of green, brown, gold whirling toward black pupils. He doesn't even blink. Makes me dizzy. Not enough air in this hot still room.

In slow motion his face comes nearer. Noses bump. Then no more waiting, no turning his head, only wet lips, sharp ridges of teeth and then the soft interior of his mouth.

I open my eyes in time to see Father's face rising over the stairwell railing, eyes bulging, mouth twisted, like an angry puppet in a Punch-and-Judy show.

I shove Randy away.

"Hey!" Bewildered, he looks around to see what I'm staring at.

He's coming at us now waving the big aluminum spatula. The flat end's streaked with brown grease and charred specks of meat.

He swings once. The spatula stings against my thigh. The metal's still hot.

"You . . . you . . ." He chokes on the word. Spittle flies from his mouth. "You can't be trusted. Always the same filthy thing."

I dart past him as he swings again. The spatula grazes my shoulder. I thought he'd come after me but he stays in the center of the room blocking the stairs.

Randy stands perfectly still, cock shriveled, arms up like he's still holding on to me.

Father stands looking at him a long time, like he's memorizing him.

"Get your clothes and get out." Randy scrambles to grab his jeans off the floor. Father gets him hard across the left buttock. The spatula leaves a brown oblong of grease.

"You're as filthy as he is. And you call yourself an athlete. Get your clothes on."

Randy's looking at his jeans like he's forgotten how
they work.

"Now!" Father bellows, brandishing the spatula.

Hopping on one leg, then the other, he pulls them
on.

"Where are your shoes?"

Randy looks around the room in a daze.

I say he wasn't wearing any.

"You shut up, goddammit. Just shut up!" He grabs
Randy's arm and drags him toward the stairs. His bare
feet squeak across the wooden floor. His shirt's half off,
half on, fluttering behind him like a pennant.

"Let's go. Now!" Father gives him a shove. I watch
his brown back going down the stairs until Father follows
after him, blocking him out.

He'll be back. Nothing to do but wait. I pull on my
bermudas and Ban-Lon and lie in the window seat looking out the window at nothing. The pain gnaws deep in
my stomach, like the Trojan boy and the fox we learned
about in Latin. Always the same pain—when he caught
me with the *Physique,* when he caught me with Paul
Herzog. Whenever he's caught me. When I close my eyes
he's all I can see—shiny chef's apron, black hair matted
across his bare chest. He's so disgusting.

Why'd we have to go upstairs to change? I knew
what would happen if we did. I knew I wouldn't be able
to control myself. We could have eaten hamburgers in
our trunks. No one would have objected to that on such a
hot day. Why go upstairs at all when I knew we'd get
carried away? So fucking stupid.

It's nearly dark when I hear his feet on the stairs. He
always waits until dark. I guess he wants me to have time
to think about what I've done. He's taken off the plastic

chef's apron. His bare shoulders glow white coming through the dark. The little blue jar's half concealed in his hand. I unbutton my bermudas and roll over.

"Not in the window seat," he says. He's calm now. His voice is low, almost soft. "I want you on the bed."

I lie down on the bed and bury my face in the pillow.

"Pull down your shorts."

I arch my ass in the air and slowly push the shorts down around my knees.

The ching of his belt unbuckling, the swish of leather through belt loops.

His fingers are cool as they slip under the elastic band of my underpants. He slowly eases them down.

The belt hisses through darkness. *One.* Like being bitten by a snake. I grind the pillow between my teeth. *Two.* The bedsprings creak as my body stiffens. *Three.* Harder this time. Maybe I should have yelled the first time. Sometimes that makes him hit harder, sometimes not. Depends on how worked up he is. I don't want him to get carried away like the time he caught me with Paul Herzog. *Four.* It burns deep inside, a red glow. *Five.* When the burning comes I know the worst is over. I know I can take it then. *Six. Seven. Eight.* I moan into the pillow. Can't help it. It just comes pouring out. *Nine.* Twitching all over. Christ. The bedsprings pop and shriek. *Ten.*

The belt buckle clatters to the floor. The springs groan. He sits down beside me, pushing damp bangs off my forehead. "What am I going to do with you, son?" His voice sounds thick, like he needs to spit. "We can't go on this way." He lays his head next to mine on the pillow. He smells of charcoal and raw meat. His cheek's wet. "I don't want to have to do this. You know that, don't you? Each time I whip you I pray to God it will be

the last time. But then you go and . . . then you're
filthy all over again." He's crying hard now, head trembling against my shoulder. I've got a crick in my neck but
I can't roll over. He'd see what I've done to the bedspread. That would make him mad all over again.

After a while he sits up, rubbing his eyes. He unscrews the lid on the little blue jar. The clean sharp smell
of Vicks Vapo-Rub means it's all over. At first it feels
cold on my ass but as he slowly rubs it in with small
circular strokes the warmth radiates right through me.
Makes me sleepy and kind of sad, like that hymn they
sing in church. "There Is a Balm in Gilead."

The bed creaks again. He stands up. He squeezes my
shoulder. I can hear his feet on the stairs, a step at a time
like he's sleepwalking through some slow ceremony. I lie
there, not moving, the pillow wet with his tears and my
saliva, the sticky damp on the bedspread between my
legs. I never cry. Never. I feel warm and calm now. And
tired. Too tired to even clean myself off. The pain in my
stomach's gone. It's over. Now I can sleep.

I called Randy from work this morning. He heard
me say hello and hung up.

"Why, Jared McCaverty. How are you, darling?"
I hadn't counted on Mrs. Muller being on duty.
Usually she's home working in her garden. Her husband
Sid fills the prescriptions and a fat girl with pimples usu-
ally takes care of the cash register.

"I'm fine, Mrs. Muller." I sniff a couple of times to
show her I'm not fine at all.

"Summer cold?" This comes out *subber code,* like
she's got one herself. For the longest time I thought Mrs.
Muller was Swedish but mother says it's just a speech

impediment. She sure looks Swedish, white-blond hair puffed up like a haystack above her shiny pink face and bright blue eyes.

"Hay fever."

"You poor thing. And in July." Her eyes open so wide the irises look like they're floating in pools of custard.

"I always seem to get it before anyone else." I rub my eyes hard to show her how much they itch.

She picks up the small glass bottle I've laid on the counter. "Sominex. That won't do much for hay fever, dear."

"I've got drops and stuff at home. But I get so stuffed up at night I can't sleep."

She takes her glasses out of the breast pocket of her powder-blue lab coat and carefully reads the label. "These may be some help. But never more than one tablet for someone your age. And never more than two nights in a row. Take them too long and they end up *disturbing* your sleep."

"Yes, ma'am. That's what I've heard. I'll be extra careful."

"I'm sure you will." She gives me a big smile and rings up the sale. She drops the bottle into a little blue paper bag. As I reach out to take it she lays one pink hand over mine. The silver ring on her middle finger has a round blue stone in it big as a robin's egg. "You're a good boy, Jared. How's that handsome father of yours?"

"He's fine, Mrs. Muller. He said to say hello." I try to pull my hand away but she's holding on tight.

"You tell him I said not to be such a stranger." She lets go, finally.

"I sure will."

When Mrs. Krapo calls up to say supper's on the table I wait a couple of minutes and then sneak down to their bathroom. Just as I'd hoped: a new unopened economy-sized bottle of Cheracol. I take it back up to my room and hide it under the window seat.

At supper Father pretends I'm not even there. That's been going on all week. Fine with me. Kind of rough on Sally though, since it means he focuses all his attention on her for a change. As far as I can tell she hasn't been eating—at all—since the Fourth. One of her girlfriends is having a big pool party next week so she's trying to lose about fifty pounds in a hurry.

Tonight he finally notices she's just scooting her food around on the plate. She's busy covering half her slice of ham with au gratin potatoes when he pounces.

"Sally, I haven't seen you take a single bite."

Sally looks down at her plate like something slimy's crawling across it. "I have."

"No, you haven't. I've been watching."

"You have not."

"I have too."

Mother, who never eats much either, rouses herself a little. "It's hard to have much of an appetite when it's this hot."

Father doesn't look at her. "Don't go making excuses for her, Helene. She has to eat or she'll get sick."

"It's when she eats that she does get sick." I know I should keep out of it but I can't resist. He doesn't seem to hear anyway. I could scream and he wouldn't hear.

"I'm fine," Sally says, spearing a string bean with her fork and holding it out in front of her.

Father leans across the table and taps the rim of her plate. "I want to see you eat everything that's on your plate."

Sally's bangs hang down in her eyes. She dangles the string bean into her mouth and gulps it whole, like a bird swallowing a worm.

"Now some ham." He taps her plate again like she needs reminding where it is.

She carves off a tiny morsel and carefully trims away a microscopic ridge of fat. She pops the ham into her mouth and starts to chew. Her face is all red and her jaw moves slowly, like she's got a pound of ham in there instead of a quarter ounce.

"That's better." Father looks over at me for the first time. "What have you got to grin about?"

"I'm not." But I was. Because somebody else is getting it for a change. Because I'm out of it at last. Who wouldn't grin?

Sally stands up so fast she knocks over her chair. She runs out of the room, big tears rolling down her red puffed-out cheeks. I can tell the ham's still in there.

"You come back here this instant," he yells.

She's already scrambling up the back stairs. The bathroom door slams.

Father wads his napkin and throws it on the table.

Mrs. Krapo comes in from the kitchen carrying four gold bowls. "Who's got room for peach cobbler?"

The note's the hardest part. I try a bunch of different ways but they all sound wrong. I don't want him to think I'm doing it because of him although he could have talked to me on the phone. But I don't blame him. Not him. I realized that tonight at dinner.

Finally I just write down the essentials:

I'm sorry you wouldn't talk to me. But I understand. It probably wouldn't have made any dif-

ference. I want you to have my jade cuff links
and my intaglio ring. It was my grandfather's.
I'll always remember you.

I guess anything like that is bound to sound silly. I've
never seen him wear cuff links. I'm not even sure he owns
a suit. Maybe he'll wear the ring. It's probably too big for
him. He has such small hands, monkey hands. Does he
know a jeweler could fix it? How's he going to get the
ring and cuff links anyway? Drop by the house and ask
for them? Fuck it. What do I care?

In the end I write it out again, except for the last
sentence since it's kind of a contradiction.

Everyone's in bed. I slip down to the morning room,
look up *Sparks* in the phone book and address the envelope.

It's a long way down to the mailbox. The crickets
get on my nerves so much I want to scream at them to
shut the fuck up. My bare feet are wet with dew. It's a
warm night but I feel chilly. I put up the red flag on the
mailbox and head back up the long drive.

Fifty pills don't seem like much until they're all laid
out on the rim of the sink. I look in the mirror a long
time. Somehow I thought I'd look different.

Finally I fill the toothglass with Cheracol. The first
ten or so are easy. After that they start sticking in my
throat. Pretty soon my mouth tastes powdery and bitter,
like I've been chewing on gravel. The Cheracol helps cut
the taste.

I take the Sominex and Cheracol bottles back upstairs and hide them under the window seat. Let him
hunt for them—he's so good at spying on me he'll get a

kick out of it. I climb into bed and pull the sheet over me. Seems kind of pointless to read so I turn out the light.

It's funny—you'd think I'd feel sad but I don't. Don't feel much of anything really. Not even sleepy. Just kind of relieved. No more hiding and worrying and feeling sick in the pit of my stomach. No more anything. Nothing. What it feels like is peaceful.

I lie there a while longer and then I start to worry. Still don't feel a thing. The pills aren't working. It's going to be just like the time he caught me with Paul Herzog. Took a whole bottle of A.S.A. and woke up next morning with a terrible headache. I can't do anything right.

Maybe I should turn on the light and read some after all. Except when I try to lift my arm I can't. I try to move my legs. They're not there. I'm so heavy I'm sinking into the mattress inch by inch. Just trying to move leaves me breathless. Dizzy. I turn my head and it rolls over onto my shoulder like it's falling off. Can't move it back either. I can smell my own skin, but like it's someone else's. Really strange. I guess this is it.

Scary. When I forget to concentrate there's all this whispering going on all around me. People have come to watch. I don't mind that so much. I'm used to being watched. Just wish they'd shut up. They get louder and louder though, rumbling in my ears like a slow freight train. I feel so heavy. My mouth's so dry. Maybe one of the whisperers will bring me water. I say the word. I know I said it. Except they can't hear me for all the whispering. I can't yell—don't want them to hear downstairs. Don't want to blow it. Not again. I can do something right. Something that'll make everybody happy. But I'm so dry. I lick my lips. My tongue's as big as a foot. Yell. I won't.

So thirsty. Water. The big pond's at the foot of my

bed. I can hear the water lapping. If someone would just scoop up a palmful and bring it to me. Water. I'm going to yell. I have to.

My head's sinking into the pillow. Try again. Water.

Whisper, whisper. Wish they'd shut up. How can anyone hear?

I take a deep breath. Air rushes in like a dry wave. Water. Yell. "Mother!"

Wrong word.

Sounded like a bullfrog croaking from the pond. I wait. Listen for their door opening. Hard to hear for all the whispering. Nothing. She can't hear either.

He's kissing me. After what happened I thought he'd never have anything to do with me again but he's kissing me all over my face, tongue cool and kind of raspy. It tickles.

"Jared, are you sick?"

My eyes are stuck shut. Something fuzzy in my face. I turn my head. *Bonk.* Something cold and hard. One eye pulls open. Shiny white. Hurts like hell. Eye, head. Other eye opens. Way too bright. Shade my eyes. Lady Jane Too's pointy little nose right in my face, pink tongue hanging out. Mother's standing over me, salmon silk robe shimmering with light.

"Are you all right?"

My neck feels broken. No, I can move. A little. I lift my head. How'd it get wedged between the toilet bowl and bathtub? My mouth tastes horrible, tongue and teeth coated with bitter moss.

I remember. Spasms in the dark, running downstairs, all of it gushing out.

I sit up and feel like lying back down. "Must have been something I ate." My head's numb and heavy. Sunlight everywhere, sharp as broken glass. Something's wrong with her face. It's blurry, out of focus.

"Feel better now?" She reaches down and touches my cheek, like she wants to make sure it's really me.

"Yeah, fine." And I am except I hurt all over. Blew it again. Well.

"You probably just needed to get the poison out of your system." She straightens up and looks away. I look down. Naked. I grab the bathmat and pull it over me. "I'd better go get ready. I don't imagine you feel up to going to church."

"No. I don't think so."

She tilts her head to one side. "Funny. No one else seems to have gotten sick."

"I had a hamburger at Dad's Root Beer."

"Well, that's just asking for trouble."

After she leaves I struggle to my feet and look in the mirror. My face is out of focus too. I lean in real close and see why. My pupils are so big and black they go right out to the edge so there's only a narrow rim of blue. Strange. I don't think anyone will notice. Who ever looks directly in your eye?

I wake up with a start in the middle of the night. The letter. I sneak down to the mailbox. Lucky no one noticed the flag was up. No mail pick-up on Sunday anyway, thank God. I tear the letter into tiny bits and let them flutter onto the gravel. That was a close call.

AUGUST

Mr. Clay drives the way he smokes. Absentmindedly. To make matters worse he tries to do both at the same time. Just when it looks like his attention's fixed on inhaling, exhaling, blowing plumes of smoke out through his nose like a dragon in a fairytale, then it's suddenly clear he's not attending at all. The ash has grown close to an inch long and is about to drop onto his trouser leg, and the Peugeot has drifted across the center line while he's pointing out how much those corn rows curving down the hill beyond the turquoise-and-orange Howard Johnson billboard remind him of Thomas Hart Benton. A Mack truck's barreling down on us and I'm thinking about ducking under the dash for safety when he gives the wheel a casual twitch. The truck thunders past with a loud blast of its horn.

"You know what they call that?"

"What?"

"The way a horn goes high-low like that."

"Scary."

He taps my shoulder with his Dunhill hand. The ash falls onto my khakis. "That, Mr. McCaverty, is called the Doppler effect. The only thing I remember from college physics."

"You took science in college?"

"Didn't I tell you? I was going to be an architect. The next Frank Lloyd Wright."

"So how'd you end up running museums?"

"Physics, my boy. Pure and applied. All those formulae were a pure mystery to me. And I couldn't apply them to save my soul. Didn't do too well with math either, so sophomore year I switched to art history. Much more civilized. The only numbers there were the endless dates we had to memorize."

"That's what I'm going to be."

"An architect?" He looks over at me and the right-hand tires of the Peugeot slide off onto the shoulder of the road, sending up clouds of yellow dust. "Really?"

"Yeah. The next Frank Lloyd Wright. Frank Lloyd Wrong, my father always says."

He doesn't laugh. "How's your math?"

"Not great. Okay, I guess."

"I wouldn't worry too much about that in any case. A red herring really. I discovered—much too late to do me any good—that math and physics aren't that crucial. That's what engineers are for: the dirty work. The architect has the vision."

"I hope so."

"If we get finished in time maybe we could run up to Oak Park and see some of Wright's buildings."

"Is it that close to Chicago?"

"I believe so. We'll have to consult a map."

We're whipping along the beltway. Mr. Clay does better in heavy traffic, darting in and out among the cars and trucks like he's in some giant pinball game. The sun's glaring off the side of the Prudential Building up ahead and I wonder why Mr. Clay doesn't get into the right-hand lane. The exit for the Loop is real soon.

"Don't we get off here?"

"What?" Mr. Clay honks his way past a long black limousine. "Oh, we're not going downtown. Di Severini's studio is farther out."

I'll say. Like another half an hour. When we finally do exit we're in a part of Chicago I've never seen before, a long way from the lake. Big yellow or red brick ware-houses alternate with deserted-looking tenements and va-cant lots strewn with broken glass and rusted-out cars.

Mr. Clay pulls up in front of a long low building and winces at the sound of a bottle popping under one of the tires. It looks like an abandoned garage, with four large slide-up doors and rows of perfectly square over-sized windows, white-washed panes screened over with chain link. Mortar oozes out between chipped maroon bricks like icing on a layer cake. When Mr. Clay invited me to come along to Chicago to pick up a piece at Mario di Severini's studio I pictured a high airy place, full of light.

"Di Severini's something of a character," Mr. Clay says, pounding hard on a big door riveted over with rusty sheet metal. "Just by way of warning." He pounds hard again.

Chains rattle, a bolt's pulled. Then another. The door scrapes open.

"Hello, Dick," Mr. Clay says, but the man filling the

doorway looks right past him, staring at me like I'm a ghost or something.

"How's Mario?" The man doesn't seem to hear. Then he looks down at Mr. Clay like he's noticing him for the first time. "Hey, Julie. How's it going? Aren't you going to introduce me to your friend?"

I thought Mrs. Clay was the only one who called him that.

"This is my assistant, Jared McCaverty. Jared, this is Richard Driver. He works for Mr. di Severini."

Richard Driver leans down—he must be seven feet tall—and sticks out his hand. "Pleased to meet you, Jared. My friends call me Dick." My hand disappears inside his. He doesn't really shake it, just holds it like it's some small animal he's afraid he might crush. Wiry black hair sprouts from his knuckles and covers his forearm like a pelt. Finally he lets go. His eyes are black as olives. He stares at me so hard I don't know where to look.

"You have a good trip up?" He winks at me.

"Very warm," Mr. Clay says.

"Mario's in back." Dick drops a heavy arm across my shoulders and practically lifts me across the threshold. It's dark and cool inside. "Watch your step." His deep voice rumbles right in my ear. Something furry brushes against my cheek. His slick black hair's pulled back into a long ponytail secured with a leather thong.

Four rows of concrete pillars run the length of the long room. The walls and pillars are painted gray to about shoulder-height and then dirty white the rest of the way up. Twisted wrecks of old cars fill the bays between the pillars. Some of the wrecks look like two or three cars crushed together, with strange chunks and cones of polished metal poking out through shattered windows. The pitted concrete floor is littered with gears, sprockets and oily chains, metal filings, wrenches and black rubber-tipped mallets, corroded batteries and coils of wire and extension cords. I can hear Mr. Clay scurrying along behind us. Dick Driver doesn't walk fast; it's just that his long legs cover more ground more quickly than anyone else's.

"How is Mario?" Mr. Clay calls, his voice sounding thin and high in the big room.

"He has his good days," Dick Driver says. "Today sure ain't one of them." He squeezes my shoulder. "But don't you pay him any mind."

After the last set of pillars we're in a big rectangular room, twice as wide as it is high and it's pretty high—three stories or more. It's neater here—a couple of long sway-backed sofas face each other at the center of the room, the brick walls are painted glossy white. This is more like it, a real artist's studio. Huge multipaned windows are set high into the walls at either end of the room. The wall directly in front of us has no windows, just two low arched doorways. Hanging high up on the wall is what looks like a giant black fly—maybe fifteen feet long —with a big crystal floodlamp where its head ought to be. The drooping black metal wings are tailfins from a '59 Cadillac. Poking out from between the wings are two corroded exhaust pipes bent to look like little kicking legs. Stuck to the ends of the exhaust pipes are two bronzed baby shoes.

"Wild!"

Dick Driver laughs hard. The air and light in the high white room seem to vibrate. "You like it?"

"Yeah. What is it?"

"Mario did that a couple of years ago. It's called 'Zeus and Ganymede.' "

Mr. Clay steps forward like he doesn't want to be

left out. "Zeus took the form of an eagle to kidnap a mortal child, Ganymede. Does it still light up, Dick?"

"Sure." Dick reaches up under the left Cadillac fin. The crystal floodlamp flashes deep red and the ruby taillights blink on and off.

"Amazing. I thought it was a big fly."

Dick laughs again and pounds my shoulder with his fist. "It does kind of resemble . . ."

A clicking sound comes from the arched doorway on the left. Then a smooth metallic purring. An electric wheelchair glides into the room. At first all I can see is the head, long and narrow like someone flattened it with a steamroller. Completely bald too. I glance over at Mr. Clay, wanting to ask him why he didn't warn me beforehand. I mean really warn me. It isn't fair springing a surprise like this. I don't know where to look. Mr. Clay rushes over to the wheelchair, arms out like he's going to hug the whole thing.

"Mario, you look wonderful."

Right. Like a crippled Mr. Potato Head. The skin on his face is all bumpy—gray-brown and kind of draped. The whites of his bulging eyes are almost the same color and all runny. His neck's thin as my wrist, wattled and spotted worse than Grandmother Fortman's.

Mr. Clay bends over the chair and hugs di Severini. Di Severini lays his big flat head against Mr. Clay's shoulder and starts to cry. "Julie, my Julie." Thick tears fast as mercury slide down his hollow cheeks. Yellowish snot runs from his narrow nostrils. His arms, really just bones wrapped in crepe paper, creep across the back of Mr. Clay's blue seersucker jacket.

"Come on, Jared." Dick Driver gives me a push toward the other arched doorway. "Let's see if there's enough beer to go around."

The kitchen's small but real neat, with rows of glass-fronted cabinets, a little white enamel two-burner stove and a white porcelain sink nearly as big as a bathtub.

"They have a lot of catching up to do." He nods toward the big room.

He doesn't make any move to look for beer, just leans back against the big sink, furry arms crossed over his broad chest. "You been working for Julie for long?"

"Five or six months."

"He's a good man."

I nod.

"Did he tell you that we were at Cooper Union together? In New York? We met in Mario's sculpture class. That was, I don't know, fifteen years ago. Before Mario's crack-up."

"What happened to him?"

"Julie didn't tell you? That's Julie all right. For such a big talker he sure can be close-mouthed. He always did like to spring things on people, see how they'd react.

"Hard to tell now but Mario was a big guy. Not as big as me but, you know, stocky. He was a marine, at Guadalcanal. Got through that okay, thought he was in the clear for life. When he was in New York he had this big old Harley. Rode it to class and everything. Liked to take it out on the highway late at night, really open her up. Wiped out on a rainy night, slid right under a semi. No one thought he'd make it but he did. That was spring of '56."

Dick Driver reaches behind his head and tugs at the leather thong until it pulls free. His thick black hair falls down over his shoulders. Makes him look like an Indian.

"Have you been working for him for long?"

He smiles like I've said something funny. "I've been with Mario since way before the smash-up. Since I was his student. Now I'm pretty much everything. I never was much of an artist—no imagination. Good with my hands though. Mario has the ideas and I hammer them together. We're quite a team."

"Does he . . . is he always like that?"

"Not always. Like I said, he has his good days. In a lot of pain most of the time. A lot of the time dope just doesn't do the trick. He didn't sleep much last night."

"Poor guy."

"You said it. But he hangs tough." He runs one meaty hand along the sink rim like the smoothness makes him calm. "You handled yourself real well. In there."

"What do you mean?"

"You didn't jump when Mario rolled in and you didn't stare at him like he was a freak."

"I looked."

"Looking's all right. You've got to look. How old are you?"

"Sixteen."

"Yeah? You look younger."

"Everyone always tells me I look older."

"Maybe. Why don't you reach down under there and grab some beers."

A little brown fridge is packed in under the counter I'm leaning against. I bend down and open it. A hypodermic needle gleams on a small aluminum tray.

"There should be some beer toward the back." He's standing right behind me. "Need some help?"

He squats down next to me. I grab three bottles and start to stand up. Dick lays his hand on the small of my back. The heat goes right through me. I start shaking and drop one of the beers. It spins round and round on the concrete floor.

Dick's lips are against my ear. His hand still presses

against the small of my back. "How old did you say you were?"

"He's fifteen, Dick." Mr. Clay stands in the doorway, stroking his striped tie.

Dick leaves his hand where it is. "He looks older. You want a beer, Julie?"

"Sure, Dick."

Mr. di Severini whirs down the center of the low dim room, chair jolting and tilting across the uneven concrete. He pulls up between two pillars in the darkest corner of the room. A dusty green tarpaulin covers an elongated shape, high at the front and long and low in back, about the size of a large dog or maybe a Shetland pony.

He looks up at Mr. Clay, moist eyes glistening. "You think your gallery's ready for a genuine di Severini?"

"Slope's is ready, Mario. It's the town I'm concerned about. But we'll bring them around, won't we, Jared?"

Di Severini signals to Dick, who sweeps off the tarp like a matador swirling his cape.

Not a dog or a pony. A three-quarter scale model of an old low-slung motorcycle. Painted black as ebony but the paint's all scratched and chipped away, the fuel tank's dented in, chromework pitted with rust. Instead of handlebars, two polished chrome horns curve out and up. Balanced on the points of the horns a small man does a handstand. At least it looks like a man. He's made out of some strange kind of metal—slate-gray and drippy, like petrified candle wax, as if the figure had somehow been poured into its lean arc above the horns.

Mr. Clay just stands there, mouth hanging open. Di Severini's watching him, flat head cocked to one side. Dick Driver's watching me.

"So what do you think, Julie?" Di Severini grabs Mr. Clay's arm.

"Stunning." Mr. Clay's face looks chalky white in the dim light.

"I call it 'Minos and After.' " Di Severini smiles and a trickle of saliva makes a snail track down his jaw.

"Pull over."

Mr. Clay swerves and bumps the Peugeot up over the curb so that we're parked half on, half off the sidewalk. "Here?"

"This is my favorite."

Mr. Clay scoots across the seat so he can look out my window. I move my arm over so it grazes his. "Really? I think I prefer the genuine Prairie Houses."

"No kidding." Oak Park is so amazing. We've been driving around for two hours and there's a Wright house on practically every block: old high-gabled ones that don't look like his work at all except for the overhanging eaves or the stucco-and-wood second stories; and then the low-slung Prairie Houses, wood-and-stucco all over, that really send Mr. Clay soaring. "The apotheosis of the horizontal," he says. They are pretty cool but the Heurtley House has always been my favorite even though till now I've only ever seen it in books.

"Why do you like this one so much?" Mr. Clay moves his arm away from mine and lights his nth Dunhill of the afternoon.

"I don't know. Because it's different. It seems warmer to me than the Prairie Houses. I guess I prefer brick to stucco."

"Stucco certainly doesn't age very well. Some of these places need a lot of work. Shocking how people can neglect a work of art."

"With this one I love the way the brick's laid in narrow bands so that at first you think it's ordinary wood siding."

"Trompe l'oeil."

"Come again."

"Fools the eye."

"Oh. And it's as horizontal as the Prairie Houses only more subtle."

"True." He sticks his head out my window to get a better look. I can see the little blond hairs inside his ear and smell his smoky breath.

"And look at the leaded windows upstairs."

"So delicate."

"And the arch over the front door."

Mr. Clay sighs. "It is awfully beautiful, isn't it? You know, Goethe said architecture is frozen music."

"I want to get out and look at this one up close."

"Jared, these aren't museums. They're private homes. People live in them. They don't want you poking about like . . ."

I'm over the low brick wall and onto the front terrace when I hear Mr. Clay's door slam. This is the house where Wright actually lived and worked.

"Jared, come on." He's wheezing from running across the narrow yard. "You're going to get us arrested."

I knock on the front door. "If you lived in Frank Lloyd Wright's very own house wouldn't you expect people to come and want to see it?"

"You know that's not the point. You can't go invading people's privacy simply because you—"

I knock again. "Nobody home."

Mr. Clay's peering into one of the narrow windows.

"This must be the dining room. Looks like they're restoring it."

I brush up against him. "Look at that beautiful grille set into the wall."

He doesn't move away. "Very art nouveau but rather squared off."

We scramble from window to window all the way around the house.

Back on the front lawn Mr. Clay points to the wide triangle of the gable. "Do you suppose that's where the playroom is? With the wonderful barrel-vaulted ceiling? God, I wish there was some way we could get inside."

"I could break a window."

"Jared!"

Unity Chapel is open. Mr. Clay swings open the heavy wooden door and we're enveloped in cool silence.

I follow him across the entry hall. "You think it's all right?" I'm whispering.

"It was open, wasn't it?" He's whispering too.

A low narrow hallway and then we're in a big cube of a room. Mr. Clay stops suddenly and I slam into him.

"Hey."

"Shit."

At the far end of the room several people in jeans and sweatshirts are gathered in front of the altar, which is completely bare—no cross, no candles, no flowers. A tieless man in a short-sleeved white shirt stands behind the altar, talking very quietly although his voice is so clear he sounds like he's standing right next to us. ". . . and then you give him the ring and he puts it on Janice's finger. Mind you don't drop it."

One of the sweatshirted figures pretends to slip a

ring onto the finger of another sweatshirted figure. Then they all burst out laughing. Looking closer I can see why. They're all young men, and Janice is a little stocky guy with curly brown hair.

Mr. Clay leans close. "I guess Janice couldn't make the rehearsal."

"Guess not." I forget to whisper.

The man in the white shirt looks up, gives us a quick close-mouthed smile and addresses the wedding party again. "Tom, you lead off when the music starts up again"—he hums a few notes of churchy music—"and then Marty, uh, Janice, you head off after him."

The big room's all rectangles and cubes of white stucco trimmed with narrow bands of dark wood. Light pours down clear and strong from a grid of skylights.

"Like a big Mondrian, isn't it?" Mr. Clay murmurs. "So geometrical and serene."

The white globes of the lamps hanging above the altar are the only curved things in the room. Mr. Clay points out the molding above the wooden grille behind the altar. I touch him on the shoulder to draw his attention to the parallelograms of light that the skylights cast on the bare stucco wall.

The wedding party divides and files up the narrow stairs on either side of the altar. The man in the white shirt remains at the altar a moment, looking about the room too. Then he gives a half bow in our direction. We bow back.

The airless late afternoon heat reminds us of how cool it was inside. On the steps Mr. Clay turns and throws his arms around me, hugging me hard. "What a man," he says, "what a great, great man."

* * *

"More wine, gentlemen?" The red-jacketed Negro waiter winks at me on *gentleman* and upends the empty bottle in the battered ice bucket.

"What do you think, Jared—can Slope's afford it?" Mr. Clay grins at me, hair falling down over one eye, and pretends he hasn't belched.

"Sure, why not?" Considering what our dinky room must be costing, I'd say Slope's could afford a whole case of wine. When Mr. Clay said we'd be staying in a hotel, I just assumed he meant the Palmer House or maybe the Drake—someplace nice. Who's ever heard of the Del Prado? It's hardly even downtown. Real handy to the Museum of Science and Industry though, in case we get the sudden urge to run over and see the first sewing machine or something.

Mr. Clay lights a Dunhill and looks about the narrow high-ceilinged room. "This place amuses me."

"Yeah?" The pink velvet wallpaper's worn so thin in places the plaster shows through. The gold-framed mirrors are spotted and cloudy.

"Like an old dowager down on her luck. Between the wars this must have been a very fashionable establishment."

"The old guys smoking their pipes out in the lobby look like they've been here ever since."

"They probably have. That's what I find so charming. A world in amber."

The only amber I've ever seen had a dead fly in it. Over near the velvet-smothered windows an old lady in a shiny black suit is lecturing our waiter about something. He grins and nods his head to everything she says. That doesn't make her any happier. Stuck away in a corner behind a mirrored pillar a younger lady, but not that young, reads a book and sips something green from a tiny crystal glass. Four of us and the waiter, and that's it. What a tomb. Hardly worth putting on a jacket and tie for.

"Don't you like any of it?" Mr. Clay smooths the tablecloth with one finger.

"The pink lampshades are kind of nice—just like at the Orpheum. And the mirrors, if you don't mind them being out of focus."

"I'm sorry, Jared. I thought this place would be an adventure for you."

"It's okay." I know he means well, but why's he have to keep harping on whether I like this dump or not?

"You seem to be in a bad mood. And after we had such a good time this afternoon."

"I'm fine." What business is it of his what kind of mood I'm in? I don't pry into every little thing he does. When we checked in the desk clerk said, "That will be a double for you and your son?" Mr. Clay nodded so I didn't say a word, not even after the bellboy showed us to our room, turned on the air conditioner, opened the bathroom door, and left. Anyway, with Mr. Clay there's no need to ask—sooner or later he explains everything. Checking the firmness of the bed closer to the window he said, "If you're my son you're free. The Family Plan."

The waiter returns with a new bottle. Mr. Clay glances at the label and nods for him to open it. When the waiter goes away he says, "Well, you've had a long day."

That's true. Feels like we've been in Chicago a week. But I'm not tired at all. Just the opposite. Wound up tight, and the wine winds me even tighter.

"What do you think of di Severini?"

"I wish you'd told me."

"Told you what?"

"You know."

"Oh, that." He waves his Dunhill like he's so used to cripples he doesn't even notice they're crippled. "Poor Mario."

"He looks terrible."

"I know. It's funny. When I'm not around him I think of him the way he was *before* the accident so each time I see him it's the same shock all over again."

"Dick said he used to be a big guy."

Mr. Clay looks at me over the rim of his glass. "Did he? Anything you want to do tomorrow before we drive back? What time do your parents expect you home?"

"They don't care. I think Dick's neat."

"Do you?" He pours himself another inch or so of wine.

"He's so big. I've never seen anybody that huge before."

"No, I suppose not. I'd like to just drop by the Art Institute if we have time. Maybe stock up on some books."

"Have you ever read *Giovanni's Room?*"

"What's that?"

"Just a book."

"By whom?"

"His name's James Baldwin."

"Oh, yes. I know his work—mainly his essays on civil rights and that sort of thing. He's an ugly fellow, looks rather like a toad. Dorcas read one of his novels. What was the title? From a Negro spiritual or something. I know. *Go Tell It On the Mountain.* What's *Giovanni's Room* about?"

"These two guys who live together in Paris. They're white."

"Oh?"

"How long have Dick and Mario known each other?"

He arches his eyebrows and looks up at the ceiling like he's doing some important calculations. "Must be close to fifteen years. You want any dessert?"

"Not especially. It's really something that Dick takes care of him and helps him with his work."

"Well, Dick never was much of a sculptor himself."

"No?"

"Lacked imagination." He carefully folds his napkin and smooths it out on the table. "You about ready to go?"

I haul the bottle out of the ice bucket and fill up my glass to the brim.

"Do you really think you should have more, Jared?"

"Who are you, my father?"

That shuts him up.

"If Dick's got no imagination, then why's he hang around with Mario?"

"Maybe because that way he's at least connected to genius."

I take a big swallow of wine. "You think that's the only reason Dick stays with Mario?"

Mr. Clay looks at me a long time, like he's not sure he heard right. Then he places his hands palms up on the table. "No, Jared, I don't think that's the only reason he stays." He sits quietly for a moment, staring at his palms while his face goes completely red. He finally looks up. "What about a brandy to top things off?"

Mr. Clay, swaying a little, strides into the elevator and announces, "Eighth floor, please, and damn the torpedoes."

The little elevator girl doesn't bother cracking a

smile as she slides the brass-trimmed doors shut. She's so small she has to stand on a small upholstered box just to reach the buttons. She's not at all like most dwarfs—her head's not big or anything. Apart from the fact that she's about three feet tall she looks perfectly normal. In fact she's really very beautiful—like a perfect little mechanical doll in her red brass-buttoned uniform and matching red pillbox hat with gold trim. I stare and stare at her but she doesn't even turn her head when she slides open the gate and says, "Eighth floor." Her voice sounds normal too, not like a Munchkin's at all.

The window-box air conditioner has been grinding away the whole time we were down at dinner but the room's stuffy, with that pine-tree smell that comes out of an aerosol can. Mr. Clay tugs off his jacket, hangs it on the closet doorknob and goes into the bathroom, carefully shutting the door behind him.

The overhead light's so bright the whole room looks flat and unreal. I switch it off and turn on the pink-shaded vanity light. Shouldn't have had so much wine. I'm not drunk but my head feels packed tight and crinkly, like it's stuffed with aluminum foil. I look in the vanity-table mirror. Strange. No matter how terrible I feel inside I always look pretty much the same in the mirror. Tonight maybe a little better than usual on account of the pink light. Does my face look thinner, or is that just shadow? I suck in my cheeks the way models do in magazines. Makes me look like a fish pressed up against the glass of an aquarium.

Draping my jacket and tie over the chair back I unbutton my shirt. Should I take it off? I can hear Mr. Clay gargling. He'll be out soon. I leave it on and take off my trousers. The shirttails hang down over my underpants so

it's like I'm wearing a button-down nightshirt. With the
shirt hiding the lumps at my waist I really do look thin.
Really. Especially when I concentrate on holding in my
stomach.

The crystal knob on the bathroom door jiggles. I
lose my courage and switch off the lamp. The door opens
and a shaft of yellow light cuts across the room. Framed
by the doorway Mr. Clay looks bigger than usual, a dark
silhouette until my eyes adjust. He's carrying his shirt
and trousers over one arm. A yellow towel's wrapped
around his waist. He's so thin. Not an ounce of fat on
him. The hair on his chest is blond and very thick.

"It's dark in here." He moves toward me and bangs
his shin against the footboard of one of the twin beds.
"Goddammit."

"You okay?"

He's doubled over, holding his shin in both hands.
His shoulders and back are smooth and hairless like a
teenager's. I reach out and touch the back of his neck. He
freezes for an instant, half crouching. Then he straightens
up: his towel juts out in front. For a second he looks me
right in the eye. Then he's looking at me all over.

"You're so beautiful. But you know that, don't
you?"

He's so crazy. Is he saying that because he feels
sorry for me, the way people tell fat girls they have pretty
faces? Or is he just making fun of me? Maybe it's his idea
of a joke. I start giggling, thinking he'll join in.

He puts his hands on either side of my face and
presses hard, like they're two halves of a vise. "You really
are, you know." But I can't stop giggling, not till he
covers my mouth with his.

Christ! the *taste*. For about a tenth of a second all

minty and cool and fresh and then—like a furnace switching on—hot, bitter, dark, gritty. Dunhills.

The funny thing is I get used to it. Fast. Mr. Clay's fast. His towel drops to the floor and the head of his cock's pressing into my open hand. Big and smooth as an egg, a goose egg maybe, and wet at the crown. He pulls his tongue out of my mouth and licks up and down my throat. He needs a shave. The whole time he's muttering, "Beautiful, so beautiful," like wishing's going to make it so. It's embarrassing.

He nibbles at the base of my neck. Partly it feels good; partly it tickles. I get the giggles again and he clamps down with his teeth.

"*Ow!*"

"Sorry."

I'd like to ask him to slow down a little but I'm afraid to interrupt. He seems to be concentrating so hard.

Without warning he tips me onto the bed. He's all over me now, like he's grown extra hands and legs. And an extra tongue. In my mouth, my ears, my *nose*. Disgusting. I never expected him to be like this. So wild. He wrenches off my shirt, almost ripping it. His cock presses into my belly, bony knees push my legs apart. It's like I'm not supposed to do anything but lie here. He's doing it all.

He's back working on my neck again. Breathing hard through his nose. He burrows down and nibbles the nape. I start shuddering all over. That really sets him off. He bites down, I arch off the bed in pain. He catches me in midair and flips me over. My face comes down in the pillow and he's covered my body with his, holding on to my shoulders like I'm giving him a piggyback ride. Weird. And all this time he's biting—real hard—my neck and shoulders and gasping, "Beautiful, beautiful."

One of his hands squirms underneath me and grabs my cock through my underpants. I can feel the fingers of his other hand in back, slipping under the elastic band.

"Oh," he says. "Oh. Oh." His hand runs over my ass, stroking, pinching, clawing. I don't know why I'm so surprised when he touches me *there*. I've read about that. I know people do that. I've just never understood how.

"Relax," he whispers in my ear. "Just relax."

Right. With his finger there.

He presses hard.

"Stop!"

He stops. Finger's gone. That's better. Now I can relax. A little. Wrong again. It's back. Wet this time. I don't like this. Things are supposed to come out of there, not go in. I grind the corner of the pillow between my teeth. He's got to stop soon. Burning. Way deep inside. Red circles of fire. I open my mouth to scream but what comes out is a thin creaking sound. The pillow's in my mouth and I'm whipping it back and forth like a dog worrying an old rag. Shit! I'm going to explode. Stop. Stop. Oh.

His finger slowly eases out.

He's up on his hands and knees behind me now like he's going to run a race. He cranes his head around and kisses me.

"Hey, beautiful."

I don't care if he's lying or teasing or joking. If he keeps calling me that, he can do whatever he wants. I mean it. He can . . . *"Owww!"*

"Come on, Jared, relax."

"It hurts like mad."

"Only because you're tense."

"I'm tense because it hurts like mad."

"You're so beautiful."

"Christ!"

"All right, all right." He collapses onto my back. "I won't move until you say so. Take your time. Get used to it."

How do I get used to that? It feels like he tore something, that first big push. Can it be torn? Can it be fixed? Oh God, let me out of here.

It's not unbearable now, now that he's stopped. The burning's fading, the rings of fire flickering out one by one. I just feel plugged up, pinned down. Can't move at all. When I do it hurts. Maybe if I just said, Look, could we try something else? he'd take the hint and . . .

"Better?" He's kissing the back of my neck. Soft, tender kisses.

"A little."

"You're so gorgeous."

"Owww!" Oh shit. Make him stop. Oh God, make him stop. Stop. Stop. Stop. Stop. At first I think it's only inside my head. Then I realize I'm actually saying it. Whispering at first, then louder till I'm practically screaming it hurts so much, plunging, burning, scraping, tearing. He doesn't even hear. Snorting away like some animal on my back. I can't believe he doesn't hear. Won't stop. Then I realize the yelling actually makes it worse. He hammers harder when I yell—the headboard bangs against the wall, the reading lamp rocks back and forth on the bedside table.

Don't yell. Count. Each stroke. Silently. One, two, three, four . . . Can't be long now. He's already been going at it forever. He can't keep up this pace. Snorting in my ear like a pig. If he goes on like this much longer he'll have a heart attack. Fine with me. Thirty-five, thirty-six, thirty-seven. I'm soaked in sweat. Must be his. I feel cold. Fifty-seven, fifty-eight, fifty-nine . . .

"Beautiful. Beautiful. Beautiful."

He falls dead on top of me. My head's pushed right up against the headboard. I can't breathe. Somebody's pounding on the wall.

SEPTEMBER

*F*lames leapfrog toward the topmost tier of tar-blackened railroad ties. Pretty soon the crisscross tower, like a giant's Lincoln Log fort, turns into a column of fire, thick black smoke billowing over the floodlit oval of the football field.

A line of cheerleaders in red sweaters and swirling red-and-white pleated skirts locomotions back and forth in front of the bonfire, red-and-white pompons rustling now and again above the crackling of the flames.

"Ashes to ashes! Dust to dust! They're a pretty good team, but they can't beat *us!*"

Homecoming. The queen and her court, tiaras glittering, shoulders draped in white bunny-fur stoles, sit crowded together on the folded-back top of a red Cadillac convertible. All blondes this year. For all I know they're all blondes every year. A tradition.

They talk a lot about tradition at Paul Dresser High School. Homecoming bonfire for instance, a mandatory tradition for entering Sophomores who want to get into a campus club. Key Club's the best club for guys. It's mainly for jocks and student-government types. Hi-Y's not nearly as good as Key Club—Hi-Y will take almost anyone—but it's still way ahead of "specialty" clubs like Chess, Chemistry and Future Farmers of America. They take all the geeks.

I personally couldn't care less about making it into any club. I'm here because I wanted to see what Homecoming's like. And I wanted to check out what Sophomores made final cut for the football team.

I've got on my class cords. Have to, if I want to be here at all. Yellow for Sophomores, blue for Juniors, red for Seniors. It's so awful—wearing the same pair of ugly pants all Homecoming Week. That's a tradition too. Then at Homecoming Bonfire, clubs choose new members by drawing the club emblem on their cords. Big fucking deal.

I figure if I stay at the far end of the bleachers near the chain link fence, no one will bother me.

Snare-drum roll. The band plows into "Happy Days Are Here Again." The crowd around the bonfire yells and whistles. The cheerleaders leap into the air and land doing the splits.

Junior and senior members of the football team run onto the field in perfect V-formation shouting *hut-hut-hut* as they run. The game's not until tomorrow night. To-night they've got on their class cords and red-wool letter jackets with leather sleeves yellowed as old ivory.

Another snare roll. The band stumbles into "Hey, Look Me Over," heavy on the xylophone, as the Sophomore team members swarm onto the field, spotless new

red-and-white jerseys extra bright in the floodlights. They
form a scraggly line across the field and stand shifting
from foot to foot eyeing the motionless V of upperclass-
men at the other end of field.

The band stops playing. The snare drum rolls a third
time. A trumpet blats out a cavalry charge. A little guy at
the far end of the Sophomore line breaks rank and
streaks across the field, head down, feet kicking hard.
Randy Sparks. Kamikaze.

The team captain, a Senior, and his best friend the
quarterback, a Junior, thunder toward him. The captain's
got blond crinkly hair and a head like a shoebox set on
end. He's too big to be fast but he doesn't have to be. His
friend the quarterback churns on ahead, dark and lean.
At the forty-yard line he grabs on to Randy's jersey.
Randy keeps going and the jersey splits right down the
back. The quarterback clamps on to his bare shoulders
and brings him down. They wrestle around a minute and
then the quarterback's sitting astride Randy's pelvis.
Randy tries to buck him off but it's no good. The quarterback pins his wrists to the ground above his head.

The captain comes loping up, barely winded, black
Magic Marker uncapped. He gets down on one knee to
draw on Randy's thigh but Randy kicks out, almost getting the captain in his boxy chin. The captain grabs his
feet and sits on his ankles. It's clear he's done for but
Randy keeps rearing and bucking while the captain
draws a wobbly black key along his left thigh.

When the captain finally stands up Randy has
stopped squirming. The captain takes a small silver flask
from the inside pocket of his letter jacket. The
quarterback's still astride Randy, pinning his wrists to
the ground. The captain squats down next to his head.
With one hand he cups Randy's chin, forcing open his

mouth. He holds the flask a foot or so above his face and pours the silver stream of liquor into Randy's waiting mouth.

The captain stands up, capping the flask. The quarterback lightly slaps Randy's cheeks and then gets up too. They help him up and flanking him, drape their arms across his shoulders and half carry him off the field. His torn jersey flutters behind him like a pennant. When they come by my end of the bleachers Randy looks right at me but I guess he didn't see me.

A girl crashes into me, knocking me against the chain link fence. A black-haired guy in a black motorcycle jacket twists her arm behind her back. She screams, "Help me! Oh, please help me!" He laughs and leans over to draw a wobbly heart on her right buttock. I didn't know that was a club.

The railroad-tie tower curves like a black spine within the orange strobing flames and topples onto the cinder track. A shower of sparks fans high into the darkness. Screaming girls dart this way and that across the football field. Walter Blechman, president of the Sophomore class, stands midfield in a ugly plaid shirt and white underpants, yellow cords around his ankles, a big grin on his face, the lenses of his black-rimmed glasses reflecting the dying flames.

A tall skinny Junior in a blue nylon Hi-Y windbreaker comes running straight for me, Magic Marker uncapped. I take off across the field. When I get close to the other side of the track I take a quick look over my shoulder. False alarm. He must have been after somebody else.

Audrey Hepburn looks up at Cary Grant with her big sad eyes. Their heads are so close their noses almost touch. How can he resist her, especially her husky voice and that strange accent that's so slight it's almost not an accent at all? But he doesn't even seem to notice. I know it's all supposed to be part of the suspense, but still, nobody's that slow.

Mr. Clay noisily unwraps his third Reese's cup since *Charade* began. He leans over and chuckles in my ear. I get a whiff of peanut butter, chocolate, and furnace mouth. "This is such wicked fun. I feel exactly like a naughty boy skipping school. I'm sure if Mrs. Mandle ever found out she'd whack our hands with a ruler."

He talks during movies. I thought only little kids and old ladies did that. He doesn't even bother to whisper. When I go to the movies I like to get quiet even before the lights go down, just to get in the mood. But he talked right through the cartoon and the newsreel. Sometimes he talks back to the screen or finishes the actors' lines before they have a chance. It's really funny but it's kind of embarrassing too. Good thing there's hardly anybody here.

He was so restless all morning, pacing about the empty galleries, shuffling Mrs. Mandle's stacks of index cards, even leafing through the visitors' book. "I can't believe it—it's almost noon and we've had a grand total of three visitors." He shook his head in disgust. "Sometimes, young man, I wonder why we bother."

I didn't have the heart to tell him that two of those visitors were a couple of little old ladies in from Champagne-Urbana who thought this was the Vigo County Historical Society. Mrs. Mandle charmed them into signing before they left. Instead I told him we should do what I always do when things are going really bad: say fuck it and go to the movies. I said it jokingly just in case he thought it was a terrible idea, but he didn't. We practically sprinted the half block to the Orpheum. Mrs. Mandle thinks we're at the framer picking out mattes for the Cocteau drawings.

He really perks up when Audrey Hepburn and Cary Grant are in a Paris hotel room and Cary Grant takes a shower with his clothes on. "Now that's funny," he says, playfully elbowing me in the ribs. "Don't you think or don't you think?" He can act like such a kid. I grab his arm and try to push it away. Pretty soon we're having an all-out tickling war.

"Stop."

"You first."

"Never."

"Please. You're killing me."

"I give."

We end up holding hands, which is nicer. And quieter. And we don't miss any of the movie. In fact what we're doing starts to seem like part of the movie. To me at least. Cary Grant says romantic stuff to Audrey Hepburn and it feels almost like Mr. Clay's saying it to me. And when she tells him she loves him I mouth the words in Mr. Clay's ear. Mr. Clay's all slumped down in his chair like he's bored or tired, except it's no longer my hand he's holding. His long thin fingers walk up and down the front of my new tweed baggies. The murderer chases Audrey Hepburn into an empty theater. She's up onstage and he's coming after her with a gun. Cary Grant's under the stage. The murderer has her where he wants her. He aims his gun. Cary Grant pulls a switch. The murderer falls through a trap door. The gun goes off. So do I.

"That was fun," Mr. Clay says when the lights come up for intermission. "Sort of pseudo-Hitchcock but fun."

"I loved it." I lean into him. "Everything about it."

He leans away. "I couldn't get past the fact that he was so much older. It all seemed so improbable—that someone that young and beautiful would fall in love with an old duffer like him."

"I don't think he looks so old."

"Then why do you think they had him keep his clothes on in the shower? Oh, Jared, it's so obvious he's old enough to be her father." The lights are going back down.

"So what?"

"So what kind of future will they have? By the time she's forty he'll be in a nursing home."

"But he's so handsome and distinguished. And he knows so much that she doesn't. He could protect her."

"And she can push him around in a wheelchair after his first stroke."

I turn to him in the dark. "But as long as she loves him, as long as they love each other, isn't that all that matters?"

Mr. Clay laughs softly. "You do love the movies, don't you? Yes, that's all that matters, especially if you're Audrey Hepburn and Cary Grant."

The Parent Trap, the second half of the double feature, isn't as good as I remembered. The first time I saw it, a couple of years ago when it was brand-new, I thought Hayley Mills was so funny playing twins. Now I don't know. She seems so fake, grinning all the time. I glance over at Mr. Clay. He looks really bored, head resting on his hand. I reach over and touch his arm. He jumps.

"Sorry. I must have dozed off."

"You want to go?"

"Gladly."

* * *

Mr. Clay's eyes roll up so only the white's visible. "Christ!" He gasps and collapses on top of me.

I'm getting used to it. Sometimes it's even all right. It's just that today for some reason I couldn't keep my mind on it. Maybe because I already had my turn at the movies. It's only right that now he should have his.

I thought Mrs. Mandle would never leave. We waited and waited in Mr. Clay's office and she kept coming in to ask about accession numbers and lading bills and all sorts of things that could just as easily have waited till Monday. Mr. Clay got more and more sarcastic with her but she didn't seem to notice.

I wish we could stay like this forever. The dropcloth Mr. Clay threw over the red horsehair settee behind the "Pietà" feels kind of gritty but it's so nice holding him in my arms. I think he must be asleep. He's drooling onto my shoulder. It's funny, he's always so fast and then— boom!—out like a light. I'd never tell him of course but I like it best when we just hold on to each other or even when we only hold hands. Or when we're in public and he suddenly reaches over and touches me on the arm or the shoulder like we're just good friends. I know there's no way to have the touching without the other. The one always leads directly to the other. It has to, that's just the way it is. Still.

The important thing to remember is that I love him. I love him so much. The fact that he's older doesn't mean a thing to me. It really doesn't. Anyway he looks so young. He's not nearly as old as Cary Grant.

He stirs a little and slips out in one quick movement. I hate it when he does that. Makes me feel so empty all of a sudden.

His eyes blink open. "Sorry."

"That's okay." Once he's awake it's not the same. I start feeling edgy, I don't know why, like something's wrong. It's so silly. I'm sure that's not the way other people feel when they're in love. Sometimes I even feel pissed off, except I can't figure out who at. Certainly not at Mr. Clay. That wouldn't make any sense. Audrey Hepburn never looked like she was truly angry at Cary Grant, not even when she was pretending to be.

"Penny for your thoughts."

I didn't realize he was watching me. I don't like it when he does that—makes me feel like he's spying on me. "Nothing. I mean I was just thinking . . ."

"Yes?" He smiles at me.

"How old are you?"

"Who wants to know?"

"Just wondering."

"I'll be thirty-six on December twenty-fourth."

Four years younger than Father. I knew he couldn't be that old. "Must be weird having your birthday on Christmas Eve."

"It's terrible."

"How come?"

"Because as you may have noticed in your brief life people are by nature incredibly stingy. If your birthday's on December twenty-fourth, they never give you one gift for your birthday and another for Christmas. Instead they buy one gift, telling themselves it's extra nice. Of course it never is. Never as nice as two separate gifts."

"What a cheat."

"Yes, life can be like that sometimes." He looks sad and like he's far away, eyelashes lowered.

"You know what?"

"What?" He sounds like he could fall asleep again.

"I'll buy you a gift for your birthday and another one for Christmas. And both will be extra nice."

He touches my nose with his index finger. "Do you know what, Mr. McCaverty?"

"What?"

"You don't have to buy me anything at all because you're extra nice all by yourself."

OCTOBER

"Oh, Jared, did you see?" Mrs. Mandle sits at the sales desk holding up the front page of the *Tribune-Star* so I can read the headline down in the lower left-hand corner: "COMMIE ART, SENATOR CHARGES."

"I saw it, Mrs. Mandle. That's why I stopped by."

Father pushed it across the breakfast table to me this morning saying, "Sounds like your Mr. Clay's got himself into a real mess. I don't want you going to that place anymore."

At first all I could see was the big picture of another crazy Buddhist monk over in Vietnam turning himself into a human torch. Then I scanned down the page to the headline and picture. Not the studio portrait they used when Mr. Clay's appointment as director was announced. This one seemed a little out of focus and he was

squinting, hair down over one eye. Looked like it might
have been taken at a reception or something after he'd
had a few glasses of champagne.

The real shocker though was di Severini's picture
next to his. If it hadn't said, "Mario di Severini, Accused
Artist," underneath, I never would have recognized him.
Neck like a bull and head to match, curly black hair,
eyebrows thick as wooly worms, dark staring eyes. When
Dick said he was handsome once I thought he was just
saying it, the way people always do about cripples or old
people.

The article itself was pretty straightforward:

The Chauncey R. Slope Museum recently spent
more than $5000 to purchase the work of a sus-
pected Communist, State Senator Cyrus T.
"Cy" Proffitt (R-Iron County) charged yesterday.

Proffitt, who also sits on the Slope board of
directors, leveled the charge last night at a special meeting of the board held at the Wabash
Avenue offices of Slope Jewelers, Inc.

"The statue 'Minos and After,' " Proffitt
said, "is the work of one Mario di Severini, who
was called before the House Un-American Activities Committee [HUAC] in 1954 as a suspected Communist."

"Instead of having the intestinal fortitude
to admit his party membership," Proffitt said,
"di Severini chose the coward's way out. He
repeatedly took the Fifth Amendment to save
his own skin and that of his fellow travelers."

Slope Museum director Julian Clay con-
firmed that in August of this year he paid $5582

for a piece of "modern" sculpture by di Severini.

"We bought 'Minos and After,' " Clay
claimed, "because it is representative of the
most forward-looking tendencies in contempo-
rary sculpture. The work, which was featured
in the April issue of *Art and Artists,* speaks for
itself in its successful blending of classical and
modern elements. Mr. di Severini's political
views, whatever they may be, seem to me to be
beside the point."

During what was often a heated meeting,
State Senator Proffitt argued that the Chicago
sculptor's politics were of real importance.
"Here we have an institution, at least partly
supported by taxpayers' hard-earned money,
which is buying the work of a so-called artist
who openly advocates the violent overthrow of
our American form of government."

The Slope board of directors, acting
against museum director Clay's recommenda-
tion that no further action be taken, asked Clay
to present at the board's next meeting a detailed
report concerning both the purchase and artis-
tic importance of the di Severini sculpture.

[see Editorial, "Red Art for Schoolkids?"
p. 4]

"Isn't it just terrible, Jared?" Mrs. Mandle's eyes are
full of tears. The pink velvet bow nesting in her silver
curls looks wilted. "Those awful, awful people attacking
Mr. Clay after all he's done. I think the di Severini is a
perfectly lovely piece, even if I don't pretend to understand it completely."

"How's Mr. Clay taking it?"

"Naturally he's very upset. When he came in this morning he was on fire. Of course I hadn't seen the article yet because we don't take the *Tribune-Star*—Charles says he won't have that Republican rag in the house. Mr. Clay made me sit down and read every nasty word of it while he paced back and forth."

"Is he still around?"

"I assume he's in his office. He's been telephoning the whole day long. His lawyer and Mr. di Severini himself of course and I don't know who else."

Mr. Clay's office is empty. He can't be far. A blue veil of cigarette smoke hangs near the ceiling. I tap on the bathroom door. With one finger I push it open. The light over the black marble sink is on. A bottle of Maalox sits on the sink rim, lid off. I look into the mirror over the sink—it reflects the mirror over the toilet so I can see right down into forever.

I take the wooden stairs to the storeroom two at a time.

He's sitting on the red horsehair settee smoking a Dunhill and looking out the window at the blank brick wall of Fort Harrison Savings & Loan.

I sneak up behind him and lay my hand on his shoulder. He jumps about a foot.

"Jesus Christ! Don't you ever do that again."

"I'm sorry, I—"

"Jared. I thought it was Mrs. Mandle, come up to offer me the milk of human kindness for the twelfth time today. I know the poor soul means well but the last thing I need right now is her clucking over me."

"I saw the paper and came as soon as I could. Is there anything I can do?"

He stands abruptly and starts circling the "Pietà."

"A fat old windbag, a piece of incompetent incontinent impotent scum who wouldn't know art if it strolled up and bit him on his flabby ass—a man like that, a state senator for God's sake, enlists the aid of a newspaper published expressly by and for subliterates and . . . It's simply too much to believe. You know that's the absolute hell of it—it's not anger or rage or outrage I'm feeling. I've been trying to put my finger on it all day. It's sheer unadulterated disbelief. I cannot believe, I refuse to believe, that this is actually happening." He turns suddenly and taps my chest three times. "Can *you* believe it?"

I nod my head. "A couple of years ago they fired a professor at Indiana State Normal for saying the American flag was just a piece of cloth."

"The American flag? They fired him?" He picks at the grime wedged under the nail of Christ's remaining big toe. "How can they fire you for stating the obvious?"

"People got all riled up over it. There was a big public hearing down at the courthouse and letters in the paper for months. He was teaching a course in symbolism, I think—this was when I was still in elementary school—and he said the flag itself had no real value. What was important was the symbolic significance people invested it with."

Mr. Clay wipes a trace of cobweb off Mary's nose. "And no one came to this poor man's defense?"

"A few people did at first. Other professors mainly. But then it came out that he was a conscientious objector during the Korean War and that pretty much finished him."

"Why didn't you warn me, Jared? I came here because I thought this was just a sleepy little hick town where nobody cared much about anything."

"Most of the time it is, but politics really tends to set

people off. You know my high school's named Paul
Dresser High? They were going to call it Theodore Dreiser High."

Mr. Clay's eyes open wide. "You mean after the nov-
elist? I'd forgotten he was from around here. Then who
the hell is Paul Dresser?"

"He was Dreiser's brother. He wrote songs. 'My Gal
Sal,' 'On the Banks of the Wabash.' He changed the spell-
ing of his name, I forget why."

"But why one brother and not the other?"

"Because everyone said Theodore Dreiser was a
Communist and believed in free love. There was also the
time a Jew tried to join the Elks Country Club. That's
not really politics, I guess, but they poisoned his English
sheepdog and sent his wife a box full of—"

Mr. Clay holds up his hand. "Enough, enough. I can
imagine. Mrs. Mandle's been taking phone calls all day.
They berate the poor woman in language as crude as it is
graphic and she sits there so prim and proper at her little
sales desk saying 'Yes' and 'No' and 'My, my' and 'Thank
you for calling.' "

He goes back to the window and traces circles on the
dusty pane. "Do you know anything about explosives?"

"You mean like dynamite or something?"

"Molotov cocktails . . . I'm not fussy. What I
think we should do is, late tonight, firebomb the office of
the *Tribune-Star.* Or perhaps we ought to do it in broad
daylight so we can be sure the place is full. I'm for elimi-
nating the complete staff and lots of innocent bystanders.
Perhaps a troop of Girl Scouts in for a tour of the printing plant. Then we abscond to Mexico with Mrs. Mandle's petty-cash box and live like kings. I'm sure a civilized country like Mexico has no extradition provisions
for firebombing a few Girl Scouts."

He can be so funny, even when things are at their worst. That's what I love about him. And I know what he loves about me. I go up behind him and slip my arms around his waist.

"Hey! None of that. What if Mrs. Mandle were to . . . Jared, this really is the last thing I need."

The Hoosier Room of the Elihu Root Hotel is standing room only. They moved the Slope board meeting here because the regular boardroom at Slope's Jewelers can't hold more than fifty people and Chauncey R. Slope stipulated in his will that all board meetings have to be open to the public. There must be about four hundred people here, most of them not the kind ordinarily found at a Slope board meeting.

Up on the dais the chairman of the board, Mrs. Puckney, is trying to call the meeting to order except no one's paying any attention to her at all. Mr. Clay's arguing with his lawyer underneath the big mural of William Henry Harrison signing a peace treaty with the Miami Indians. On the other side of the room, underneath the panel showing James Whitcomb Riley putting the finishing touches on his poem, "Little Orphan Annie," Senator Proffitt's lecturing a clutch of reporters, one of them here on special assignment all the way from the *Indianapolis Journal.* And over by the windows a group of fat old men in American Legion uniforms are draping a banner over the smiling bronze statue of Johnny Appleseed. Unfurled the banner reads REAL ART, NOT RED ART.

Mrs. Puckney bangs her gavel so hard her feathered soup-bowl hat slips over to one side. "Do you think we could please get started?" she squawks into the microphone. "I've got a husband who'd like to have me home for supper."

That gets a lot of laughs and scattered applause. Mr. Clay's lawyer claps him on the back and darts away, and Mr. Clay takes a seat at the long table. The chancellor of Indiana State Normal leans over and shakes his hand. The rest of the board members, mainly rich old ladies in bright-colored dresses, smile and nod in Mr. Clay's direction.

Senator Proffitt's the last to take his seat, waving to the crowd as he lumbers onto the dais.

"Give 'em hell, Cy," somebody yells and practically the whole audience bursts into applause with lots of extra hooting, whistling and stamping.

"With the board's permission," Mrs. Puckney shouts over the noise, her voice a little quavery now, "I'd like to dispense with the reading of last week's minutes and old business. Otherwise we'll be here all night and anyone who can read a newspaper knows what went on at last week's meeting."

More hoots and hollers. One of the lady board members leans over and whispers something in Mrs. Puckney's ear. Mrs. Puckney straightens her hat and continues. "Between that meeting and this a number of board members got together and hammered out a compromise motion that they hope will prove acceptable"— she looks pointedly to her left at Mr. Clay and then to her right at Senator Proffitt—"to all parties concerned. Mrs. Lacey, would you be so kind as to read the motion?"

Mrs. Lacey, a tall stringy old lady in a bright red suit with black buttons and a black hat struggles to get up and immediately sits back down. Senator Proffitt gives her an arm for her second try and she makes it, although she's still swaying a little as she reads in a surprisingly deep voice: "Be it resolved that a special committee of the board be established to conduct a full and independent study of the propriety of the purchase of the sculpture 'Minos and After' and of the character of its creator, the Chicago artist Mario di Severini. Be it further resolved that the committee report its findings to the board at large no later than one month from today."

Mrs. Lacey's hardly finished reading when the room erupts into boos, shrill whistling and cries of "sell-out" and "whitewash." Somebody at the back of the room shouts, "No More Reds! No More Reds!" and pretty soon the whole room's roaring with it. Mr. Clay puts his hands over his ears and looks down at the tabletop. Mrs. Puckney tries to calm the crowd but her gavel can barely be heard above the chanting. "No More Reds! No More Reds!"

Senator Proffitt slowly rises from his chair and strolls over to Mrs. Puckney. They talk quietly for a couple of minutes. Senator Proffitt does most of the talking with Mrs. Puckney nodding her head a lot and looking doubtful. Then Mrs. Puckney stands up and goes over to talk to Mr. Clay. He listens, head tilted to one side, one hand tugging at his hair in exasperation. At last he nods and Mrs. Puckney goes back to Senator Proffitt and nods to him. Senator Proffitt smiles broadly and lifts his arms like Charlton Heston getting ready to part the Red Sea. The crowd quiets down at once.

Mrs. Puckney clears her throat. "I believe the board is ready to accept this motion by acclamation if two slight modifications can be made. Number one, the special committee will submit its findings in two weeks rather than one month from today, and two, that Senator Proffitt will chair this committee. Is this agreeable to everyone?"

Mrs. Lacey booms out, "So moved," and after a lot of talking about Robert's *Rules* the motion's acclaimed.

The Hoosier Room's three-quarters empty by the time Mrs. Puckney bangs her gavel and says, "And now perhaps we can get on with the more usual business of the Chauncey R. Slope Museum."

Out in the lobby Mr. Clay's sitting all alone on a scuffed brown leather sofa. His face is kind of gray and pinched and up close his hair looks like it hasn't been washed in a week. He looks old.

"You think it will be all right?"

He looks up like he didn't even see me approach. "Are you kidding? With that penny-ante fascist running things? No, Jared, I think the writing's on the wall. I think we're rapidly approaching the end of my tenure at the Chauncey R. Slope Museum and *Marché aux Puces.* And I can't say I'm sorry to see it come."

I hate it when he talks like that. I sit down beside him, close enough that my shoulder rests against his. "Don't give up yet. Senator Proffitt isn't the only person on the committee. There's Mrs. Lacey and the chancellor and Wilhelmina Laudermilk. They all like you."

He reaches inside his jacket for his Dunhills. He flips back the top of the little red-and-gold box. Empty. He crushes the box, flips it toward a sand-filled bronze ashtray, and misses. "Perfect end to a perfect day." He looks at his watch. "I'm late. I'm supposed to meet the chancellor and Wilhelmina for drinks and a strategy session." He looks straight into my eyes. "I'm sorry to sound so bleak. They're just wearing me down a little, that's all. I've got to run." He grasps my shoulder and shakes my hand, looking like he'd like to do more. Maybe a lot more. "And if you hear about any job openings for a rapidly aging museum director, let me know. Okay?"

He gets up and heads across the empty lobby, head down, hands in pockets, but walking fast.

He surely doesn't mean that. About leaving, I mean. He couldn't think of leaving, just like that. What would he do? Where would we go?

With all this going on, school seems completely unreal. I still go of course but I'm not really there. Even my grades have started slipping. That's *never* happened before. I totally blew my history of modern Europe test even though I knew the material backward and forward. I simply could not concentrate at all. It just didn't seem very important. It's funny too—I thought screwing up in such a major way would be humiliating. It wasn't though. When Mr. Greenwood handed back my test with a big B— scrawled in red on it, it didn't mean a thing to me. Nothing at all. Not next to what Mr. Clay and I are going through.

Most days everything seems so far away. Muffled. A teacher stands up at the front of a classroom and talks and gestures or writes things on the blackboard or demonstrates how to turn on a Bunsen burner and suddenly I realize I'm not hearing anything. I can shut it all out.

Life's actually kind of neat with the sound turned down, like those silent movies they show on TV sometimes. Everyone looks kind of silly and rushed, as if what they're doing is the most important thing in the world. Except it's only important to them. That's why it looks so silly.

English Honors is the only class where that doesn't happen. It comes through loud and clear. That's because Miss Angle's completely crazy. Everybody knows it. And because everybody knows she can say whatever she wants and nobody much minds.

Today when she comes it it's easy to see she's running on high. She's pretty old, fifty at least, but when she's in a good mood she really sways her hips when she walks. I don't think she's trying to be sexy. It's more like when Rex and Louis are really happy to see someone and they wag not just their tails but their whole bodies.

She slaps her book down on the lectern and fiddles for a moment with the collar of her blouse. She dresses like it's still 1945—long gray tweed skirts and these filmy blouses that show what kind of bra she's got on. She runs one bony hand through her tarnished silver hair and shakes her head to one side a couple of times like she's just been swimming and can't get the water out of her ear. Then she props her elbow on the lectern, chin on her fists, and slowly surveys us all. "Can anyone hear that buzzing?" Her voice is sharp and clear and sort of sing-song. "It's been driving me crazy all morning. You don't? Isn't that odd. Do you suppose it's only me? Wouldn't that be hysterical!" She throws her head back and laughs like a crow cawing, like being crazy's more fun than anything else in the whole wide world. "It's a very low buzz really. Almost a drone. It was there when I woke up this morning and it's been following me everywhere I go. You're sure you don't hear it?"

Most kids don't say much in Miss Angle's class. Most don't know what *to* say. They just watch real close like they're scared to death they're going to miss the next crazy thing she does. Meanwhile I'm back in the corner near the window cracking up as quietly as I can.

"You hear it, don't you?" She nods in my direction but generally enough so it could be anyone in my part of the room. "I can tell you do. The buzzing of the spheres." She claps her hands together. "Oh, I can't wait to learn all your names so I won't have to call everyone *you.* Although I do find it adds that touch of mystery to the teaching of English literature, don't you? A touch of ambiguity? When I say *you,* it could mean everyone or one person in particular or perhaps no one at all. What we call the indefinite *you,* as in 'You could have heard a pin drop.'

"Mr. Empson in today's assignment tells us there are seven types of ambiguity, but that may not do some of you a lot of good, especially those of you who haven't read Mr. Empson or simply don't know what *ambiguity* means. Of course not knowing the meaning of the term probably constitutes an eighth type of ambiguity for Mr. Empson to worry over, but perhaps somebody who does know should tell us *exactly* what *ambiguity* means, if that isn't an out-and-out contradiction."

The pony-tailed girl in the front row who answers practically every question whether she's called on or not shoots up her hand and says, "Not clear."

Miss Angle puts her hands on her hips and rocks back and forth on her heels, pursing her lips like she's about to whistle a happy tune. "Well, that's one way of looking at it, isn't it? Although I've often thought ambiguity a somehow richer concept than that. Could we cast it as a positive rather than a negative? Clear in too many ways, like a prism? Does that help at all? No, I can see it doesn't." She picks up her book and carefully examines its corners. Then she slaps it down again. "Wordsworth, page two hundred sixteen. Can't get much more unambiguous than old Wordswords, one would have thought."

Without waiting for everyone to find the right page she plunges into the poem. Most English teachers put on a special holy voice when they read poetry, like they're being goosed by God or something. Miss Angle though just sings it out like it's some brand-new song, fast and loud. I always read the day's assignment beforehand. It's the only schoolwork I still bother with but it's like I haven't even seen the poem, let alone understood it, until Miss Angle belts it out.

"So what does he *mean*?" she says, stretching out *mean* like it's a big thick rubber band that's about to snap. "What's he getting at when he, or perhaps his persona, his mask, says 'Up, up! my friend and quit your books'? When he calls books 'barren leaves' and says nature makes the better teacher—is he being serious here?"

The ponytail girl waves her hand like she's drowning. "I don't see how he could be serious, Miss Angle. He's a poet. A man of learning. He *writes* books."

Miss Angle smiles broadly and her eyes drift sideways like she's hearing secret harmonies. Or maybe just the buzz. "That's quite true. But when he says, 'Come forth into the light of things,' he implies that books are things of darkness. You must admit that's a fairly sharp note for a writer of books to strike. And look, just look!" She flings out her arm in a wide dramatic arc that takes in the six tall windows. Forty pairs of eyes swivel leftward to study the rippling tops of maple trees, white cumulus clouds against a blue October sky.

"Couldn't it be that Wordsworth feels ambivalent about books and learning? Remember that word from last week? Ambivalent. Literally, to be strong in both. To entertain two contrary emotions at the same time and feel them to be equally true. I'm sure Wordsworth had equally strong and positive emotions concerning both books and nature, but on a day like today the choice must look pretty clear: words on a page in a stale airless classroom or the last bright days of autumn. Which will it be?"

Henry Noble, president of Student Council, answers without raising his hand. "Aren't you oversimplifying a complex issue, Miss Angle? Doesn't it depend on what your goals are? If Wordsworth wanted to be a poet more than anything else, wouldn't it be more pragmatic of him to sacrifice the pleasures of the moment in order to achieve something of lasting importance?" Henry thinks he's such hot shit. He's going to be a politician.

Miss Angle smiles so wide her gold inlays in back show. She combs her fingers through her hair once more so it splays out around her face like wrinkled tinfoil. "Yes, yes, yes. We must be pragmatic in this world, otherwise we won't survive. But if he doesn't get out there and experience the pleasures of the moment, what's he going to have to recollect later, in tranquility? What's he going to write about? And also, what if you sacrifice and put off and deny and you don't achieve your goal anyway? What if, because you have no strong emotions to recollect, you end up a lousy poet and you miss out on nature too? Then where will you be?"

"Dead."

Everyone turns around. I thought I said it to myself.

"Exactly. For instance. Some of you are studying hard so you can become Juniors, and the Juniors among you are studying hard so they can become Seniors, and the Seniors are all studying hard so they can graduate and the next stop is rice paddies and getting shot at in Vietnam." She claps her hands together hard and laughs. "Don't you think that's just hysterical?"

Henry Noble's face goes brick-red. "You don't think it's our duty to fight for our country?"

"Oh, by all means. It's everybody's patriotic duty as an American citizen to get out there knee-deep in the rice paddies and fight for the American way in an undeclared war. Who would disagree with that? Certainly not I. But Wordsworth isn't really talking about duty here. Or rather he's talking about a different kind of duty: *carpe diem."* She turns around and scrawls it across the blackboard so it's six feet long at least. "Seize the day. Up, up! from your books. What are you waiting for? It's out there, not in here. What's holding you back? You're not afraid, are you?" She turns her head from right to left, left to right, slowly scanning the room like a lighthouse beacon. She ends up looking straight at me. She's not smiling anymore. "You can walk out of here and take your chances, or you can stay here and take what you get."

I gather up my books and walk to the front of the room. Everyone's looking at me. Miss Angle too, propping her chin on her hands. She smiles a little as I walk past her lectern, heading for the door. "You. You're not indefinite at all."

NOVEMBER

*F*ather shoves the *Tribune-Star* across the table so
hard it almost knocks over my orange juice. I glance
down at the headline—"SLOPE SCULPTOR PER-
VERT"—but don't pick up the paper. I wouldn't give
him that satisfaction. He pushes back his chair and
stands up. "If I'd known what that place was all about
I'd never have let you work there. Like putting a monkey
in a banana factory."

On his way out he crashes into Mrs. Krapo bringing
in my scrambled eggs. She presses herself up against the
sideboard. "There's plenty more sausage, Doctor."

Sally reaches for the paper but I grab it first.
"Mother!" she squeals but mother's already on her feet
and heading for the morning room.

They've blown up di Severini's picture so it covers

three columns and looks real fuzzy. The article beside it covers three more:

Chicago artist Mario di Severini, 51, named by the House Un-American Activities Committee [HUAC] as a hostile witness, is also a known homosexual, according to Chicago police reports.

This information, revealed at last night's City Council meeting concerning the Chauncey R. Slope Museum's purchase of a di Severini sculpture, was unearthed by a special committee of the Slope Museum's board of directors investigating the artist's political past.

According to Slope board member and special-committee chairman State Senator Cyrus T. "Cy" Proffitt (R–Iron County), di Severini was arrested on a morals charge in 1955 in Cook County.

"Chicago police apprehended di Severini," Sen. Proffitt informed City Council members, "in a raid on a bar on the city's north side. This bar, a notorious gathering place for deviants of all stripes, was raided numerous times during the fifties until the police obtained a court order to close it down in 1958."

According to Sen. Proffitt, police records also reveal that di Severini was a founding member of the Chicago cell of the Mattachine Society. "The Mattachine Society is a Communist-affiliated organization dedicated to the recruitment of homosexuals and the promulgation of their sick beliefs. It is on HUAC's list of the hundred most dangerous subversive organizations operating in America today."

Proffitt called for the immediate removal of di Severini's statue, "Minos and After," from public view at the Slope Museum. He also urged that Slope director Julian Clay be held fully accountable for the purchase of a piece of public sculpture by an artist who is both "a Communist agent and a dangerous invert known to the police."

"Minos and After" cost $5582, approximately $500 of that coming from an annual municipal grant to the Slope Museum to help defray the cost of new acquisitions.

Clay, who Proffitt says was also a student of di Severini's in the early 1950's at an art school in New York City, was not available for comment at presstime.

[see Editorial, "Setting Our House in Order: Clay Must Go," p. 4]

The blue-and-white police car's parked half on, half off the sidewalk, passenger door wide open, cherry on top flashing as it revolves. I race up the stairs. What have they done to him?

No one at the sales desk. I'm heading for his office when Mrs. Mandle comes in from the South Galleries. She's crying, jaw jutting out like she wishes she weren't. Two cops are following her, looking like they wish she weren't either.

"Oh, Jared, I'm so glad you're here."

"What's going on? Where's Mr. Clay?"

She takes a handkerchief from the sleeve of her purple dress and dabs at her streaked rouge. "He's at a luncheon meeting of the board. I can't think how I'll ever tell him . . ."

The older cop coughs into his hand. "If that's all here, Mrs. Mandle, we'd best be on our way. The detectives will be by after lunch to take a full report."

The tears have stopped. She puts her palms together like a hostess saying good night at the end of a party. "Thank you for coming, Officers. You've been a great help."

The younger officer looks at me closely. "You work here too?"

"Jared helps out on weekends," Mrs. Mandle says.

"Right. Well, it might be better if you could arrange to have two people on duty at all times. Maybe even think about hiring a security guard. Full time."

"I'm sure we'll give it some thought." Mrs. Mandle's still trembling all over but she's got it so under control I don't think they notice.

The cops touch the bills of their hats and head down the long stairs.

"What's going on, Mrs. Mandle?"

She shakes her head and clicks her false teeth twice. "Come." I follow her back through the South Galleries. She stops in front of the doorway to the Flower Gallery. "Prepare yourself."

For vandalism it's real careful work: the eyes cut out of every single Cocteau drawing. With a razor blade or something. Small perfectly rounded smooth-edged holes, each one about the size of a quarter. Whoever did it must have taken his time, taking each picture down, removing the backing, sliding out the matte, slicing out the eyes and then putting it all back. Eighteen drawings. Must have taken an hour at least.

"When did it happen?"

Mrs. Mandle looks down at the oatmeal-colored carpet. "It was all my fault. I can't believe I was so naive. It was slow this morning, not anywhere near the numbers of visitors we were having when this whole thing first flared up. But then about ten a group of young men came in. There must have been six or seven of them. Very nicely dressed. Big strapping fellows, athletic-looking. They wandered around the North Galleries some and I was so busy with my index cards I guess I lost track of them. Then two of them came over and started talking to me. We had a very pleasant chat. They wanted to know how much it costs to become a member, how many members there were, that kind of thing. They said they were new in town, students at the university.

"Even after they'd all left I didn't think a thing about it. They seemed so *normal,* and you know the odd ones we've been getting lately. At eleven-fifteen or so I came back to check on the dehumidifier and . . ." She looks about the room, eyes panicky because there's no safe place to look, and stares back down at the carpet.

"Oh, Jared, I could just kill myself. I could. These beautiful elegant drawings. Who could do a thing like that? I suppose they went after them because there wasn't much they could do to 'Minos and After' without making a lot of racket.

"What hurts the most is that they were Mr. Clay's discoveries. Up in the storeroom all these years and we didn't even know they were there. It took somebody with his eye to tell us what we had right under our noses. He's done so much for this place. How will I ever tell him?"

"It's not your fault, Mrs. Mandle. You can't run the sales desk and watch the galleries at the same time."

"Still, I feel so responsible. And all this on top of this morning's article."

"Did you talk to Mr. Clay about it?"

"Of course I called him at home the minute I saw it. I thought he'd be livid but instead he was quite calm. Like all the fight had gone right out of him, poor man. The article's what the board meeting's all about. I'm almost certain they're going to ask for his resignation."

"What do you think he'll do?"

"What can he do at this point? Until this morning I felt sure he'd fight them to the bitter end. But now I don't know. I'm sure by now he thinks the whole town's against him." She looks up at the drawings again and winces. "He may be right."

"When he gets back, Mrs. Mandle, would you tell him I've got to talk to him? Tell him it's urgent."

Mrs. Mandle looks at me and her face brightens. "Do you think you can persuade him to stay and fight the good fight?"

"Just tell him I need to see him desperately, and that I'll be back."

I leave her standing in the Flower Gallery, encircled by eyeless faces.

Grandmother Fortman takes forever to answer the door. "This is a surprise. Two visits in the same week. To what do I owe this honor?"

I bend down to kiss her.

"Not on the lips."

"Where's Brigid, Grandmother?"

"She's around somewhere. Poor thing's getting deafer than I am." Grandmother rattles her throat and leads me into the front parlor. The fire's down to almost nothing. "You want to give that a poke for me," she says as she settles into her platform rocker. "And if you look in that box on the mantelpiece there you'll find a little surprise."

I open the heart-shaped silver box. "Butterscotch balls! Where'd you find them?"

"Brigid got them for me up in Twelve Points. Get a handful for yourself and bring me one while you're at it."

I hand her one and pop another in my mouth. "Mmmm. I haven't had these since I was a kid."

"I suppose you think you're such a grown-up now." Any other time she would have said that mean but today she's smiling all over. She thinks I'm here to see her. "Just look at that hair of yours. Do you suppose you'll ever get it cut again?"

"I don't know, Grandmother. I kind of like it like this." She knows I'm kidding her. Her squinty eyes shine behind her silver-framed eyeglasses.

"Way down over your ears like that. It's indecent. But I suppose the girls like it."

I just nod and pop another butterscotch ball into my mouth.

She leans forward in her platform rocker. "You know I don't like nosey Parkers, but if I were to ask you something, purely in confidence, would you answer me honestly?"

How am I supposed to say yes to something like that if I don't know what it is in advance? "What do you want to know?"

"I worry about you, Jared. You're a fine handsome boy and you have everything money can buy and more, but sometimes you seem just plain lonesome to me. Always by yourself, never the merest mention of a friend."

I don't see what business that is of hers. "I've got friends. I just don't bring them over here."

"I'm not asking you to do that, honey. Who'd want

to come to see a decrepit old woman like me? But I would like to know, are you seeing anyone?"

Seeing anyone what? Why can't she just keep out of it? "What do you mean?"

"Is there some special girl you care a lot for?"

For a moment I think about letting her have it right between the eyes. "Yeah, I guess there's someone kind of special."

Grandmother throws back her head and laughs till all her wattles shimmy. "I knew it. I knew all along. As long ago as last summer, isn't it? I told your mother at your birthday party I thought you were acting kind of moony. Can you tell me a little something about her?"

"What do you want to know? I mean, there's really not that much to tell."

"Now you're being evasive. Sometimes you're so like your mother—I could shake the pair of you. When she was a teenager I never could get a thing out of her either. Even now it's hard to know what's on her mind. Well, still waters run deep. Did I ever tell you about the time she came to see me all in tears?"

I shake my head and settle into the couch. At least the interrogation's over. The eight-day clock says four-thirty. No matter where he's been during the day Mr. Clay usually goes back to Slope's at around five to see if there's any urgent business.

"I don't think she and your father had been together for more than a few years when she came to me bawling her eyes out saying she had to leave him. You couldn't have been more than three or four at the time. Can you imagine that, your mother leaving your father? I told her pretty squarely, 'No matter what he's done it's your job to forgive him. That's what marriage is all about. For better or for worse. Fortmans don't divorce.'

"And that only made her cry all the more. 'But you don't know what he's done,' she'd say over and over, the tears pouring from her eyes. And I'd say, 'Tell me, Helene,' but she'd just cry some more and say, 'It's too terrible, Mother, I can't.'

"You know it's always too terrible when you're first married, men being what they are. And you know she never did tell me. All she could say was, 'Are you going to send me back to him?' Of course I sent her back to him. What else could I do? A marriage is a marriage."

She shakes her head in amusement. "At the time I wondered if I was doing the right thing—she seemed so miserable. But I'm glad I held my ground. Only time will tell with something like that, and look how happy a couple your mother and father are now."

I guess. The clock strikes the quarter hour. "Listen, Grandmother, I'd better be going."

"So soon?"

"I just remembered I left my Latin book at school. And I've got an exam tomorrow."

"Well, if that's the case, you'd better go while the going's good."

In the entry hall she reaches up and gives my shoulder a squeeze. "Come back when you can stay longer. Next time maybe you could stay for dinner. But I suppose three visits in one week is too much to ask."

"I don't know, Grandmother. Friday's a definite possibility."

"Brigid doesn't need much advance warning. Just time to throw on an extra chop."

I stand in the entry hall, pulling on my camel's hair. "If anyone calls to see where I am could you say I came here after school and that I had to go back to school to get something?"

She opens her eyes wide and points a bony finger at me. "I'm on to you, mister. You're seeing your sweetheart after school before you come to see me, aren't you? Just using your poor old grandmother."

I can feel myself blushing.

She pinches my cheek. Hard. "Well, I can't say I mind very much being used for love. You're that mother of yours all over. Close-mouthed to the bitter end."

Mr. Clay pulls a drawer out of his desk and empties it into a large cardboard box. "At this stage of the game I don't know what you could do, Jared. I'm not sure what anyone could do."

"There must be something."

He slides the drawer back into its slot and sits on the corner of the desk, crossing one leg over the other. He's got on one burgundy sock and one brown one. This probably isn't the time to tell him. The skin under his eyes is gray and pleated. "I think it's far better to face the fact that my career, as they say in the better magazines, is in ruins." He gives a dry laugh and lights a Dunhill. "You know, this was supposed to be just a stop along the way. A couple of years' drudge work in the provinces, turning a hole-in-the-wall curio shop into a respectable regional showcase. Then on to bigger and better things. Still in the Midwest of course for the next rung up the ladder, but someplace bigger—Kansas City, Louisville, Milwaukee maybe. And finally back East to relative glory and something substantial. It all looked like such a smoothly charted passage at the time."

I don't understand how he can take it so calmly. "But none of this is your fault. You didn't know what it was like here. How could you know Senator Proffitt would latch on to something like this? Or the *Tribune-Star*? Your job's art, not politics."

"I'm an administrator. The first rule of administration, whatever you're doing, is Don't Make Waves. Keep it all running smoothly. Foresee and if possible forestall all potential difficulties. In a way, you know, I brought all this on myself. I tried to move too fast. I didn't prepare the groundwork with sufficient care. I was so cocksure I didn't even consult the board on a major purchase like 'Minos and After.' The Greeks had a word for my affliction."

"Hubris."

"That's not quite how they taught us to pronounce it at Amherst but yes, hubris. Luckily I don't have to gouge out my eyes or anything equally dire. My dismissal here simply means another few years in some equally dismal place. Some worse place perhaps, although I doubt that's possible. I hear there's an opening in Nashville."

"God."

"Precisely. My period of atonement. I'm sure more awful things have happened to far better people. At the moment though, I'm at a loss to say what."

"But don't you want to fight it? Fight them? It isn't fair."

He gets up and walks over to the glass-brick window. He stands looking at the wavy bricks a long time, like he can see right through them. "What do you think I've been doing these last few months? I know when I'm licked. Another place, I might have been able to tough it out, but here . . . I can't take on the whole town. Do you know what the chancellor of the State Normal said to me today at the board meeting? 'I was willing to stand by you all the way, Julian, so long as it was a question of freedom of expression, but I'll have no truck with perversion.' Pompous ass."

I wish he'd turn around. "So you're just going to walk away and let people like that win?"

"They have won. Can't you see that? They'll always win in a little two-bit town like this."

I go over and stand right behind him. "And you think it's going to be better the next place you go?"

"Probably not. But I intend to keep my nose clean and my head down. Survival's the only name of the game now. Till I can get back to something like civilization."

I try to make a joke out of it. "And you're just going to leave me here?"

He turns around looking kind of startled, like he missed the joke. "What?"

"You're going to leave me here to fight them on my own?"

He laughs softly, like he finally got it, and rubs his hands together slowly. "Jared, Jared. I am sorry. Here I am going on about me. All this does leave you rather high and dry, doesn't it? But you'll see, things will work out for you. Another couple of years and you'll be going away to college. You'll be getting out too. It's only a matter of time."

I hate it when people pretend to be cheery to make me feel better when it's actually to make them feel better.

"Is Dorcas going with you?"

That wipes the smile off his face. He looks at his cigarette closely and purses his lips. "Of course she's going with me. What else would . . ." He stubs out the half-smoked cigarette in the Sphinx ashtray and looks straight at me for the first time since I entered his office. "What's this all about?"

He's such a hypocrite, just like everybody else.

"Nothing."

"Jared, come and sit down." He pats the back of his chair.

"I'm fine."

"You know you're not. I can see you're terribly upset." He sits back down on the corner of his desk. "What happened between us . . ."

Now he's talking at the ceiling. And I'm thinking, I could shut you off in a minute if I wanted to, just like I do at school. But not yet. Let him drone on.

". . . don't want to say I regret it because in some important way I don't. I know I oughtn't to have done it. It was very foolish of me, very unwise, but I don't regret it. It would have been better if it hadn't happened. I know that. We—that is, I—got carried away.

"You're a remarkable boy. Really and truly remarkable. And you have such a bright future ahead of you. So smart, attractive, perceptive. You'll shoot right to the top, whatever you choose to do with your life. Don't turn away from me, Jared. Please don't turn away.

"You're too young to know what you feel. What you're going through right now is just a phase. Boys your age get crushes. If it hadn't been me it might have been one of your teachers. I remember when I was sixteen—" He suddenly needs another cigarette. Fast. He starts patting all his pockets at once.

"Behind the inkwell."

"What? Oh, so they are. What I'm trying to get at is, someday you'll meet the right girl, the way I met Dorcas, and all this will seem unimportant to you."

"All those things you said. You were lying."

He turns red faster than anybody I've ever seen. "What things?"

"You wouldn't have said those things if you didn't mean them."

Little bubbles of spittle form at the corners of his mouth. "I honestly don't remember what I said. People say a lot of things when—"

"You're just a coward, aren't you?"

"Jared, that's enough." He stands up. He's shaking all over.

"A fucking hypocrite, just like everybody else."

I see his hand coming but I don't feel it strike, just my head jerking back. My upper lip tingles. I can taste blood.

He stands there looking silly, holding his own hand, face absolutely white. "I'm sorry, Jared. I didn't mean . . . Here, take my handkerchief."

"I'm fine." I head for the door.

"You can't go out of here looking like that."

"Sure I can."

He grabs my arm and tries to drag me to a chair.

"There's no reason why we can't talk this over calmly, like two . . . like two friends."

"There's nothing to talk about."

He holds me by my shoulders and talks right into my face. It's all I can do to keep from spitting on him. "Please listen to me. I know this may not make any sense to you now but when you're a little older maybe you'll understand. I'm perfectly conscious of the decisions I've made in my life and if I had it to do all over again I'd do it all exactly the same way." He smiles slightly as he speaks, like a doctor trying to get an important point across to an idiot patient. He lets go of my shoulders and takes his handkerchief to try to wipe my mouth but I pull my head back.

"You're a liar. It's what you like. Don't tell me it isn't."

He lowers his voice like he hopes that will make me do the same. "What I'm trying to tell you is that I've made my choices and I'm comfortable with them. What happened between us was a momentary lapse that—"

"—that you liked." I'm shouting now. I don't care who hears. "Tell me you didn't like it."

"All right, Jared. I didn't like it."

"Liar, liar, liar!"

"If you'll just lower your voice I'll try to explain. The first time, in Chicago, I was very drunk. I honestly didn't know what I was doing. The other times, up in the storeroom, well, I went along with it because . . . because I didn't want to hurt your feelings." He reaches out and takes hold of my hand. "That's the truth, Jared, the honest-to-God truth. I didn't know how to tell you without hurting you."

I yank my hand away and start for the door again. "You didn't care about hurting me in Chicago or up in the storeroom. All the same shit. 'Beautiful, beautiful, you're so beautiful.' I'm not going to listen to any more of your lies."

He sits back down on the edge of his desk and crosses his arms over his chest like he's finished listening even if I'm not finished talking. I open the door and look at him for a moment. He looks so puny sitting there. Not like Cary Grant at all.

"I'm going home and I'm going to tell my father exactly what you did to me."

I can tell by his face that he really thinks I would. It stops him dead.

*   *   *

Grandma McCaverty says it was almost exactly a year ago today that Kennedy got shot.

"It was too damn bad," Grandpa McCaverty says, "even if he was a Catholic."

"I can still see those poor little children standing by the coffin," Aunt Lily says.

Grandma McCaverty says, the way she always does when she hears about a father dying, that it reminds her of when her dad got crushed in the coal mine when she was only nine.

Sally comes in late, looking pale, a film of sweat across her forehead. She smells sour. She sits down at her place and Uncle Fox leans over and says, "How's my college girl?" I can see his big hand going under the tablecloth so he can give her a squeeze. She jumps about a mile and squeals, "Uncle Fox!" He gives a low juicy laugh. Sally turns red and giggles. His hand stays down there.

". . . and we heard a thud out on the front porch and Mae and Sarah and I ran out just in time to see the wagon from the mine pulling away. Dumped his body right there on the bare boards. No covering or anything. Can you imagine the like? And do you know that to this day there isn't a day in my life I don't see his broken body lying there?"

And there isn't a holiday we don't hear about it.

"That's a very sad story, Mrs. McCaverty," Mr. Popoff says, reaching for the basket of pocketbook rolls.

"Very sad," Grand-aunt Hermione says, watching the light flash off the big diamond ring on the third finger of her left hand. She gets up quickly and slips out of the room.

Mr. Popoff watches her go. He looks like he's about to get up and go after her when he notices he's still holding the bread basket. He starts to put it back where he found it, next to the crystal cornucopia vomiting wax fruit, but Sally jerks it out of his pudgy hand. She plops two rolls onto her bread plate and breaks and butters a third. Her plate's a swamp of turkey and oyster stuffing swimming in gravy, mashed potatoes with big dabs of butter on top, shoelace noodles in bright yellow broth, cranberries bleeding into candied yams. She stuffs half the roll into her mouth. Her pale cheeks are so full she can hardly chew. Well, she's got a lot to be thankful for.

Grandmother Fortman's down at the far end of the table, next to mother. They think they're talking softly but I can hear nearly every word they say. I always can when people are talking about me.

"He looks kind of blue to me," Grandmother Fortman says.

Mother stares up at the chandelier for a moment, like she's wondering if it doesn't need a good washing, pendant by crystal pendant. Then she says something to Grandmother Fortman that I can't hear. Grandmother makes a sour face and rears back in her chair like she's bitten into a raw persimmon.

"He *what*?"

"I said they say it was a suicide."

"And he did it there? At that place?"

Mother nods and glances down the table at me. I pick up my water goblet and take a long drink.

Grandmother runs one gnarled hand over the back of the other like she's trying to smooth out all the wrinkles. "I don't want to say it, Helene, but maybe the poor man's better off out of it." The she starts to cry. Not a lot. Just two or three tears slowly running down her cheeks. I don't know what right she has to cry. She didn't even know him. Mother sits quietly, mouth clamped shut, looking kind of helpless.

They're wrong. I'm not sad. Not at all. I haven't cried either. Haven't even thought about it. It would be silly to cry anyway. Especially since it was my fault. I killed him. I know that. He was a fucking hypocite and a lying coward and I killed him. I didn't mean to. I only wanted to scare him a little. But I killed him just the same as if I'd taken a gun and shot him through the head.

The grandfather clock bongs out three-thirty and gets twenty or so replies from throughout the house. Instead of chiming, the wall clock over the sideboard makes a rattling noise like pebbles in a tin can. Father gets up to see what's wrong.

"I don't know how you keep them all going," Aunt Lily says as he adjusts the brass pendulum.

"And I don't know why," Father says, grinning a little as he closes the clock's glass-paned door.

I didn't even know there was a Unitarian church in town. Kind of stupid to call it a church anyway when it's only a room stuck away in the basement of the Student Union down at Indiana State Normal. It's real plain, with no stained glass, flowers, candles or anything. No body either. Because it's a memorial service instead of a real funeral. The wood paneling's kind of nice, smooth and dark gold like butterscotch. Over the altar hangs a big crimson banner with a gold Aladdin's lamp emblazoned on it. Maybe it's the lamp of knowledge.

The altar's not really an altar, just a wooden lectern like the one Miss Angle uses, except it's a little fancier and has a green-shaded reading lamp fixed to it. No organ music because there's no organ. When all the people are settled into their seats, plush fold-down ones just like

at the Orpheum, a man in a baggy blue serge suit gets up
and goes to the lectern. He's carrying a small brown spiral notebook.

He switches on the lamp and adjusts the green glass
shade. "I didn't know Julius Clay very well. He wasn't
with us long enough for friendship or even close acquain-
tance to spring up between us, but I do remember
that . . ."

He doesn't remember diddly-shit. He could at least
have gotten the name right. I turn down the volume and
start sliding in and out of what he's saying, just like I do
at school. Not a whole lot of people here. Mrs. Mandle
and Charles at the other end of my row. She's wearing a
black velvet hat like a flying saucer with a black speckled
veil that ties under her chin. Down in front Mrs. Clay
isn't wearing any hat at all. Her hair's short as ever, with
a little cowlick in back. She could be a boy sitting there.
The nape of her neck looks kind of naked. I don't know
any of the rest of the people. Some of the men have white
smudges on the sleeves or backs of their rumpled jackets
so they're probably professors at State Normal.

The guy at the lectern sounds like he's winding
down, reading something that sounds famous:

O may I join the choir invisible
Of those immortal dead who live again
In minds made better by their presence.

He closes the spiral notebook and turns off the lamp. Got
through the whole thing and never once mentioned God
or Christ or anything, not even Death. Strange. I look
around to see if other people are getting ready to get up
and leave. That's something Grandmother Fortman
taught me when I was real little: in church never be the
first one up.

The music ripples out like a fountain somebody suddenly turned on. I look over my shoulder. Back by the
door Mrs. Sparks sits on a little stool, a big gold harp
between her knees. Her short fingers flutter up and down
the silvery strings, sometimes plucking, sometimes moving in soft circular strokes. Something slow and sad as
"Sarabande" at first but then sweetly cracking, trickling,
rushing like an icy river in thaw. For a minute I feel like
I'm not going to be able to hold it in. But I do. I don't
deserve to cry. Not after what I did.

The receiving line's so short I'm at the front before I
know it. Mrs. Clay doesn't look like she's been crying or
anything. Her emerald-green suit's made of some shiny
material, kind of bright for the occasion, but so pretty
with her short black hair and pale pale skin. Her hand's
hot and damp and strong. "Jared, I'm so glad you could
come. I didn't know if you would. Won't you come by the
house now? You remember where it is."

Mrs. Sparks is over in the corner, crouching down as
she zips her harp into its brown canvas cover. I think I
managed to slip past without her seeing me.

"And to think I didn't even know he was in the
building. He must have let himself in early that morning.
I know I must have passed his office half a dozen times.
Of course it wasn't until late afternoon, when the day had
drawn in, that I noticed the light under his door. Once I
opened it something told me to go straight to his bathroom. To the end of my days I know I'll wish I hadn't.
Not that he wasn't very neat about it, towels spread on
the floor and everything. A cigarette had burned itself out
in the soap dish. I never liked that bathroom to begin
with. So dark. And black marble's so hard to keep nice.
Now all I can see is black and red, the ivory-handled

straight razor on the edge of the sink and those shiny black tiles simply dripping with—"

"Now, Catherine, the boy doesn't want to hear that kind of thing." Charles Mandle puts his arm around Mrs. Mandle's narrow shoulders and she starts sobbing, black mascara running behind her speckly veil.

There are a lot more people here than at the service. Lots of them didn't even know enough to take off their shoes at the door and are scuffing up the grass mats. Mr. Clay would have a fit. An old Negro in a white jacket stands behind a bridge table over by the fireplace, pouring out drinks. I don't see anyone I know so I go over to the window and look out at the bare front lawn.

"Can I get you a drink?"

Same long burlap dress but new jewelry, lots of it— copper and onyx, silver and turquoise, barrel-shaped ceramic beads and dangling from a leather thong a big gold medallion that looks like the hood ornament from a Mercedes Benz. "Hi, Bronwyn. How's Berkeley?"

She swings her long mane of brown hair back over one shoulder. "Didn't you know? I left Berkeley almost immediately upon arriving. I'm in New Mexico now. A place called Taos. Near Taos, really. Way up in the clouds."

"That's nice."

"And how are things on the middle-school front?"

"I'm in high school now."

"Are you? So how are things in high school?"

"About the same."

"I can see you're as forthcoming as ever. You're absolutely sure you wouldn't care for a drink? Don't know if they've got any sake but I could ask."

"That's okay." What a bitch.

"I'm sorry, Jared. You didn't deserve that. It's been a very trying day, as you can imagine."

"I didn't see you at the memorial service."

"No, I stayed here. Housebreakers watch the obituary notices like vultures."

"Well, my two favorite people. So far." Mrs. Clay comes up and drapes one arm around Bronwyn's neck, the other around mine. She's changed into black silk hostess pajamas and black sequined slippers. "I believe I'm getting mildly pissed."

"What a splendid idea." Bronwyn ducks out from under her arm. "Maybe I'll go and see if the bartender can do the same for me."

Mrs. Clay keeps her arm around my neck and guides me across the room. "I'd like to talk to you, if you don't mind, preferably in private."

She leads me past the long black-and-white paper screen into the kitchen where three middle-aged men and a young woman in a bright purple cocktail dress are laughing softly together. They stop when we come in.

"Don't mind us—just passing through," Mrs. Clay says and drags me down a dark hallway. She throws open a door. Two guys—they look like university students—are sitting in the middle of the bed. One of them's lighting a small brass pipe. The air's already blue with smoke and there's a funny smell. They look up, surprised. Mrs. Clay shuts the door softly.

"One place left," she says and leads me back through the kitchen and out the back door. Her black pajamas ripple in the wind. It's not that cold for the end of November but my teeth start chattering. The Peugeot's in the driveway. She opens the door on the driver's side.

"What about the other cars?" A VW bug, a gold Corvette and a rusty green Mustang block the drive.

"It's okay. We're not going anywhere."

I shut my door and it's like being inside a big pack of Dunhills. The car reeks of him.

"You want the heater on?"

I shake my head.

She tilts her head. "What's that funny clicking noise?"

"My teeth."

"Then I'd better turn on the heat. Damn. My keys are inside."

"I'm all right. Honest."

She slumps down in her seat, hands at ten and two on the steering wheel. "Sometimes I even surprise myself. I feel so calm. I suppose I'll fall apart afterward or something dramatic like that. I've always suspected that only happens in the movies."

She takes her hands off the wheel and shifts in her seat so her back's against the door and she's looking right at me. "I simply cannot fathom it. Can you? Can you think of any reason why he'd do such a thing? I've been mulling it over all day. And all last night. Ever since they told me. Instead of falling apart I started trying to work it all out. Except it doesn't work out. Like a jigsaw puzzle with one piece missing.

"I know he was depressed over the witch hunt. He tried so hard for this godforsaken town and look how they rewarded him. But I can't believe it was only that. He never contemplated staying here, I'm sure you're aware of that. Certainly leaving in disgrace wouldn't have made it any easier at the next place. Still, we're young. It's not as though this is our last chance." She looks up at the felt-upholstered ceiling and laughs. "Well, I guess it was, wasn't it?"

Without any warning she reaches over and grabs my arm. With both hands. She twists it like she wants to give me an Italian burn. Her black eyes are sharp as darts. "Don't you find this bewildering, as bewildering as I do?"

I can't say no. I nod.

She squeezes harder. "Then say it. Say you find it bewildering."

"I find it bewildering."

She lets go. "And not even to leave a note. I'll never understand that. Never. It makes me so angry. Such a betrayal. I don't think I adequately can express just how furious that makes me feel." She puts her face in her hands and starts to cry. No, she's giggling like a little girl. "If he were alive I'd give serious thought to killing him."

She lifts her head to look at me. "I was about to say, But you don't understand what I'm talking about. Except it suddenly occurred to me that you do understand all this, don't you?"

"All what?" The wind's picking up. Dead leaves spin along the front walk.

"Everything. Everything I've been saying to you. You sit there with your big blue eyes wide open, taking it all in. Talking to you is exactly like talking to an adult. To an extremely sensitive adult. I imagine you've always been like that, haven't you? Even as a child, I'll bet, like one of those sad-eyed boys in an Italian film.

"Now I wish I'd talked like this to you before. Of course it was always Julie and you, wasn't it? Did you know he loved you very much? He was always talking about you. Coming home at night to tell me the funny things you'd done or said. 'That boy has such a wicked wit,' he'd say and laugh and laugh.

"He was tremendously impressed by you. I think you may have reminded him of himself as a child—intelligent, isolated, a little cold. He always claimed you were far smarter than he ever was.

"It's a shame we couldn't have had children. I think Julie would have made an excellent father. Just excellent. That depressed him, I know, not being able to have children. A great deal more than he was ever willing to admit.

"The funny thing was, that depression stopped completely when we moved here. And I always wondered why. He even stopped talking about wanting to adopt. I suppose I knew why even while I was wondering. He found his son in you, didn't he?"

Actually it's getting hot in here even without the heater. The smell's starting to make me sick. I roll down my window a little way.

Mrs. Clay shivers. "I probably ought to be getting back inside. People seem a bit cheerier than at the memorial service. The reader seemed like such a nice man. He warned me it would be a standard text, seeing as he hardly knew Julie, but Christ, I would have had no text at all if I'd known it was going to include George Eliot. Julie hated her with all his soul."

She puts her hands on the back of her neck and arches her head as far back as it will go. "All the tension seems to accumulate right at the back of my neck. Maybe another drink would help. Probably not. Today it seems to be going right through me with only brief moments of anything like intoxication. You know, that's one of the few things of value, maybe the *only* thing, I learned from my sainted mother. Somebody dies, first call the mortuary, then the liquor store. Words to live by."

She gets out of the car and stares up at the blank

gray sky. "It would be nice to be able to believe he was up there somewhere, don't you think? But after what he's done, what he did to me, I'm not sure I can even believe in *nice* anymore."

"A large Buttercup, double butter, please, and a giant Coke, two Clark bars, a Reese's cup and a jumbo box of Root Beer Barrels."

The snack-counter girl moves like she's under water. She floats over to the popcorn machine, scoops a striped barrel full, squirts it twice with warm butter, brings it back. Then she drifts back over to the soft-drink spigots —right next to the popcorn machine—fills my Coke, brings it back. Anyone other than a total fool would have done it all in one trip.

Now she's squatting down behind the counter, sliding open doors and drawers and rooting around. Finally she stands up and puts her hands on her hips. "Can't think of where they got to."

"What?"

"The little cardboard trays. For your stuff. You know, collapsible? There was a whole stack of them yesterday and now . . ."

She's so dumb she deserves the birthmark. "Look, I don't need a tray. Just give me my Root Beer Barrels. I'm going to miss the start."

"It's a lousy picture anyway."

"You've seen it already?"

"Only about a dozen times. The ending's really stupid."

"I'd prefer to be able to judge that for myself."

"Well, la-di-da."

Pretty good crowd for a three-o'-clock show. Two women in fur-collared plaid coats are settled into the Royal Box so I go into the one across the aisle.

Something must be wrong with the heat. I've kept my camel's hair on and I'm still shivering. Must be from sitting in the Peugeot for so long. I thought she would never shut up.

I don't know when I've felt this hungry. Like it's gnawing at my stomach. Haven't had a Reese's cup in ages. I strip off the orange wrapper, take out the chocolate disc and bite into it. Yuck. The peanut-butter filling tastes rotten. Sort of smoky. Weird. I throw the rest of it on the floor.

All those questions. Sometimes it felt creepy, like she knew everything. But she couldn't have—otherwise she wouldn't have been asking. Did she really think I'd tell her? For a second or two I did think about just letting it rip, spilling everything. It's not like it would be that big a deal, considering what I've already done. To him, I mean. Might even be kind of nice to tell her. Nice for me. But try to explain one thing to her and I'd have to explain everything. She's better off not knowing the things he did.

I'm halfway through my Buttercup when the Scrooge McDuck cartoon ends. The burgundy curtains swoop shut and then slowly creak open again. Shit. Black-and-white. But the title's so neat. It's why I came: *Dr. Strangelove: Or How I Learned to Stop Worrying and Love the Bomb.*

At first it's just like a regular old war movie except with atom bombs. Then this crazy cowboy rides a big bomb down to the target like it's a bucking bronco, waving his Stetson and shouting "Whoo-ee!" I about fall out of my seat.

The neatest thing of all's the mad scientist in a wheelchair, Dr. Strangelove. He has this one black-gloved hand he can't control that's always jerking up to give the Nazi salute.

The first time he does the *Sieg heil!* bit one of the ladies in the Royal Box says very loudly, "That's not funny, not funny at all." I'd tell the old sow to shut her trap but hardly anyone else in the whole theater is laughing, only me and some guy with a high-pitched giggle sitting way down front.

Pretty soon every time something really funny happens the bitch in the box says, "That's not funny" or "This is disgusting." And when Dr. Strangelove's own hand goes completely out of control and tries to strangle him, she stands up and says real loud, "Come along, Myrtle. I won't stand for another minute of this."

The giggler down in front leaps to his feet. He turns around and shakes his fist at the Royal Box. "Shut up, you crazy fool!" But the ladies are so busy gathering up their coats, scarves, purses and shopping bags they don't even notice someone's shouting at them.

The rest of the movie's pretty uneventful, at least in terms of the audience. At the end, when the mushroom clouds start sprouting up all over the place like big gray flowers and the lady's singing, "We'll meet again, don't know where, don't know when," the giggler down in front leaps to his feet again and claps his gloved hands together hard, shouting, "Bravo, bravo!" in a high reedy voice. Really strange.

Water streams endlessly down the side of the long porcelain trough. The sluicing sound echoes off the pink tile walls. The basement washroom of the Orpheum is like being inside a big seashell.

The stall doors all slant open at exactly the same angle but not far enough to see if anyone's inside. I go to the far end of the trough, away from the stalls.

The door wheezes open. A man with a navy-blue overcoat draped over his shoulders positions himself at the other end of the trough, legs apart. I keep my head down, concentrating hard, but it's no good. I can't go if someone else is around.

He stands there a long time. I can't tell if he's going because of the sound of the rushing water. Finally I look over. He's looking down, concentrating hard too. His black hair's long, down over the collar of his coat. He's younger than I thought. He looks over. I look down.

He zips up and steps back from the trough. I zip up and step back too. He looks over, I look up at the grimy ceiling.

I hear him heading for the door, footsteps gritty on the black-and-white mosaic floor. He stops.

"Beautiful coat." His voice is high but hoarse.

I look around. "Beg your pardon?"

"A beautiful coat you wear."

I can feel myself blushing. "Thanks. I was just about to say the same thing about yours."

He looks down at his navy-blue lapels. His nose is small and very sharp. His lip curls. "Very old. I detest this coat. Disgusting."

"No, no. It's really very nice."

One heavy eyebrow arches up. "Perhaps we must make an exchange?"

Why not? But how would I explain it to mother?

His giggle's almost a shriek. He must be the guy from down in front.

"I make a joke."

I laugh a little.

He indicates the ceiling with his thumb. "You will rise up?"

"What?"

"You will go up?"

"Upstairs?"

"Yes, upstairs."

"Yes."

He holds the door for me and together we climb the narrow stairs to the lobby.

He stands at the exact center of the lobby and slowly turns on his heel. "Very beautiful." He walks over to examine the plaster of paris male torsos holding up the coffered ceiling. "Very rococo."

"Yes."

He extends his arm straight from the shoulder. "I am sorry. I think I am quite rude. My name is Alexandre." He shakes my hand once, short and quick, without bending his elbow. "And you?"

I tell him my name.

"Please?"

I say it again.

He tries it. It sounds very foreign. I like that. He touches my elbow lightly. "Come along, Zher-id. We go for a coffee at the Pharmacy Gillis. You know?"

"Yeah. I don't know. I mean I don't know if I should. I told my mother I'd be home by six."

He consults his watch, which is silver and complicated-looking. "But it is five only. You live far?"

"Not far. You're from France?"

"Grenoble."

"Where?"

"Grenoble. Home of Stendhal."

"Who?"

"Stendhal." His eyebrow shoots up again. "You

don't know Stendhal? He is called also Marie-Henri Beyle?"

"No." I hold the door for him and he strides out, long hair flapping like dark wings in the cold wind.

"Americans do not know very much of French literature. Very ignorant people." He smiles slightly, like he's enjoying insulting me.

"So how much do you know about American literature?"

He purses his lips and blows a narrow stream of air through them. "There is little I do not know. That is why I come here. I study at the university."

"American literature?"

"Samuel Clemens, Booth Tarkington, Dos Passos, Theodore Dreiser, Hemingway, Hart Crane, Sinclair Lewis, Sherwood Anderson. All American writers living in the Middle Wests." He stops at the corner and looks north along The Boulevard at the dark gray granite and lighter gray limestone office buildings, at the shapeless gray-skinned shoppers plowing past in their colorless clothes, at the thick gray motionless clouds above. "I think," he says, giggling, "that I make a great mistake to come here."

"How long are you here for?"

"One entire year. I will die here."

"You don't like it at all?"

He grimaces, showing his sharp bright teeth. "Worse than Grenoble. So flat."

"Yes."

"And many fat people."

"Yes."

"And ugly."

"Yes."

"Many ugly fat people." He stops midsidewalk for a

moment, like he's considering the accuracy of his description. Two Negro ladies with legs as thick as his waist lumber by, thin coats pulled tight across their big bellies. "And many poor also."

"You think so?"

"We have not so many poor in Grenoble."

"Not everyone here is poor and ugly and fat."

"No, I can see with my eyes open. Some are very handsome and *fils à papa.*"

"What's that mean?"

He looks into my eyes. "I tell you with coffee."

We cross The Boulevard and head up Seventh.

"And you, you are at the university also?"

"High school."

His eyebrow darts up again. "You are how old?"

"Seventeen." There's no way he'll find out I'm not. "And you?"

"Twenty. Very old."

I stop in front of Slope's brass doors and point at the bronze plaque. "Do you know what that is?"

He studies the brass grilles over the narrow windows set into the doors. "It looks like a bank."

"It's a museum."

He purses his lips and blows. "For art?"

"Yes."

"Now *you* make a joke."

"No joke. You want to go in?"

He points at the black-bordered card taped to the inside of one of the narrow windows. For once Mrs. Mandle's copperplate is plain and readable: CLOSED FOR FUNERAL.

"That's okay. I've got a key. I work here." I turn the key in the lock and swing open the heavy door. I feel kind of odd, but it's not like this is any worse than anything I've already done. So I'll go to hell.

He steps into the little entry hall and looks up the three tiers of black marble steps. "And our coffee?"

"We can have coffee here."

He winks at me. He has the longest darkest eyelashes I've ever seen. "And the mother who waits?"

"I'll call her and tell her I won't be home."

Printed in the United States
by Baker & Taylor Publisher Services